"Thank you,"
Kristin said simply.

The stranger turned to her, and she felt color flood her face as he smiled. She clutched her torn clothing around her, but her rescuer didn't gallantly look away. Instead he stared at her without disguising his bold appraisal.

She moistened her lips, willing her heartbeat to cease its erratic beating, and she tried to meet his eyes, but she couldn't. The day was still, the sun bright and the sky clear and blue, yet she felt as if this was the calm before the storm. She could sense something in the air, an elusive crackling, as if lightning were sizzling between them. Something tense and potent was searing her senses.

"Think you might offer a stranger a meal, Miss...?" he asked.

"Kristin. Kristin McCahy," she offered softly.

"Kristin," he echoed. And then he touched her....

"Ms. Pozzessere sets a high standard..."
—*Romantic Times*

D0180000

Heather Graham Pozzessere

Dark Stranger

MIRA BOOKS

ISBN 1-55166-079-2

DARK STRANGER

Printed in U.S.A.

Dark
Stranger

PART 1

The Stranger

1

The hoofbeats were the warning. The relentless, pounding hoofbeats. The sound of them sparked a sense of primal fear deep inside Kristin. Strangely, before she'd first felt the staccato rhythm through the ground, she hadn't contemplated such a danger. The day had been too ordinary, and perhaps she had been too naive. She had expected a storm, but not of the magnitude that was to come.

It began with the stillness in the air. As she came along the path through the orchards from the river, Kristin paused. The breeze had dropped. The day had gone dead still. The sudden calm gave her a strange feeling, and she searched the sky. Overhead, she saw blue, a beautiful blue. No clouds marred that endless blue.

It was the calm before the storm, she thought. Here, on the Missouri side of the Kansas-Missouri border, storms were frequent and vicious. Blue skies turned to smoke, and vicious twisters whirled out of nowhere.

Then she heard the hoofbeats.

She looked out across the plain that stretched away from the house. A tumbleweed caught by a sudden gust of wind blew across a patch of parched earth.

Bushwhackers.

The word came unbidden to her mind, and raw fear swept through her, fear and denial. Please, God, no...

Pa! Matthew, Shannon...

Kristin began to run. Her heart began to race, thundering along with the sound of the hoofbeats.

Pa was already dead, she reminded herself. They'd already come to kill him. They'd come, on a cloudless day, and they'd dragged him out in front of the house. He had drowned in a pool of his own blood while she had stood there screaming. There had been nothing, *nothing* she could do.

Matthew was safe. He'd gone off to join up with the Union Army near the Mississippi. He had said she would be safe. After all, they'd already killed Pa in his own front yard, killed him and left him bleeding.

Bleeding. They called it "bleeding Kansas," and though they were on the Missouri side of the border here, the blood ran thick and deep. The War Between the States had boiled down to a barbarian savagery here. Men did not just fall in battle here, they were cruelly, viciously executed—seized, judged and murdered. Kristin had few illusions; one side was almost as bad as the other. The dream of freedom, the dream of endless land and a life of dignity and bounty had drowned in rivers of blood. The dream was dead, and yet it seemed that was all she had left to fight for. Her father had died for it, and they thought she would flee, but she wouldn't. She couldn't. She had to fight. There was nothing else to do.

Shannon.

Cold dread caught in her throat. Shannon was up at the house. Young, frightened, vulnerable.

Her feet slapped against the dry earth as the hoofbeats came closer. How many of them were there? Maybe twenty, like the day they had come to kill Pa? Maybe not so many. Maybe they knew that Matthew had gone off to fight in the war and that no one remained behind but the girls, the foreman, a maid and a few young hands. She almost felt like laughing. They'd tried to take Samson and Delilah the last time they had come. They didn't understand that the two were free, able to make their decisions. Pa wasn't a fanatical abolitionist; he had just liked Samson, plain and simple, so he had freed them on the occasion of their marriage. Little Daniel had been born free, and they'd all come here together in search of the dream . . .

Kristin stumbled and fell, gasping for breath. The riders were just behind the trees to her left. She heard screams and shouts, and she knew they were slaughtering whatever cattle they could lay their hands on. This wasn't war.

This was carnage.

She staggered to her feet, smoothing back stray tendrils of hair still damp from her early-morning swim in the river.

They could hold the attackers off. She would be prepared this time. She wouldn't assume that some of these men would be old friends and acquaintances. She wouldn't assume that they were human, that they knew anything about morals or ethics or simple decency. She didn't think she would ever trust in such things again.

Suddenly, while Kristin was still several hundred yards from the house, the horsemen burst through the trees.

"Samson!" she screamed. "Samson! Get me Pa's six-shooter. Samson!"

Samson, a tall, dignified black man, burst through the front door. He glanced at Kristin, then at the horsemen racing through the corn, trampling the tender green stalks.

"Run, Miss Kristin, run!"

She could hardly breathe, could hardly speak. "Pa's Colt, get me the Colt! Tell Shannon to get to the cellar!"

"Samson, what is it?"

Samson turned to see Shannon standing behind him in the hallway.

"Bushwhackers," he said grimly. "Where's Delilah?"

"Out back, feeding the chickens."

She was in the barn. His wife was in the barn. God, he prayed silently, give her the good sense to stay there!

"Shannon," he told her, "you get yourself in the cellar."

She turned away, and Samson hurried back to the hallway, then paused. He thought he'd heard something around back. When the sound wasn't repeated, he looked out the front door again. He could see the riders, and he could see Kristin running.

There were about twenty men, Samson reckoned. Just an offshoot of a bigger raiding party, probably. Some of Quantrill's raiders.

Quantrill himself was a damned butcher. He sanctioned the horror, and the death. Once upon a time he'd been friends with Gabriel McCahy, Kristin and Shannon's father, but one of his henchmen, a man named Zeke Moreau, had wanted Kristin. She hadn't wanted anything to do with him though. She was in love with Adam Smith. But Adam was dead now, too. Dead like her pa, dead like hundreds of men.

Now Zeke Moreau was coming back. He was coming for Kristin. Samson was sure of it.

"Samson!"

Her eyes met his, desperate, pleading.

Those might be God-fearing gentlemen out there, but if they captured a black man after he had leveled a Colt at them, even in his own defense, they would skin him alive.

It didn't matter. Gabriel McCahy had been the most decent man Samson had ever met. He would lose his skin over old Gabe's daughter if he had to.

He swung around, ready to rush into the house and get the guns. Then he paused, his eyes going wide and his throat closing up, hot and dry.

Zeke Moreau was already in the house. He was standing in the hallway, on the polished oak floor, and he had a double-barrelled shotgun leveled right at Samson.

A slight sound caught Samson's attention. He turned swiftly to see that another man was holding Delilah, one arm around her waist, a hand tight against her mouth.

"Watch it, Samson," Zeke said. "Be quiet now, or I'll hang you, boy. Hang you 'til you're dead. Then I'll see that your woman and your kid wind up on the auction block down Savannah way."

Zeke Moreau smiled slowly. He was dark-haired, with a dark, curling moustache, and Samson thought he would look more at home on a riverboat with a deck of cards than he did now, standing there in chaps and a vest, holding a shotgun. He was a good-looking man, except for his eyes. Cold, pale eyes, just like Kristin had always said.

Samson smiled back. "You murdered Gabriel, didn't you?"

Zeke rested his shotgun against his thigh. Samson was a big man, a good six-foot-six, and he was all muscle. But Zeke knew Samson wasn't going to move. Not while Delilah was being held.

"Now, Zeke, Gabe was my friend. He had some bad acquaintances, and he shot off his mouth too much, but I was mighty sorry to hear what happened to him. And it hurt me, hurt me bad, to hear about young Matthew running off to join up with them Yanks."

"Samson!"

He spun around at the sound of Kristin's voice. Just as she reached the steps, her voice rose in a sudden scream.

The horsemen had reached the steps, too and Kristin was trapped. She was choking in a cloud of dust as they circled her, chasing her back into the center of their trap every time she tried to elude them.

As Samson watched, she cried out and ran again. An Appaloosa ridden by a yellow-toothed scavenger in a railroad man's frock coat cut her off completely. She turned again, and the man rode closer, reaching down to sweep her up. She clawed at him, and Samson saw the blood run down the man's cheek. Kristin cursed and swore, fighting like a tigress. The Appaloosa reared and shrieked as its rider wrenched hard on the reins. The man struck out with a whip, and Kristin fell. As Samson watched, the Appaloosa reared again and again, its hooves just missing Kristin's face.

She didn't move, didn't flinch. She just stared up at the man, hatred in her eyes.

Samson charged toward the door, but Zeke stepped up behind him, slamming his head hard with the butt of his shotgun.

Kristin cried out as she saw him fall through the doorway, blood trickling down his forehead.

Then she saw Zeke. He stepped over Samson's body and onto the porch. A man came from behind, holding Delilah. She screamed, and the man laughed, then threw her down on top of Samson. Sobbing, she held her husband.

The horses around Kristin went still, and the men fell silent.

Kristin got to her feet and stared at the man. She even managed a semblance of a smile.

"Why, Mr. Moreau, what a pleasure." Her voice dripped with sarcasm.

Zeke Moreau let out a long sigh. "Dear, dear Kristin. It just never seems to cross that little mind of yours that you're in deep trouble, girl."

"Trouble, Zeke? I'm not in any trouble. Trouble is something that's hard to handle. You're just a fly to be swatted away, nothing more."

"Look around, Kristin. You know, you've always been a real sassy piece of baggage. The boys and me, we think it's about time you paid for that. You *are* in trouble, honey. Deep trouble." He started walking toward her.

Kristin held her ground. She'd never known what it was like to hate before. Not the way she hated Zeke. Her hatred for him was fierce and intense and desperate. She stared at him and suddenly she knew why he had come, knew why he was moving slowly, why he was smiling. This was vengeance, and he meant to savor it.

She didn't give a damn. She wasn't even really frightened. She knew that she would scratch and claw and fight just as long as she was still breathing, as long as her heart was still beating. He couldn't understand that she had already won. She had won because she hated him so much that he *couldn't* really touch her.

Zeke kept walking toward her, his smile still in place. "Fight me, Kristin," he said softly. "I like it that way."

"You disgust me," she hissed. She didn't tell him that he would pay, didn't threaten revenge. There was no law to make him pay, and whatever revenge she dealt out would have to be now.

"You know, once upon a time, I wanted to marry you. Yeah, I wanted to head out to the wild, wild west and make you my wife. I wanted to hit the gold fields out in California, and then I wanted to build you a fine house on a hill and make you into a real lady."

"I am a real lady, Zeke. But you're just dirt—and no amount of gold could make you anything but."

She raised her chin slightly. There was a hard core of fear inside her, she realized. This man didn't want her to die. He wanted her to pay. He wanted her to cry out in fear, wanted her to beg for mercy, and she was afraid that he could make her do it.

Zeke would never, never be prosecuted. No matter what he did to her.

He smiled and lunged toward her, and his men hooted and called from the backs of their mounts.

Kristin screamed. Then she grabbed a handful of the loose Missouri dirt, cast it into Zeke's eyes and turned to run.

The Appaloosa came at her again, with its dead-eyed rider. She tried to escape, but the animal reared, and she had to fall and roll to avoid its hoofs.

She heard Zeke swearing and turned to see that he was almost upon her again. The dirt clung to his face, clumps of it caught in his mustache.

She leaped up and spun toward him. The catcalls and whistles from the mounted men were growing louder and more raucous.

Escape was impossible. Zeke caught hold of her arms. She slammed her fists against his chest and managed to free herself. In a frenzy, she brought up her knee with a vengeance. Zeke let out a shrill cry of pain; his hold on her eased, and she broke free.

Someone laughed and before Kristin could gain her breath the back of Zeke's hand caught her. Her head swam, and she felt his hands on her again. Wildly, she scratched and kicked and screamed. Sounds rose all around her, laughter and catcalls and cheers. Her nails connected with flesh, and she clawed deeply. Zeke swore and slapped her again, so hard that she lost her balance and she fell.

He was quick. He straddled her while her head was still spinning. The hoots and encouraging cheers were growing louder and louder.

She gathered her strength and twisted and fought anew. Zeke used his weight against her while he tried to pin her wrists to the ground. Gasping for breath, she saw that while she might be losing, Zeke's handsome face was white, except for the scratches she had left on his cheek. He was in a cold, lethal rage, and he deliberately released his hold on her to slap her again with a strength that sent her mind reeling.

She couldn't respond at first. She was only dimly aware that he had begun to tear at her clothing, that her bodice was ripped and that he was shoving up her skirt. Her mind cleared, and she screamed, then began to fight again.

Zeke looked at her grimly. Then he smiled again. "Bitch," he told her softly. He leaned against her, trying to pin her mouth in a savage kiss while his hands roamed over her.

Kristin twisted her head, tears stinging her eyes. She could probably live through the rape. What she couldn't bear was the thought that he was trying to kiss her.

She managed to bite his lower lip.

He exploded into a sound of pure rage and jerked away, a thin line of blood trickling down his chin.

"You want it violent, honey?" he snarled. "That's the way you're going to get it then. Got that, Miss High-and-Mighty?"

He hitched up her skirt and touched her bare thigh, and she braced herself for the brutality of his attack, her eyes shut tight.

Just then the world seemed to explode. Dirt spewed all around her; she tasted it on her tongue.

Her eyes flew open, and she saw that though Zeke was still posed above her he seemed as disoriented as she was.

Even the men on horseback were silent.

A hundred yards away, stood a single horseman.

He wore a railroad man's frock coat, and his hat sat low over his forehead, a plumed feather extending from it.

He carried a pair of six-shooters, holding them with seeming nonchalance. Yet one had apparently just been fired. It had caused the noise that had sounded like an explosion in the earth. Along with the six-shooters, there was a rifle shoved into his saddle pack.

His horse, a huge sleek black animal, began to move closer in a smooth walk. Finally he paused, only a few feet away. Stunned, Kristin stared at him. Beneath the railroad coat he wore jeans and a cotton shirt and he had a scarf around his throat. He wasn't wearing the uniform of either army; he looked like a cattleman, a rancher, nothing more.

Or a gunfighter, Kristin thought, bewildered.

His face was chiseled, strong. His hair was dark, lightly dusted with gray. His mustache and beard were also silvered, and his eyes, beneath jet-black brows, were silvergray, the color of steel.

"Get away from her, boy," the stranger commanded Zeke. His voice was deep, rich. He spoke softly, but the sound carried. It was the voice of a man accustomed to being obeyed.

"Who's gonna make me?" Zeke snarled.

It was a valid question. After all, he was surrounded by his men, and the stranger was alone.

The man tipped his hat back from his forehead. "I'm telling you one more time, boy. Get off the lady. She doesn't seem to want the attention."

The sun slipped behind a cloud. The stranger suddenly seemed no more than a silhouette, an illusion of a man, atop a giant stallion.

Zeke made a sound like a growl, and Kristin realized that he was reaching for his Colt. She inhaled to scream.

She heard a sound of agony rend the air, but it wasn't hers. Blood suddenly streamed onto her chest. In amazement, she realized Zeke had cried out, and it was Zeke whose blood was dripping down on her. The stranger's bullet had struck him in the wrist.

"Fools!" Zeke shouted to his men. "Shoot the bastard."

Kristin did scream then. Twenty men reached for their weapons, but not one of them got off a shot.

The stranger moved quickly. Like double flashes of lightning, his six-shooters spat fire, and men fell.

When the shooting stopped, the stranger dismounted. His guns were back in his gun belt, but he carried a revolver as he walked slowly toward her.

He tipped his hat to Zeke. "I don't like killing, and I do my damnedest not to shoot a man in cold blood. Now, I'm telling you again. Get away from the lady. She doesn't want the attention."

Zeke swore and got to his feet. The two men stared at one another.

"I know you from somewhere," Zeke said.

The stranger reached down and tossed Zeke his discarded Colt. "Maybe you do." He paused for just a moment, arching one dark brow. "I think you've outworn your welcome here, don't you agree?"

Zeke reached down for his hat and dusted it furiously against his thigh, staring at the stranger. "You'll get yours, friend," he promised softly.

The stranger shrugged in silence, but his eyes were eloquent.

Zeke smiled cruelly at Kristin. "You'll get yours, too, sweetheart."

"If I were you," the stranger said softly, "I'd ride out of here now, while I still could."

Furiously, Zeke slammed his hat back on his head, then headed for one of the now riderless horses. He mounted the animal and started to turn away.

"Take your refuse with you." The stranger indicated the dead and wounded bodies on the ground.

Zeke nodded to his men. A number of them tossed the dead, wounded and dying onto the skittish horses.

"You'll pay," Zeke warned the stranger again. Then his mount leaped forward and he was gone. The stranger watched as the horses galloped away. Then he turned to Kristin and she felt color flood her face as she swallowed and clutched her torn clothing. She stumbled to her feet.

"Thank you," she said simply.

He smiled, and she found herself trembling. He didn't look away gallantly. He stared at her, not disguising his bold assessment.

She moistened her lips, willing her heart to cease its erratic beating. She tried to meet his eyes.

But she couldn't, and she flushed again.

The day was still again. The sun was bright, the sky blue. Was this the calm before the storm?

Or had some strange new storm begun? Kristin could sense something in the air, an elusive crackling, as if lightning were sizzling between them. Something tense and potent, searing into her senses.

And then he touched her, slipping his knuckles beneath her chin.

"Think you might offer a drifter a meal, Miss—"

"McCahy. Kristin McCahy," she offered softly.

"Kristin," he murmured. Then he smiled again. "I could use something to eat."

"Of course."

She couldn't stop staring at him now, searching out his eyes. She hoped fervently that he couldn't feel the way she was trembling.

He smiled again and brushed her fingers with a kiss. Kristin flushed furiously, suddenly aware that her breast was almost bare beneath her torn chemise and gown. She swallowed fiercely and covered herself.

He lowered his eyes, hiding a crooked smile. Then he indicated Samson, who was just coming to in the doorway. "I think we should see to your friend first, Kristin," he said.

Delilah stood up, trying to help Samson. "You come in, mister," she said. "I'll make you the best meal this side of the Mississippi. Miss Kristin, you get in here quick now, too. We'll get you some hot water and wash off the filth of that man."

Kristin nodded, coloring again. "Shannon?" She whispered softly to Delilah.

"Your sister's in the cellar. Things seem to be all right. Oh, yes, bless the heavens, things seem to be all right."

The stranger started toward the steps, and Kristin followed, watching his broad shoulders. But then she paused and shivered suddenly.

He had come out of nowhere, out of the dirt and dust of the plain, and he had saved her from disaster and despair.

But Zeke Moreau had ridden away alive.

And Zeke Moreau would surely ride back, once the stranger had ridden on and she was alone again.

It wasn't over. Zeke had come for her once, and he would come again. He wasn't fighting for Missouri, for the South, for the code of chivalry. He was in this to loot, to murder, to rob—and to rape. He would come back for her. He sought out his enemies when they were weak, and he would know when she was weak again.

They would have to leave, she thought. This was her home, the only home she could remember. This land was a dream, a dream realized by a poor Irish immigrant.

But that immigrant lay dead. Gabriel McCahy lay with his Kathleen in the little cemetery out back. He lay there with young Joe Jenley, who had tried to defend him. The dream was as dead as Pa.

She couldn't just give it up. She had to fight the Zeke Moreaus of the world. She just couldn't let Pa's death be in vain.

But she had fought, and she had lost.

She hadn't lost, not this time. The stranger had come.

Kristin straightened, squared her shoulders and looked after the tall, dark man who was moving up her steps with grace and ease. The man with the set of six-shooters and the shotgun. The man who had aimed with startling, uncanny precision and speed.

Who was he?

And then she knew it didn't matter, she just didn't care. Her eyes narrowed pensively.

And she followed the curious dark stranger into her house.

2

A fire burned warmly against the midmorning chill in the enormous kitchen. Even with her head back and her eyes closed, she could imagine everything Delilah was cooking from the aromas that surrounded her over the rose scent of her bath. Slab bacon sizzled in a frying pan along with hearty scrapple. There would be flapjacks, too, with melted butter and corn syrup. Delilah was also going to cook eggs in her special way, with chunks of ham and aged cheese. They were usually careful about food these days. If Quantrill's raiders didn't come looking to steal horses and cattle—or worse—the Union side would come around needing supplies. Kristin had long ago been stripped of all her illusions about the ethics of either side. There were men on both sides who claimed to be soldiers but were nothing but thieves and murderers. This wasn't a war; it was a melee, a bloody, desperate free-for-all.

It was amazing that the family still had enough to eat. There was the secret cellar, of course. That had saved them many a time. And today it didn't matter. Today, well, today they all deserved a feast.

The stranger deserved a feast.

The kitchen door was pushed open, and Kristin sank deeper into the bubbles that flourished in the elegant brass bathtub, an inheritance from Kristin's mother, who had dragged it all the way over from Bristol, in England.

She needn't have feared. It was only Delilah. "How you doin' there, child?" she demanded. She reached into the cabinet above the water pump and pulled out a bottle of Kristin's father's best Madeira. She set the bottle and a little tray of glasses on the counter and pulled the kettle off the kitchen fire to add more steaming water to Kristin's bath.

Kristin looked into Delilah's dark eyes. "I feel like I'm never going to get clean, Delilah. Never. Not if I wash from here to doomsday."

Delilah poured out the last of the water, warming Kristin's toes. Then she straightened and set the kettle down on the hearth. She walked over to the stove to check the bacon and the scrapple. "It could have been a lot worse," she said softly, staring out the window at the now deceptively peaceful day. "Thank the Lord for small miracles." She looked back at Kristin. "You hurry up there, huh, honey?"

Kristin nodded and even managed a small smile. "Do we have a name on him yet?"

The kitchen door burst open again. Kristin shrank back and Delilah swung around. It was Shannon, looking flushed, pretty and very excited.

"Kristin! You aren't out of there yet?"

Kristin looked at her sister, and she didn't know whether to be exasperated or relieved. She was still shaken by the events of the morning, but Shannon had put them all behind her. Of course, Shannon had been down in the cellar. And that was what Kristin had wanted. It seemed that everyone here had lost their innocence. The war didn't let you just stay neutral. Man or woman, a body had to choose a side, and you survived by becoming jaded and hardened. She didn't want that for Shannon. She wanted her sister to retain a certain belief in magic, in fantasy. Shannon had turned seventeen not long ago, and she deserved to be able to believe in innocence. She was so young, so soft, so pretty. Blue-eyed and golden blond, a vision of beauty and purity. Kristin didn't think she'd ever looked like that. When she looked at herself in the mirror she knew that the lines and planes and angles of her face were hard, and that her eyes had taken on an icy edge. She knew she looked much older than eighteen.

She had aged ten years in the last two. Desperation had taught her many lessons, and she knew they showed in her face.

"I'm coming out in just a minute, Shannon," Kristin assured her sister.

"Slater," Delilah said.

"Pardon?" Kristin asked her.

"Slater." Shannon came over to the bathtub, kneeling beside it and resting her elbows on the edge. "His name is Cole Slater."

"Oh," Kristin murmured. Cole Slater. She rolled the name around in her mind. Well, that had been easy enough. Why had she thought it would be so difficult to drag the man's name out of him?

Shannon jumped to her feet. "Kristin's never coming out of this old tub. Shall I get the Madeira, Delilah?"

"Sounds like someone's got an admirer," Kristin murmured.

"I'm trying to be polite," Shannon said indignantly. She arranged the little glasses on a silver serving tray. "Honest, Kristin, he's a right courteous fellow, and he told me I shouldn't rush you, says he understands you might feel you need a long, long wash. But I think you're just plain old rude and mean. And you know what else I think? I think you're afraid of him."

Kristin narrowed her eyes at her sister, tempted to jump from the tub and throttle her. But it was far more serious than that. "I'm not afraid of Zeke Moreau, or even Bill Quantrill and all his raiders, Shannon. I just have a healthy respect for their total lack of justice and morality. I'm not afraid of this drifter, either."

"But you *are* beholden to him," Delilah reminded her softly.

"I'm sorry," Shannon murmured.

When Kristin looked at her sister, she saw the pain that welled up in her eyes, and she was sorry herself. Shannon had lived through the same horrors she had. She just wasn't the eldest. She wasn't the one with the responsibility.

She smiled at Shannon. "Bring the Madeira on in, will you please? I'll be right out."

Shannon smiled, picked up the tray and went out of the kitchen. Kristin grinned at Delilah. "Pa's Madeira, huh? You must think highly of this drifter."

Delilah sniffed as she fluffed out the clean petticoat she'd brought down from Kristin's room. She sent Kristin a quick glare. "He ain't no ordinary drifter. We both know that. And you bet I think highly of him. Moreau might—just might—have left you alive, but he'd have hanged Samson. Slater kept my husband alive and he kept me from the block at the slave market. You bet I think highly of him."

Kristin grinned. From what she remembered of her lovely and aristocratic mother, she knew Kathleen McCahy would have been shocked by such blunt language. Not Pa, though. Pa had made himself a rancher and a farmer; he'd learned all the rough edges of the frontier. He'd have laughed at the plain truth of her statement. Then he'd have been grateful to have Delilah safe and sound, because she and Samson were part of the family, too.

"Want to hand me a towel, Delilah?" Kristin said, thinking again about the stranger who had arrived among them just in the nick of time. No, he wasn't any ordinary drifter, not judging by the way he handled a weapon. What was he, then? A gunslinger from down Texas way, maybe? Perhaps he'd come from farther west—from California, maybe. Somewhere he'd learned to make an art of the use of his Colts.

He made an art of the simple act of walking, too, she thought. She shivered suddenly, remembering the silence that had followed the sudden burst of gunfire. She remembered the way his eyes had looked as he'd ordered Zeke away from her. Slate-gray eyes, steel eyes, hard and merciless. She remembered the way his frock coat had fallen along the length of his tall body, remembered his broad shoulders, remembered the way he'd looked at her. A heat that didn't come from the water seemed to flutter to life deep inside her.

It hadn't been a romantic look, she reminded herself. She knew about romantic looks. She knew about falling in love. It was easy and gentle. It was slow and beautiful. It was the way she had felt about Adam, and it was the way he had felt about her. When he had looked at her, he had looked into her eyes. He had held her hand, awkwardly at first. He had stuttered sometimes when he had spoken to her, and he had whispered tenderly to her. That was romance. That was love. She had never felt this shameful burning inside when she had been with Adam. She had been content to hold his hand. They had been content to sit and dream. She had never once imagined him . . . naked.

Appalled by her thoughts, she swallowed hard. She hadn't imagined any man naked, and certainly not this stranger. No, he had not given her any romantic looks. What he had given her was an assessment. It had been just as if he were studying a horse and liked what he saw, good bones and decent teeth. And then he had smiled, if not tenderly, at least with a certain gentility.

Still, the way he had looked at her . . .

And he had seen her nearly naked.

Color seemed to wash over her body. She rose to reach for her towel, then fell back into the water again, shamed by the way her breasts swelled and her nipples hardened. She prayed that Delilah hadn't noticed.

"You cold?" Delilah asked her.

Delilah had noticed.

Kristin quickly wrapped the big towel around herself. "A little," she lied.

"Get over by the fire. Dry off good and I'll help you get your clothes on."

Kristin nodded, rubbing her pink flesh dry. The fire warmed her, the flames nearly touching her. At least she would have an excuse for being red.

When she was finished she sank into the old rocker by the fire and Delilah brought over her corset, pantalets and stockings. Kristin quickly slid into the knit stockings and pantalets, and Delilah ordered her to hold her breath while she tied up the corset.

Kristin arched a tawny brow when she saw the dress Delilah had brought down for her. It wasn't one of her usual cotton day dresses. It was muslin, with soft blue flowers and double rows of black-and-white lace edging along the puff sleeves, the bodice and the hem. It was one of her best dresses.

"Delilah—"

"Put it on, child, put it on. We are celebrating here, remember?"

"Oh, yes." Kristin grinned, but then she started to shiver again. She was afraid she was going to burst into tears. They were never going to be done with it. They couldn't ignore it, and they couldn't accept it. Pa had been murdered, and the same—or worse—could have happened today. Today could have been the end of everything.

They had been saved today, but it was only temporary. Zeke would be back.

"Lordy, Lordy," Delilah said. She and Kristin hugged one another, holding tight.

"What are we going to do?" Delilah said.

"We—we have to convince him to stay around a while," Kristin said softly.

"Think he needs a job, maybe?" Delilah said hopefully.

"Does he look like he needs a job?" Kristin said, smiling shakily as she pulled away. She turned her back to Delilah. "Hook me up, please."

Delilah started with the hooks, sweeping Kristin's bountiful hair out of the way. When she was done she stepped back, swirling Kristin around. She surveyed her broadly, then gave her a big smile. "Miss Kristin, you're the prettiest little thing I ever did see!"

Kristin flushed. She didn't feel pretty these days. She felt tired and old and worn most of the time.

"Brush your hair now. Your little Chinese slippers are by the door. Slip them on. And go out there and see what else you can find out about that man beyond his name."

"Yes, yes," Kristin murmured. Delilah searched her pockets for a brush. Kristin stood on tiptoes to stare into the small mirror on the kitchen door. She combed out her hair, leaving it thick and free and a little wild. She looked too pale, she thought. She pinched her cheeks and bit her lip. Then she thought about the man beyond the door again and all the color she could have wanted flooded into her face.

"Thanks," she said, handing the brush back to Delilah. Then she pushed the door open and hurried out.

She went through the family dining room first. Ma had always wanted a dining room, not just a table in the middle of everything else, as in so many ranch homes. Dining rooms were very proper, Ma had thought. And it was nice, Kristin decided now. The Chippendale table was covered with a lace cloth and with Ma's best silver, crystal and Royal Doulton plates. The table was set for three. The four young ranch hands they had remaining ate in the bunkhouse and she couldn't let a stranger know that she and Shannon usually just sat down with Samson and Delilah. Of course, they didn't use the silver or the crystal or the Royal Doulton every day, either.

After the dining room she came to the parlor. There was another big fireplace here, and a braided rug before it, over the hardwood floor. Large windows looked out on the sunshine. Ma had liked things bright, even though there were heavy velvet-and-lace curtains in crimson softened by white that could be closed at sunset to hold in the warmth. The furniture here was elegant, a small settee, a daybed and fine wood chairs, and a spinet that both girls had learned to play. It was a beautiful room, meant more for a lady than for a man. Kristin knew she would find the stranger and her sister in the next room, Pa's office and library. That was a far more comfortable room, with rows of books, a huge oak desk and a pair of deacon's benches that drew up to the double-sided fireplace.

Kristin was right. When she came through the parlor doorway, she saw that the stranger—no, Cole, his name was Cole Slater, and she had to stop thinking of him as the stranger—was indeed in this room. It was a great room. It smelled of pipe tobacco and fine leather, and it would always remind her of her father.

Cole Slater looked good here, as if he fit the place. He'd removed his plumed hat, his spurs and his railroad coat. Kristin paused, annoyed that she was trembling again just at the sight of him. He was a handsome man, she thought, though not in any usual way. He was far from pretty, but his steel-gray eyes were arresting, and what his face lacked in actual beauty it made up in strength. It was fine-boned yet powerful, sensual yet hard. And Kristin thought that she saw still more in his face. Cole Slater was another one who had lost all his illusions. She saw it when their eyes met. She studied him, and it was several long moments before she realized that he was studying her, too.

His knee was up, and his booted foot was resting against one of the footstools that seemed to have been cast haphazardly alongside the rows of books in the study. His boots were high, like cavalry-issue boots. His trousers hugged his long legs, betraying the lean muscles there, the trim line of his hips and the contours of his strong thighs and buttocks. His shoulders were broad, and he was tightly sinewed, and yet, he gave the appearance of being lean. A tuft of dark hair showed where his shirt lay open below his throat, and Kristin thought that his chest must be heavily matted with it.

Then she saw that his gaze was resting on her chest, too, and that just the hint of a smile was playing at the corners of his mouth. She almost lowered her lashes. Almost. She kept her eyes level with his and raised her chin a fraction. Then she inclined her head toward the glass of Pa's that he held—the little pony glass seemed ridiculously small contrasted with the size of his bronzed hand and the length of his fingers—and smiled graciously. "I see that Shannon has been taking good care of you."

He grinned at Shannon, who sat on one of the deacon's benches with a happy smile glued to her features. "Your sister is a most courteous and charming hostess."

Shannon colored with pleasure at the compliment. Then she laughed and jumped to her feet with the curious combination of grace and clumsiness that always reminded Kristin of a young colt. "I'm trying, anyway," she said. "And you two haven't been properly introduced. Miss Kristin McCahy, I give you Mr. Cole Slater. Mr. Slater, my sister, Miss Kristin McCahy."

Cole Slater stepped forward. He took Kristin's hand, and his eyes met hers just before his head lowered and his lips touched her hand. "I'm charmed, Miss McCahy. Quite charmed."

"Mr. Slater," she returned. She tried to place his accent, but she couldn't. He didn't sound as if he came from the deep South, and he didn't sound as if he came from any of the New England states. He wasn't a foreigner, but he didn't speak with the twang of the midwesterner, either.

He was still holding her hand. There was a feeling of warmth where his lips had touched her flesh, and the sensation seemed to seep into her, to enter into her bloodstream and head straight for the coil of liquid heat that churned indecently near the very apex of her thighs.

She pulled her hand away.

"We really don't know how to thank you, you know," she said, remaining still and seeking out his eyes again.

"I don't want to be thanked. I stumbled along at the right moment, that's all. And I'm damned hungry, and everything cooking smells damned good. A meal will make us even."

Kristin raised a brow. "You'll forgive me if I find my life, my friends, my sister, my sanity, my—"

"Chastity?" he offered bluntly.

"My person," she returned quietly, "are worth far more than a meal."

"Well, now..." He set his empty glass down, watching her thoughtfully. "I reckon that you are worth much, much more, Miss McCahy. Still, life isn't like a trip to the dry-goods store. I don't sell my services for any price. I was glad to be here when I was needed. If I helped you—"

"You know that you helped me. You saved all of us."

"All right. I helped you. It was my pleasure."

His voice matched his eyes. It wasn't quite a baritone, but it was still deep and full of the same hard, steely confidence. A drifter, a man who knew his guns. He had faced death out there today almost callously. Where did such a man come from?

Kristin stepped back. He was a tall man, more than six feet, and she was no more than five foot two. She felt more comfortable when there was a little distance between them.

And distance helped keep her heart from pounding, helped keep her blood from racing. Dismayed, she wondered what it was about him that made her feel this way. She never had before, not even with Adam.

Of course, not even Shannon could be completely innocent here. This was a working ranch, after all. Her father's prize bulls were the most valuable possessions he had left behind, and no matter how many of their cattle were stolen, Kristin knew they could start over with the bulls. But because of them and the other animals on the ranch, none of them could escape the details of the act of procreation.

Of course, watching the bulls made it all seem horribly crude. And nearly falling prey to the likes of Zeke Moreau made the bulls look like gentlemen of quality. She had never—never—imagined that a woman could actually wonder about what it would be like with a man, think about his hands touching her, think of his lips touching places other than her mouth.

She wanted to scream. She wondered suddenly if Cole could read her mind, for he was smiling again, and his smile seemed to reach into the heart and soul and heat of her. He knew.

She scowled and spun around, forgetting that he had saved her from a fate worse than death.

"I believe the meal that is worth so much to you is just about on the table, Mr. Slater. Shannon . . . let's all come along, shall we?"

Cole Slater followed his hostess through the parlor and into the formal dining room, suddenly and keenly aware of the soft scent of roses wafting from her flesh.

Then he noted that the fragrant flesh was as soft and smooth and tempting as cream silk. Her hair, loose around her shoulders, was like spun gold. And her eyes were level and filled with a surprising wisdom.

She was a very beautiful woman.

Outside, not so long ago, he had seen her differently. He had seen the Missouri dirt that had clung to her, and he had seen her spirit, but he had seen someone very young then. A girl, over-powered but fighting madly. Memory had clouded his vision, and he had seen the world through a brilliant red explosion.

He should have killed the bastard. No matter what his own past, no matter his codes when it came to dealing out death, that was one bastard he should have killed. Zeke Moreau. He had recognized Cole. Well, Cole had recognized Zeke, too. Zeke was one of the creatures that had been bred here in this den of blood, creatures that could shoot an unarmed man right between the eyes without blinking.

Zeke wanted this girl bad. No, this woman, he thought, correcting himself. She really wasn't a child. What was she? Twenty, perhaps? Older? Her eyes spoke of age, and so did the grace of her movements, and the confidence with which she spoke.

She was built like a woman.

Longing, hard and desperate, like a lightning bolt out of a clear blue sky, suddenly twisted and seared into him, straight into his groin, with a red-hot heat that was even painful.

He was glad he was walking behind her and Shannon. And he was glad his button-fly trousers were tight.

He clenched his teeth as another pain sizzled and burned in the area around his heart. This was a decent woman, this girl who had fought a strong man so desperately. Decent and still innocent, he imagined—thanks to his timely arrival.

This was the kind of girl men married.

Exhaling through clenched teeth, Cole wondered if there was a bordello anywhere nearby. He doubted it. There was probably a cold river somewhere, though. He would eat and then head out and hit that river.

Damn her, he thought suddenly, savagely. So she was innocent—maybe. The way she had looked at him had been too naked. He had seen too many things in her eyes. Too much that was sensual and tempting. He could have sworn she had been wondering about things that she shouldn't have been wondering about.

He would eat and then get out. And he would bear in mind that his range of experience far surpassed hers. Did she think she could play cat and mouse with him? She might not know it, but she was the mouse.

Still, when she seated herself at the head of the table, he felt the lightning again. It filled the air when she spoke. It raced through him when she lightly brushed her fingers over his hand as she reached for the butter. It filled him when their knees brushed beneath the table.

"So…" She handed him a plate of flapjacks. "Where do you hail from, Mr. Slater?"

Kristin watched as the stranger helped himself to the flapjacks. He buttered them lavishly, then poured what seemed like a gallon of syrup over them. He shoveled a forkful into his mouth, chewed and swallowed, then answered her.

"Oh, here and there."

Here and there. Kristin sat back, dissatisfied.

Delilah came into the room, bringing more coffee. "Mr. Slater," she said, filling his cup again, "can I get you anything else?"

"Thank you, Delilah, no. This is one of the finest meals I've ever had."

Delilah smiled as if someone had just given her the crown jewels. Kristin sent her a glare over Cole's bowed head as he sipped his coffee.

Delilah nudged her firmly. Kristin sighed inwardly, and her eyes answered Delilah's unspoken question. She knew as well as Delilah that they needed Cole Slater.

"Where are you heading, Mr. Slater?" she asked.

He shrugged. "Just drifting at the moment, Miss McCahy."

"Well," Kristin toyed idly with her fork. "You certainly did drift into the right place for us this morning, sir."

He sat back, studying her in a leisurely fashion. "Well, ma'am, like I said, I'm right glad to be of service." She thought that was all he was going to say, but then he leaned forward, his elbows on the table, his steel-gray eyes on hers.

"How did you get on the wrong side of this Moreau man?" He paused again, just for a split second. "Isn't he one of Quantrill's boys?"

Kristin nodded.

Shannon explained, "She turned him down, that's what happened. Pa used to know Quantrill. The bastard—"

"Shannon!" Kristin protested.

Shannon ignored her. "They act like he's Jesus Christ come back to life, some places in the South—"

"Shannon! What would Pa say! You're supposed to be a lady!"

Shannon grimaced in exasperation and submitted reluctantly to Kristin's chastisement. "Oh, all right! But Mr.

Slater, Quantrill is a bloody traitor, that's all!'' She insisted. "He used to be a jayhawker out of Kansas, preying on the Southerners! Then he led a band of abolitionists down here, pretended he was spying out the terrain and turned on his own people! He got out of it by passing out a lie about his older brother being killed by jayhawkers. He didn't have an older brother, but those stupid fools fell for it!''

Kristin looked at her plate. "Quantrill is a murderer," she said softly. "But he usually leaves women alone. He won't let them be murdered."

"But Zeke would," Shannon said. "Zeke would kill anybody. He wants to kill Kristin now, just because she turned him down. She was in love with Adam, you see."

"Adam?"

"Shannon!"

"Adam, Adam Smith. Adam was like Pa. He had no stake in this war. He just wanted to be a rancher. But when the bushwhackers came and killed Pa, Adam went out with a group of jayhawkers to find Zeke's boys. Kristin didn't know about it, not until they sent her back his horse. They killed him down southwest somewhere, and we don't even know where they left his bones. At least Pa is buried out back."

Kristin felt his eyes on her again. She looked up, but that steel-hard gaze was unreadable.

"So this was no random raid here today," he said. It was a statement, not a question.

"No," Kristin admitted. She felt as if she were holding her breath. He must realize that once he left they were all at the mercy of Zeke's bushwhackers again.

"You should get out," he told her.

"What?"

"You should get out. Pack your bags, get some kind of an escort and get the hell out."

It was a cold, callous statement. But what could she say in reply? He had stumbled upon them and he had saved her, but it had happened almost by accident. He didn't owe her a thing. She already owed him.

"I can't get out. My father died for this land. I owe it to him to keep it for him."

"To keep it for what? Your father is dead, and if you stay you'll probably wind up that way, too."

"That's all you can say?"

"What do you want me to say? I can't change this war, and I can't change the truth. Trust me. I would if I could."

For the first time she heard the bitterness in his voice. She wondered briefly about his past, but then she saw that he was rising, and panic filled her. He couldn't be about to ride away.

She stood. "You're not leaving?"

He shook his head. "I saw a few cigars in your father's study. Mind if I take one out back?"

Kristin shook her head, speechless. He wasn't leaving. Not yet.

She heard his footsteps as he walked through the dining room, heard them soften as he walked over the braided rug by the stairs. A moment later she heard the back door open and close.

"Kristin, are you all right?"

Kristin saw that Shannon was watching her, grave concern in her eyes.

"You're all pale," she said.

Kristin smiled, biting her lower lip and shaking her head. She squeezed Shannon's hand. "Help Delilah with the chores, won't you?"

Shannon nodded. Kristin turned around and followed the path the stranger had taken out of the house.

He was out back, puffing on one of her father's fine Havana cigars, leaning against the corral and watching as a yearling raced along beside its mother.

He heard Kristin and turned his fathomless gray gaze on her as she approached. He waited, his eyes hooded and curious.

Kristin wasn't at all sure how to say what she had to say. She folded her hands behind her back and walked over to him with what she hoped was an easy smile. Once she had thought she had the power to charm the male of the species. Once. She had been able to laugh and tease and flirt, and at any dance she had been breathless and busy, in unending demand.

Those days seemed so long ago now. Now she felt very young, and totally unsure of herself.

She had charmed boys, she realized. This was a man.

Still, she came over to him, leaning against the wooden gate of the corral.

"It's a good ranch," she told him.

He stared at her relentlessly, she thought. He didn't let a woman use her wiles. He didn't let her smile or flirt or tease.

"It's a good ranch," he agreed.

"Did I tell you just how much we appreciate your timely arrival here?"

"Yes, you did." He hiked himself up suddenly and sat on the gate, staring down at her. "Spit it out, Miss McCahy," he demanded, his eyes hard. "You've got something to say. Say it."

"My, my, you are a discerning man," she murmured.

"Cut the simpering belle act, Kristin. It isn't your style."

She flashed him an angry glance and started to turn away.

"Stop, turn around and tell me what you want!" he ordered her. He was a man accustomed to giving commands, she realized. And he was a man accustomed to his commands being obeyed.

Well, she wasn't going to obey him. She had paused, but she straightened her shoulders now and started to walk away.

She heard his boots strike the dirt softly, but she didn't realize he had pursued her until she felt his strong hands on her shoulders, whirling her around to face him. "What do you want, Miss McCahy?" he demanded.

She felt his hands, felt his presence. It was masculine and powerful. He smelled of leather and fine Madeira and her father's fine Havana cigar. He towered over her, and she wanted to turn away, and she wanted to touch the hard planes of his face and open his shirt and see the dark mat of hair that she knew must cover his chest.

"I want you to stay."

He stared at her, his eyes wary, guarded. "I'll stay until you can get some kind of an escort out of here."

"No." Her mouth had gone very dry. She couldn't speak. She wet her lips. She felt his eyes on her mouth. "I—I want you to stay on until—until I can do something about Zeke."

"Someone needs to kill Zeke."

"Exactly."

There was a long, long pause. He released her shoulders, looking her up and down. "I see," he said. "You want me to go after Zeke and kill him for you."

Kristin didn't say anything.

"I don't kill in cold blood," he told her.

She wanted to lower her eyes. She had to force herself to keep meeting his demanding gaze.

"I—I can't leave this ranch. I can give you a job—"

"I don't want a job."

"I—" She paused, then plunged on desperately. "I can make it worth your while."

He arched a brow. Something brought a smile to his lips, and suddenly his face was arrestingly handsome. He was younger than she had thought at first, too. But then he was talking again.

"You—you're going to make it worth my while."

She nodded, wishing she could hit him, wishing he would quit staring at her so, as if she were an unproved racehorse.

"Come here," he said.

"What?"

"Come here."

"I—I am here."

"Closer."

He touched her. His hands on her shoulders, he dragged her to him. She felt the steely hardness of his body, felt its heat and vibrancy. Through his pants and through all her clothing she felt the male part of him, vital and pulsing, against the juncture of her thighs. She still stared at him, wide-eyed, speechless, her breasts crushed hard against his chest as he held her.

He smiled crudely. Then his lips touched hers.

Curiously, the touch was very, very light. She thought she might pass out from the feel of it, so startling, so appealing. His lips were molded to hers....

Then hunger soared, and his tongue pressed between her teeth, delving deep, filling her mouth. She was engulfed as his mouth moved over hers, his lips taking hers, his tongue an instrument that explored her body boldly and intimately. Her breasts seemed to swell and she felt her nipples harden and peak almost painfully against his chest. He savaged her mouth, moving his tongue as indecently as he might have moved another part of his hard body...

Something inside her exploded deliciously. Heat coursed through her, filling her. She could not meet the power of his kiss, but she had no desire to fight it. It was shameful, maybe more shameful than what had happened to her this morning.

Because she wanted it.

She savored the stream of liquid sensations that thrilled throughout her body. Her knees shook, and the coil deep inside her abdomen that was so much a part of her womanhood seemed to spiral to a peak, higher and higher. She wanted to touch him. To bring her fingers against him, exploring. To touch him as his tongue so insinuatingly invaded all the wet crevices of her mouth...

Then he released her. He released her so suddenly that she nearly fell, and he had to hold her again to steady her.

He stared down at her. Her lips were wet and swollen, and her eyes were glazed. He was furiously angry with himself.

"Worthwhile?" he asked.

Kristin's mind was reeling. What did he mean?

"You don't even know how to kiss," he told her.

"What?" she whispered, too stunned to recognize the anger rising inside her.

"I'm sorry," he said. His voice was softer now.

"Damn you!" Kristin said. "I'll make a bargain with you! If you'll just stay—"

"Stop it!" he said harshly. "I'm sorry. I just don't have the time or the patience for a silly little virgin."

"What?" She stepped back, her hands on her hips, and stared at him. The insolence of him! She wanted to scream and she wanted to cry.

"I don't want a love affair, Miss McCahy. When I do want something, it's a woman, and it seldom matters who she is, just so long as she's experienced and good at what she does. Understand?"

"Oh yes, I understand. But I need help. I need you. Doesn't that mean anything?"

"I told you, I don't want a virgin—"

"Well then, excuse me for an hour, will you?" Kristin snapped, her eyes blazing. "I'll just run on out and screw the first cowhand—oh!"

She broke off in shock as he wrenched her hard against him. "Shut up! Where the hell did you come up with language like that?" he demanded heatedly.

"Let me go! It's none of your business! It's a rough world here, Slater!" she flailed desperately against him. He didn't feel her fists, and he didn't even realize that she was kicking him.

"Don't ever let me hear you say anything like that again!"

"Who do you think you are, my father?" Kristin demanded. She was very close to bursting into tears, and she was determined not to, not here, not now—not anywhere near this drifter. He had made her feel as young and naive and foolish and lost as Shannon. "Let me go!"

"No, I'm not your father. I'm a total stranger you're try-ing to drag into bed," he said.

"Forget it. Just release me and—"

"You just stop, Miss McCahy!" He gave her a firm, hard shake, then another. At last Kristin stopped fighting. Her head fell back, her hair trailing like soft gold over his fin-gers, her eyes twin pools of blue fire as she stared into the iron-gray hardness of his.

"Give me some time," he said to her very softly, in a tone that caused her to tremble all over again. "I'll think about your proposition."

"What?" she whispered warily.

He released her carefully. "I said, Miss McCahy, that I would think about your proposition. I'll stay tonight. I'll take my blanket out to the bunkhouse, and I'll give you an answer in the morning." He inclined his head toward her, turned on his heel and started off toward the house.

3

When she walked back into the house, Kristin was in a cold fury. She didn't see Cole Slater anywhere, and for the moment she was heartily glad.

He had humiliated her, plain and simple. She'd been willing to sell honor, her pride, her dignity—and he hadn't even been interested in what she'd had to sell. She wished fervently that she wasn't so desperate. She'd have given her eyeteeth to tell the man that he was a filthy gunslinger, no better than all the others.

Yet even as she thought of what she'd like to be able to say to him, she realized it would be a lie. He'd saved her from Zeke, from the man who had murdered her father. She owed him.

And she'd paid, she thought drily. With humiliation.

Shannon wasn't around when Kristin reached the dining room. Delilah was there, though, humming a spiritual as she carefully picked up the fine crystal and china on the table. She glanced Kristin's way curiously and kept humming.

"Where's Shannon?" Kristin asked.

"Out feeding the chickens," Delilah said.

Kristin decided to help clear away the remains of the meal, but when her fingers clenched too tightly around a plate, Delilah rescued it from her grip. "Sorry," Kristin muttered.

"Kristin, for the sake of your mama's fine things, you go do something else here this morning, hm?"

Kristin stepped away from the table, folding her hands behind her back.

"You didn't ask where Mr. Slater had gotten himself off to," Delilah said.

"I don't care where Mr. Slater has gotten himself off to," Kristin replied sweetly.

Delilah shot her a quick glance. "The man saved our lives," she said sharply.

Kristin strode furiously across the room to look out the window. "He saved our lives . . . and he really doesn't give a damn."

"He's riding out?"

Kristin exhaled slowly. She could see Shannon by the barn, tossing feed to the chickens. If she had any sense she would leave. Shannon was precious to her, just as Delilah and Samson were. She should do whatever was necessary to protect them.

But the dream was precious, too. The dream and the land. And where would she go if she did leave? She could never embrace the Southern cause—she had been treated too cruelly by the bushwhackers here for that—nor could she turn against Missouri and move into Yankee territory. She wanted desperately to fight, but she was helpless.

It didn't matter where she went, Richmond, Virginia or Washington, D.C. Nowhere was life as cruel and violent as it was here on the border of "bleeding Kansas." Nowhere else did men murder each other so callously.

"Kristin?" Delilah said.

"Slater . . ." Kristin murmured. Her pride was wounded, she realized. She had offered up her finest prize—herself— and he had informed her crudely that he wasn't interested.

"Kristin, if you're mad at that man for something, you remember the rest of us here. You understand me, missy?" Delilah came toward her, waving a fork. Kristin tried not to smile, because Delilah was deadly serious. "Quantrill's men get ahold of us and they'll think nothing of a hanging. You saw what they did to your pa. I got a baby boy, Kristin, and—"

"Oh, Delilah, stop! I'm doing my best!" Kristin protested. She tried to smile encouragingly. She couldn't quite admit to Delilah yet that she had offered her all and that it hadn't been enough. She hadn't even tempted the man.

She clenched her teeth together. She'd like to see him desperate, his tongue hanging out. She'd like to see him pining for her and be in the position to put her nose in the air, cast him a disdainful glance and sweep right on by. Better yet, she'd like to laugh in his face. If it hadn't been for this war, she could have done just that. She could have had any rich young rancher in the territory. She could have had—

Adam. She could have had Adam. A numbing chill took hold of her. Adam had loved her so much, and so gently. Tall and blond and beautiful, with green eyes that had followed her everywhere, and an easy, tender smile.

Adam was dead. The war had come, and Adam was dead, and she had few choices. Yes, Slater had humiliated her. But part of it was the fire. Part of it was the feeling that he had embedded in her, the hot, shameful longing for something she didn't know and didn't understand. She had loved Adam, but she had never felt this way when she had been near him. Never. Cole Slater *did* frighten her. She didn't like the feelings he evoked in her. They shattered her belief in her own strength.

"Cole Slater is staying tonight," she told Delilah.

"Well, glory be!"

"No, no," Kristin said. "He's bunking with the hands for the night. He'll, uh, he'll probably be gone by morning."

"By morning?" Delilah repeated blankly. "Kristin, I don't want to suggest anything that ain't proper, but chil', I'm just sure that if you tried being friendly to the man..."

"Delilah," Kristin murmured, her sense of humor returning at last, "I'm sure I don't remember what proper is anymore. I tried. Honest to God, I tried." She shrugged.

"I'm not going to do you any good around here. I'll see you in a bit, huh?"

She hurried toward the stairs, giving Delilah a quick kiss on the cheek as she passed. She felt the older woman's worried gaze follow her, but by the time she reached the landing, she had forgotten about her.

The house felt so empty now.

Delilah and Samson and their baby had the rooms on the third floor. Kristin's and Shannon's were here on the second floor. But Matthew's room was empty now, as was the big master bedroom where her father and mothers had slept. The two guest rooms were empty, too. They hadn't entertained guests in a long, long time.

Kristin walked down the hallway, not toward her own room but toward the room that had been her parents'. She opened the door, stood there and smiled slowly. Her mother had been dead for years, but her father had been unable to part with the big Bavarian sleigh bed that his wife had so cherished. After her death he'd slept in it alone. And it was beautiful still. Delilah kept the mahogany polished and the bedding clean, as if she expected Pa to come back anytime.

Kristin walked into the room. There were giant armoires on either side of the window. One still held Pa's clothes, and the other still held her mother's.

We don't take to change easily here, Kristin thought. She smiled. It was the Irish blood, Pa had always told her. They were too sentimental. But that was good. It was good to hold on to the past. It helped keep the dream alive. Someday Pa's grandchildren would have this room. Matthew's children, probably.

If Matthew survived the war. It couldn't be easy for him, a Southern boy fighting in the Yankee army.

Kristin turned away. If Zeke Moreau had his way, none of them would survive the war. And when he was done torturing and killing, he would burn the house to the ground.

She started to close the door. Then she hesitated and turned back. She could suddenly see Cole Slater stretched

out on that sleigh bed. It was a big bed, plenty big enough
for his height and for the breadth of his shoulders. She could
imagine him there, smiling lazily, negligently. Then suddenly, a whirlwind, a tempest of heat and fire . . .

She gritted her teeth, closed her eyes tightly and swore.
She was sick of thinking about Cole Slater, and she was sick
of remembering how grateful she had to be to a man who
made her feel this way.

She slammed the door to her parents' room and hurried
to her own. She threw her good dress on her bed and did
likewise with her silk slippers and her corset. She slipped on
a chemise, a cotton shirt, a pair of breeches and her high
leather boots, and headed straight for the stables. She didn't
bother with a saddle, but grabbed a bridle from a hook off
the wall for Debutante and slipped into the stall to find her
horse.

Debutante was an Arabian mare, a gift to Pa from one of
the men he'd done business with in Chicago. She was a
chestnut with white stockings, a deep dish in her nose and a
tail that rode as high as the sun. Kristin loved her. She was
amazed that the horse hadn't been stolen yet, but so far she
had managed to have the horse out in the far pasture when
the various raiding parties had swept through.

"Hello, you beautiful thing," Kristin whispered as she
slipped the bit into the mare's mouth. Debutante nudged
her. Kristin stroked the horse's velevety nose, then leaped on
her back. Debutante nudged the stall door open, and Kristin gave her free rein as they left the stables behind.

It felt good to ride. It was good to feel the wind strike her
cheeks, to feel the coolness of the air as it rushed by her. She
was glad she had come bareback. She could feel the power
of the animal beneath her, the rhythm of her smooth gallop, the great constriction and release of superbly toned
muscle. Kristin leaned close to Debutante's neck. The
horse's mane whipped back, stinging her cheeks, but she
laughed with delight, glad simply to be alive.

Then Kristin realize she was being followed.

She wasn't sure how she knew she was being followed, except that there was an extra beat to the rhythm churning the earth, something that moved in discord.

She tried to look behind her. Her hair swept into her face, nearly blinding her.

There was a rider behind her. A lone figure, riding hard.

Panic seized her. She was already riding like the wind. How much harder could she drive the mare?

"Debutante! Please! We must become the wind!" She locked her knees more tightly against the animal's flanks. They were moving still faster now. The Arabian mare was swift and graceful, but the horse behind them seemed to be swifter. Either that, or Debutante's stamina was fading.

"Please!"

Kristin leaned closer to the mare's neck. She conjured up a mental image of the terrain. Adam had once owned this land. Ahead, just to the right, was a forest of tall oaks. She could elude her pursuer there.

The trees loomed before her. She raced the mare into the forest, then reined in when the trees became too dense for a gallop. She moved to the right and to the left, pushing deeper and deeper into the maze of foliage. Then she slid from the mare's back and led her onward.

Kristin's heart was pounding as she sought shelter.

If Zeke had come back, if he found her now...

She would pray for death.

But he was alone this time, she thought, praying for courage. She could fight him.

A twig snapped behind her. She spun around. She couldn't see anything, but she knew that her pursuer had dismounted, too, that he was still following her.

The branches closed above her like an arbor. The day was not bright and blue here, it was green and secretive, and the air was cold. She began to shiver.

She wasn't even armed, she realized ruefully. She was a fool. After all that had happened this morning she had rid-

den away from home without even a pocketknife with which
to defend herself.

Kristin searched the ground and found a good solid
branch.

Another twig snapped behind her. She dropped the mare's
reins and crouched down against an oak. Someone was
moving toward her.

Someone was behind her.

She spun around, the branch raised, determined to get in
the first blow.

"Son of a bitch!" he swore.

She had gotten in the first blow—just barely. The man
had raised his arm, and the branch struck it hard.

The impact sent her flying, her hair in her eyes. She
landed in the dirt, and he was on top of her in an instant.
She slammed her fist into his face, and heard a violent oath.

"Stop it! Kristin!"

He caught her wrists and straddled her.

She blinked and went still. It was Cole Slater.

"You!"

He rubbed his jaw. "You pack a hell of a punch."

"A hell of a punch?" she repeated. "You—you—" She
was trembling with fear and with fury. She didn't mean to
strike him again but she was nearly hysterical with relief, and
she moved without thinking, slapping him across the face.

She knew instantly it was a mistake. His eyes narrowed,
and everything about him hardened. Kristin gasped and
looked around her for another weapon. Her fingers curled
around a branch, and she raised it threateningly.

Cole wrenched the branch from her grasp and broke it
over his knee, then pulled her roughly against his chest.

"What do you think you're doing?" he asked.

She had never seen him so furious, not even when he had
gone up against Zeke and his gang of bushwhackers. Then
he had seemed as cool as a spring stream. Now his eyes were
the dark gray of a winter's sky, and his mouth was a white
line of rage.

Kristin clenched her teeth hard, struggling to free herself from his grip. "What am I doing? You scared me to death."

He pulled her closer, and when he spoke again, his words were a mere whisper. "You're a fool, girl. After a morning like this you take off into the woods, without a word, without a care."

"I'm not a fool, and I'm not a girl, Mr. Slater, and I'd appreciate it, sir, if you would take your hands off of me."

"Oh, great. We have the grand Southern belle again."

Kristin gritted her teeth, wishing she could stem the rising tide of rage within her, rage and other emotions. He was too close. He was touching her, and she could feel the power of his anger, the strength of his body, and she was afraid of her own reactions.

"Let go of me. Just who the hell do you think you are?"

"The man who saved your life."

"I'm getting tired of eternal gratitude."

"Gratitude? A crack with a stick?"

"I didn't know it was you! Why didn't you say something? Why didn't you let me know—"

"You were running that mare a little fast for casual conversation."

"Why were you chasing me?"

"Because I was afraid you were going to get yourself in trouble."

"What were you afraid of? I thought you'd decided I wasn't worth the effort."

"I hadn't made any decisions yet. You are a girl, and you are a fool. You didn't give Moreau's men a chance to get far enough away. I didn't save you this morning for a gang rape this afternoon."

"Well, Mr. Slater, I wouldn't have been an annoying little virgin then, would I?"

Kristin was stunned when his palm connected with her cheek. Tears stung her eyes, though she wasn't really hurt. She hadn't expected his anger, and she hadn't imagined that she could humiliate herself this way again.

"Get off me!" she demanded.

"I don't want to hear it again, Kristin. Do you understand me?" He stood and reached down to help her up. She
ignored his outstretched hand, determined to rise unaided,
but he wouldn't even allow her to do that. He caught her
arms and pulled her up. She hated him at that moment. She
hated him because she needed him. And she hated him because this heat filled her at his touch, and this curious longing grew within her. She was fascinated by the scent of him,
amazed by her desire to touch his face, to feel the softness
of his beard....

To experience the sweeping wonder of his kiss once again.

She jerked free, and the leaves crackled under her feet as
she whistled for Debutante. He followed behind her, dusting his hat off on the skirt of his coat.

"Kristin..."

She spun around. "You know, I've been wondering where
you come from. You certainly aren't any Southern gentleman."

"No?" he queried. They stared at one another for a moment. Then his lips began to curl into a rueful smile. "I'm
sincerely beginning to doubt that you're a Southern lady—
or any kind of a lady, for that matter."

She smiled icily. She could manage it when he wasn't
touching her. Then she turned away from him, squared her
shoulders and walked toward her waiting mare.

"Sorry. I haven't had much time lately for the little nice-
ties of life."

When she reached Debutante, he was there beside her. She
didn't want his help, but he was determined to give it anyway. He lifted her onto the mare's back and grinned up at
her.

"I may have to accept your generous offer."

"My generous offer?"

"Yes." His eyes suddenly seemed dazzling. Smoke and
silver. His smile lent youth and humor to his features. He

laughed. "I may have to bed you yet. To save you from yourself."

She wanted to say something. She wanted to say that her offer was no longer valid, that she would rather go to bed with Zeke and every single one of his raiders, than spend a single night with him, but the words wouldn't come. They weren't true. And it didn't matter, anyway, because he had already turned away. He picked up the reins of his big black horse and leaped upon the animal's back with the agility of long practice.

Kristin started out of the forest, heading for the house. She didn't look back. She rode ahead all the way. He rode behind her, in silence.

By the time they reached the house she was trembling again. She didn't want to see him, she didn't want to talk to him. The whole thing had been a deadly mistake. He needed to get his night's sleep and head out in the morning.

She didn't even know who the man was! she reminded herself in dismay.

When they had dismounted she spoke at last, but without looking at him. "The hands eat out in the bunkhouse at about six. Sleep well, and again, thank you for rescuing us all. I really am eternally grateful."

"Kristin—"

She ignored him and walked Debutante toward the stables. Her heart began to pound, because she imagined that he would follow her. He did not.

She didn't rub Debutante down as she should have. She led the mare into the stall and removed her bit. In a worse turmoil than she had been in when she had left, she walked to the house.

Cole Slater was no longer in the yard. Kristin walked into the house. It was silent, and the drapes were drawn against the afternoon sun. Kristin bit her lip, wondering what to do. Depression suddenly weighed heavily upon her. It was all lost. She would have to leave, and she would have to be grateful that they were alive and accept the fact that nothing else of their life here could be salvaged.

She wasn't sure it mattered. They had already lost so much. Pa. Adam. Her world had been turned upside down. She would have done anything to save it. Anything. But anything just wouldn't be enough.

With a soft sigh, she started up the stairway. At the top of the stairs, she paused, her heart beating hard once again.

There was someone there, on the second floor with her.

There was someone in her parents' bedroom.

She tried to tell herself it was Delilah, or Shannon, but then she heard Delilah calling to Shannon below and heard Shannon's cheerful answer.

"Oh, God," she murmured, her hand traveling to her throat.

Something inside of her went a little berserk. She couldn't bear it if Zeke or one of his cronies had managed to enter that room. Her father's room, a place he had cherished, a place where all his dreams remained alive.

She ran toward the doorway. If Zeke had been in the room, she might have managed to kill him with her bare hands.

But it wasn't Zeke. It was Cole Slater. He had his blanket laid out on the comforter, and he was taking things from it. He looked up at her in surprise as she stared at him from the doorway. He frowned when he noticed the way her breasts heaved and noticed the pulse beating hard at the base of her throat. He strode to her quickly.

"Kristin, what happened?"

She shook her head, unable to speak at first.

"I—I didn't expect you. I mean, I didn't expect you to be here," she said.

He shrugged and walked back into the room, taking a shirt from the blanket and striding toward her father's armoire. "I didn't intend to be here. Delilah insisted there was plenty of room inside the house." He paused and turned back to her. "Is there something wrong with that? Do you want me out of here?"

She shook her head and had to swallow before she could speak again. "No...uh, no. It's fine." He was going to come toward her again. Quickly, before he could come close enough to touch her, Kristin turned and fled to the sanctuary of her own room.

She didn't know what seized her that afternoon. She didn't dare sit and think, and she certainly couldn't allow herself to analyze.

She went out in the early evening to speak with the hands. There was Jacob, who was nearly seventy, and his grandsons, Josh and Trin, who were even younger than she was. Their father had been killed at Manassas at the beginning of the war. And there was Pete, who was older than Jacob, though he wouldn't admit it. That was all she had left—two old men and two young boys. Yet they had survived so far. Somehow they had survived so far.

Cattle were missing again. Kristin just shrugged at the news. Zeke's boys had been through. They had simply taken what they wanted.

Pete wagged a finger at her. "We heard what happened, missy. I think it's time you got out of here."

She ruffled his thin gray hair. "And what about you, Pete?"

"I've gotten along this far. I'll get along the rest of my days."

She smiled at him. "We'll see."

"Hear tell you've got a man named Slater up at the house."

Kristin frowned. "Yes. Why? You know him, Pete?"

Pete looked down at the wood he was whittling, shaking his head. "Can't say that I do."

She thought the old man was lying to her, and she couldn't understand it. He was as loyal as the day was long.

"You just said his name. Slater."

"Yeah, I heard it. From someone. Just like I heard tell that he managed to get rid of the whole lot of the thieving gutter rats." He looked up, wagging his knife at her. "You can't beat the likes of Zeke Moreau, Kristin. He doesn't have a breath of mercy or justice in him." He spat on the floor. "None of them do, not the jayhawkers, not the bushwhackers. It's time to get out."

"Well, maybe," Kristin said distractedly. She stood from the pile of hay she'd been sitting on. "Maybe."

"Your Pa's dead, Kristin. You're smart and you're tough. But not tough enough to take on Zeke on your own."

He looked at her expectantly. She felt like laughing. Everyone thought she could help. Everyone thought that all she had to do was bat her eyelashes at Cole Slater and he'd come straight to their rescue. If they only knew.

"We'll talk about it in the morning," she told him.

When she returned to the house, it was dinnertime.

Delilah had set out the good china and fine crystal again. She'd made a honeyed ham, candied yams, turnip greens and a blueberry pie.

Shannon and Cole Slater talked all through the meal. There might not have been a war on. There might not have been anything wrong with the world at all, the way the two of them talked. Shannon was beautiful and charming, and Cole was the perfect gentleman.

Kristin tried to smile, and she tried to answer direct questions. But all she could remember was that he had rejected her—and that she needed him desperately. She hated him, yet trembled if their hands so much as brushed when they reached for something at the same time.

She drank far too much Madeira with dinner.

When he went out back to smoke a cigar afterward, Kristin decided to take another bath. She hoped Delilah would think she hadn't been able to wash away the miserable stench of the morning.

Shannon was a sweetheart, tender and caring. Kristin realized when Shannon kissed her good-night that her sister was suffering more then she had realized. She was just taking it all stoically, trying to ease Kristin's pain with smiles and laughter.

Shannon went to bed.

Kristin dressed in her best nightgown. It had been part of her mother's trousseau. It was soft, sheer silk that hugged her breasts in a pattern of lace, then fell in gentle swirls around her legs.

She sat at the foot of her bed in the gown, and she waited. She was still, but fires raged inside her.

She had to make him stay, no matter what it took.

This was something that she had to do.

She heard his footsteps on the stairs at last. She heard him walk down the hallway, and then she heard the door to her parents' room open and close.

She waited, waited as long as she could, as long as she dared. Then she stood and drifted barefoot across the hardwood floor. She opened her door and started across the hall. She nearly panicked and fled, but something drew her onward. She wondered if she had gone mad, wondered if the world really had been turned upside down. Nothing could ever be the same again.

She hated him, she told herself. And he had already turned her down once.

One day she would best him.

She placed her hand on the doorknob and turned it slowly. Then she pushed open the door.

The room was dark. Only a streak of moonlight relieved the blackness. Kristin stood there for several seconds, blinking, trying to orient herself. It was foolish. She had waited too long. He was probably fast asleep.

He wasn't asleep. He was wide awake. He was sitting up in bed, his chest bare. He was watching her. Despite the darkness, she knew that he was watching her, that he had been waiting for her and that he was amused.

"Come on, Kristin," he said softly. He wasn't whispering like a man afraid of being caught at some dishonorable deed. He was speaking softly out of consideration for the others in the house, not out of fear. He wouldn't give a damn about convention, she thought. And yet he seemed to expect her to respect it.

Men.

"I, uh . . . just wanted to see if you needed anything."

"Sure." He smiled knowingly. "Well, I don't need anything. Thank you."

The bastard. He really meant to make it hard for her.

"That's a nice outfit to wear to check on your male guests, ma'am." He said the last word with a slow, calculated Southern drawl, and she felt her temper flare. Where the hell was he from?

"Glad you like it," she retorted.

"Oh, I do like it. Very much."

This was getting them nowhere. No, it was getting *her* nowhere.

"Well . . ."

"Come here, Kristin."

"You come here."

He grinned. "If you insist."

She should have known he would be lying there nude beneath the sheets.

Well, she had come to seduce him, after all.

She just hadn't imagined his body. The length of it. She couldn't remember what she had imagined. Darkness, and tangle of sheets... She had known it involved a naked man, but she hadn't known just how a naked man could be.

She tried to keep her eyes on his, aware that a crimson tide was rushing to her face. She wished she had the nerve to shout, to run, to scream, but she didn't seem to be able to do anything at all.

Her eyes slipped despite her best efforts, slipped and then widened. She knew that he saw it, and she knew that he was amused. But she didn't move and she didn't speak, and when he stood before her at last, his hands on his hips, she managed to toss her head back and meet his gaze with a certain bravado.

He placed his hands against the wall on either side of her head. "Like what you see?" he inquired politely.

"Someone should really slap the living daylights out of you," she told him sweetly.

"You didn't do badly."

"Good." She was beginning to shake. Right now it was a mere tremor, but it was growing. He was so close that…that part of his body was nearly touching the swirling silk of her gown. She felt his breath against her cheek. She felt the heat radiating from him. She bit her lip, trying to keep it from quivering.

He pushed away from the wall. He touched her cheek with his palm, then stroked it softly with his knuckles. She stared at him, unable to move. She knew then that he could see that she was trembling. His eyes remained locked with hers. He moved his hand downward and cupped her breast.

The touch was so intimate, so bold, that she nearly cried out. He grazed her nipple with his thumb, and sensations shot through her with an almost painful intensity. She caught her breath, trying desperately to keep from crying out. And then she realized that he was watching her eyes carefully, gauging her reactions.

She knocked his hand away and tried to push by him, but he caught her shoulders and threw her against the wall.

"I hurt your feelings before. But then, I don't think that you were lacking in self-confidence. You must know that you're beautiful. Your hair is so golden and you have the bearing of a young Venus. Kristin, it isn't you. It's me. I haven't got any emotion left. I haven't got what you need, what you want. Damn it, don't you understand? I want you. I'm made out of flesh and blood and whatever else it is that God puts into men. I want you. Now. Hell, I could have wanted you right after I ripped another man away from you. I'm no better than he is, not really. Don't you under-stand?"

She drew herself up against the wall. She hated him, and she hated herself. She had lost again.

"I only know that I need you. Emotion! I saw my father murdered, and Adam . . ."

"Yes, and Adam."

"And Adam is dead, too. So if you're worried about some kind of emotional commitment, you're a fool. I want help against Zeke Moreau."

"You want me to kill him."

"It's worth any price."

"I told you . . . I don't murder men in cold blood."

"Then I just want protection."

"How badly?"

"Desperately. You know that."

"Show me."

She stepped toward him and placed her hands around his neck. Suddenly she realized that she hadn't the least idea of what to do. Instinct guided her, instinct and nothing more.

She stepped closer, pressing against him so that she could feel the length of his naked body through the thin silk of her gown. She wound her arms around his neck and came up on tiptoe to press her lips against his, summoning up the memory of the kiss he had given her. She felt him, felt the instrument of his desire pulsing against her. She felt the muscles of his chest and belly and thighs. Then she felt his arms, powerful around her.

Then she plunged her tongue into his mouth and the world began to spin. She had come to seduce him, and she was ready to fall against him, longing for him to sweep her away.

To help her . . .

She felt the passion in him as he held her, and for a moment, victory was hers. She burned, she longed, with an astonishing hunger, and she could not know where it would lead. His lips held hers, his mouth devoured hers, and with each second that passed she entered deeper into a world that was pure sensation. Her pulse soared, and there was a pounding in her ears that was like the rush of the sea. His kiss was her life, his body was her support. She was afraid, and she was ecstatic.

And then he suddenly pushed her away.

His breathing was coming rough and ragged.

He watched her for a long, long moment. She felt his eyes on her, felt them as she would have felt an approaching storm. Then he shook his head.

"Go to bed, Kristin."

She inhaled sharply, furiously. "You let me make a complete fool of myself and then you— Damn you!"

Kristin slammed her fists against his shoulders, catching him off guard. He staggered, and she found the doorknob. Throwing the door open, she tore across the hall. She threw herself onto her own bed, tears hovering behind her lashes, fury rising in her throat.

The door crashed open behind her, and she spun around. He had followed her across the hall without even bothering to dress.

"Get out of here!" she snapped, enraged.

He ignored her and strode calmly toward the bed. Kristin shot up, determined to fight. It was all to no avail. His long stride quickly brought him to her. She came to her knees hastily, but he joined her on the bed, grabbing her hands and pressing her down.

"I should scream!" she told him. "Samson would come and—"

"Then scream."

She held her breath. He pressed her down on the bed and straddled her.

"Why won't you leave me alone?"

"You wanted to make a deal," he said harshly.

"What?"

"You said you wanted to make a deal. All right. Let's talk. I'm willing to negotiate."

PART 2

The Lover

4

Kristin was glad the room was steeped in darkness. His features were shadowed, his body was shadowed, and she prayed that her own emotions were hidden by the night. She wanted to hate him. She could not. She wanted to think, to reason, and she could think of nothing but the hard male body so hot and intimate against her own.

He had come here, naked, to accept her proposition, it seemed. And yet he was angry again, angrier even than before. Hard and bitter and angry.

Moonlight cast a sudden soft glow over the room. She saw his features, and they were harsh, taut, almost cruel, as if he were fighting some inner pain.

"Negotiate?" she whispered.

"First, Miss Kristin, if you're going to play a game of chance, make sure you're playing with a full deck."

"I don't know what—"

"Exactly. That's why I'm going to explain things to you. I'll meet any man in a fair fight, but I won't go out and commit murder, not for you, not for myself, not for anyone. Do you understand?"

She nodded. She didn't understand him at all, but she was suddenly too afraid to do anything else. She had lost her mind. The war and the bloodshed had made her insane. She, Kristin McCahy, raised to live up to the highest standards of Southern womanhood, was lying on her bed with a naked stranger.

And she wasn't screaming.

"No involvement, Miss Kristin." The mock drawl was back in his voice, making her wonder again where he hailed from. She was filled with awareness of him. His muscled chest was plastered with crisp dark hair. She thought of how quickly he had drawn his Colts and his rifle, and she shivered. He carried with him an aura of danger that drew her to him despite her best intentions.

His sex pulsed against her belly, and she fought wildly to keep her eyes glued to his. It was all she could do to remember that she had intended to seduce him, to leave him gasping and longing and aching, his tongue hanging out for her.

He would never long for her that way, she realized now. Nor would he be denied. He had mocked her, but now he was determined to have her, and she felt sure he must despise her more with each passing second.

She steeled herself and whispered harshly, "No involvement. You needn't worry. I need a gunslinger. I could never love one."

A slight smile curved his lip. "This deal is made on my terms, lady. No involvement, no questions. And I won't murder Zeke. I'll go after him when I can. I'll do my damnedest to keep you and Shannon safe and your place together. But I've got other commitments, too, Kristin. And I can't forget them."

She didn't say anything. She didn't know what to say or do, didn't know where to go from here. This was so easy for him. He was so casual. He didn't even seem to know he was naked.

He touched her cheek, brushing it with his fingertips. "Why?" he said suddenly.

She shook her head, uncomprehending. "Why what?"

"This is all Zeke wanted."

"I hate Zeke. I hate him more than you could ever imagine. He killed my father. I'd rather bed a bison than that bastard."

"I see. And I'm a step above a bison?"

"A step below."

"I can still leave."

Panic filled her. She wanted to reach out and keep him from disappearing, but her pride wouldn't let her. Then she realized that he was smiling again, that he was amused. He leaned down low and spoke to her softly. His breath caressed her flesh, and the soft hair of his beard teased her chin. "There's one more point to this bargain, Miss Mc-Cahy."

Her heart was suddenly pounding mercilessly, her body aching, her nerves screaming.

"What's that, Slater?"

"I like my women hungry. No, ma'am, maybe that's not enough. I like them starving."

Words and whispers could do so much. As much as his slow, lazy, taunting smile. Fever ran through her, rife and rampant. She wanted to strike him because she felt so lost, and in spite of herself, she was afraid. She wasn't afraid he would hurt her. She might have gone insane, but she believed with all her heart that he would never hurt her. And she wondered, too, if this madness hadn't been spawned by the very way he made her feel, alive as she had never been before, haunted and shaken and...hungry, hungry for some sweet sensation that teased her mind and heart when he was near.

And yet she lay stiff and unyielding, numbed by the fear that swept through her, the fear that she would be unable to please him, the fear that she didn't have what it would take to hold him. Women... He had used the plural of the word. He liked his women hungry....

No, starving.

She didn't know him, and she didn't want involvement any more than he did, and yet this very intimacy was involvement. Even as she lay there, unable to move, she felt a painful stirring of jealousy. She had sacrificed so very much pride and dignity and morality for this man, and he was herding her together with every other female he had ever known.

He touched her chin. Then he brushed her lips with his, with the soft sweep of his mustache.

"Hungry, sweetheart." She sensed his smile, hovering above her in the dark. "This is as exciting as bedding a large chunk of ice."

She struck out at him blindly, but he caught her arms and lowered his weight onto her. She clenched her teeth as his laughing eyes drew near.

"Excuse me, Mr. Slater. My experience is limited. You wouldn't let me run out and screw a ranch hand, remember?"

"Kristin, damn you—"

"No, damn you!" she retorted, painfully close to tears. This couldn't be it. This couldn't be the night, the magic night she had wondered about in her dreams. No, it couldn't be, she thought bitterly. In her dreams this night had come after she had been married. And Adam had been in her dreams. And there had been nothing ugly or awkward about it. There hadn't even been any nude bodies, except beneath the sheets, and even then she had been cloaked all in white and he had whispered about how much he loved her and how beautiful she was and it had been wondrously pure and innocent....

She hadn't known these feelings then. And she hadn't known she could sell herself to a man who didn't even really want her.

"Please!" she cried suddenly, trying to escape his touch. Tears were beginning to sting her eyes, and she didn't want him to see them. She couldn't bear any more humiliation. "Just leave me alone. I—I can't be what you want, I can't—"

"Kristin!"

She went still when she heard the pained tenderness in his voice. He touched her cheek gently. Then he lay beside her and swept her into his arms.

She was stunned to realize that he was trembling, too, that his body was racked by heat and fever. He murmured her name again and again, and his lips brushed over her brow, as light as air. "Don't you see? I don't want to need you like this. I don't want to want you!"

There was passion in his voice, dark and disturbing. There was bitterness in it, too, pained and fervent, and as he continued to touch her, his emotions seemed to burn and sear her along with his touch. His hands were tender, then demanding, then gentle again.

"I don't want to want you," he murmured, "but God help me, I do."

Then he kissed her, and there was nothing left to worry about, for she was suddenly riding swiftly across the dark heavens and there was no time to think, no time for reason. She could only hold tight.

It all seemed to come together, everything she had felt since she had first set eyes on the man. Hungry...his mouth was hungry, and he was devouring her. His lips molded and shaped hers, and his tongue seemed to plunge to the very depths of her being, licking her deep, deep inside, taunting her, arousing her still more.

His hands roamed her body with abandon, abandon and a kind of recklessness. He caressed her tenderly, even delicately, then touched her with a force that told her that he wanted to brand her, wanted to leave his mark on her.

She never knew where the awe and the trembling and fear ceased and something entirely different began. She didn't even know when she lost the elegant nightgown brought west in her mother's trousseau, for his touch was so sweeping, so swift, so heady. She knew only that her breast was suddenly bare and his mouth was upon it. He cupped the soft mound of flesh with his hand, his lips hard around the nipple, drawing, suckling, raking the peak with his teeth as he demanded more and more.

She nearly screamed. She had never imagined such intimacy, and she never dreamed that there could be anything like the sensation that gripped her now with burning fingers, drawing a line of raw excitement down her spine and

into her loins. She clutched his shoulders, barely aware that
her nails were digging into him, that she was clutching him
as if he were a lifeline in a storm-swept sea.

And still the tempest raged. His lips found her throat, and
he raked his palm down the length of her, kneading her
thigh and her buttocks. He moved swiftly, and she tried to
follow, but she could not, for she was breathless, gasping in
shock and amazement at each new sensation. He began
anew. He touched her, held her, all over again. His lips
trailed a line down the valley between her breasts to her navel, and the soft, bristling hair of his mustache and beard
taunted her naked flesh mercilessly. She felt his knee force
her thighs apart, and she knew that she was close to the
point of no return, to being changed forever, and even then
she could not keep pace with the winds that buffeted her.

And then he stopped. His palms on either side of her
head, he caressed her with that curious tenderness he possessed and lowered his head to hers, whispering into her
mouth.

"Hungry?"

She didn't want to face it. It was too new, too startling.
She lowered her head and nodded, but it wasn't enough, not
for him.

"Kristin?"

"Please..."

"Tell me."

"Oh, God!" she cried, trying to twist away from him. His
palms held her fast, and her eyes were forced to meet his.
Her lips were moist and her hair was a mass of gold between them, startlingly pale against the darkness of his
chest.

He smiled at her, watching her as he drew his hand down
to the pulse at her throat, then over her breast, down, down,
to draw a circle on her abdomen and then plunge lower. He
kept his eyes on her as he stroked her upper thigh. Then,
suddenly, he swept his touch intimately inside her, moving
with a sure, languorous rhythm.

She cried out again and tried to burrow against him, but he held her away from him. He watched her eyes, watched the rise and fall of her breasts, watched her gasp for air.

He caught her lips with his own, caught them and kissed them, and then he whispered against them again.

"Yes. You are . . . hungry."

Was this it? Was this the hunger he demanded, this burning sensation that filled her and engulfed her? She was grateful for the darkness, for the night, for with the moon behind a cloud, she could believe that all her sins were hidden, all that she had bartered, all that she had given so freely. She couldn't believe how she lay there with him, and yet she would not have changed it for the world. A soft cry escaped her, and she threw her arms around his neck, hiding against his chest at last. Something surged within her, and she gasped and murmured against his chest, barely aware that her hips were pulsing to his rhythm, that he hadn't ceased taunting her, that his strokes were growing more enticing.

Cole knew vaguely that he shouldn't be there. He should have told her that morning that nothing could make him stay, nothing could make him help her. She was the last thing in the world he needed. He had commitments of his own, and come heaven or hell or death itself, he meant to see them through.

And this innocence . . .

This, too, was the last thing he needed. She was hardened, and there were jagged edges to her. War did that. War and death and pain and blood. But the innocence was still there, too. He had thought he could make her run, and he had thought he could be strong enough himself not to touch her. He was used up. He knew that. He was used up, and she deserved more than that. He was still alive, though, still breathing, and she touched every raw cord of desire within him. Maybe he had known what was to come, and maybe he hadn't expected it at all, but now that it was happening, he couldn't even try to deny it. She spun a golden web of arousal and passion as soft and silky and luxuriant as the long strands of hair that tangled around them both, dampened by the glistening sheen of their bodies. She had beautiful features, exquisite features, fine, high cheekbones, a small, slim nose and eyes like an endless blue sky, darkly fringed with rich lashes and glazed now with blossoming passion. And her mouth...it was full and giving, sensual in laughter, sensual when her lips parted beneath his own. She was soft, she was velvet and she was created for desire, with high, firm breasts, a slim waist and flaring hips, and smooth, fascinating buttocks. He hadn't meant to stay. He hadn't meant to come here, and he hadn't meant to stay. He hadn't meant to touch her....

But he had.

And she moved. She moved with exquisite grace. She made sweet, soft sounds that entered his loins and caused the blood to pound in his head so that he could think no more. Only one thought guided him, and that was that he had to have her, had to have her or go mad. Her nipples pressed against his chest, and she arched against his hand. Despite his best efforts, the agony of the past was erased, the vengeance of the future forgotten. Even the present meant nothing at all. All that mattered was this woman, and she was hot and wet and begging for release.

He pulled her to him almost roughly. Her eyes widened, and he commanded her to hold tight. He caught her lips in a heady kiss and swept his hands beneath her. He fought hard to remember her innocence. He kissed her with sweeping ardor, and then he entered her.

He was slow, achingly slow, and she was sleek and damp, a hot sheath ready to encase him, and still he felt her shudder, heard the sudden agonized cry that she muffled against his chest.

He'd heard it before. On his wedding day.

The irony, the bitter, bitter irony touched him for a moment, and for a moment he hated her and himself. For a moment he was still. Then he felt her shudder again and thought she might be crying, and then he was whispering things without thinking.

Yes . . . he'd been here before. Making love tenderly to a woman for the very first time. Her very first time.

He held her, caressed her, promised to help her. And then he moved again, slowly at first, carefully, tenderly.

And then she was moving beneath him, subtly at first. She was taking him in, and the tears were gone, and the shock was gone, and the desperate tension was growing again.

Care and consideration left him. A thirst that he was frantic to slake ripped through him and into his loins. He couldn't remember ever being so fevered, and still the sensations grew. He touched her breasts, struck anew by their beauty. He inhaled the clean, sweet scent of her tangled hair and the fever soared higher and higher. He wrapped her legs tightly around him and cupped her buttocks, and rocking hard, filled her with himself again and again. He threw back his head and rough sound tore from him as the relief began to shake and convulse through his body. Again and again he spilled into her. She cried out, her voice ragged. He was aware that she had reached some sweet satisfaction, and he was pleased. She fell still, and the last of the fever raked through him. He thrust deep, deep inside her one last time. It was shattering, and he couldn't remember when he had known such a deeply satisfying climax.

He fell to her side, covered with sweat, breathing heavily.

She was silent. He touched her cheek and found tears there.

Suddenly he was furious with himself and with her. This should never have happened. She should have married some young buck and worn white, and she should have been loved, not just desired.

She twisted away from his touch, and he let her go. She turned her back on him, and he wondered if she was crying again. Maybe she had a right to, but it was damned insulting. He'd taken even greater care with her than he had with—Elizabeth. With Elizabeth.

There. He dared to think her name.

Though he gritted his teeth and wished it away, agony gripped him from head to toe. He wondered if the pain would ever leave him.

"You can...you can go back now," Kristin said suddenly.

"What?" His voice was sharp.

"Our deal." She spoke softly, her voice a mere whisper, as if tears hovered behind her words, tears and just a touch of anxiety. "It's—it's made now, isn't it?"

He hesitated before he answered her. "Yes, your bloody bargain is made, Miss McCahy."

"Then you could...you could go back. Across the hall."

He didn't know what demon seized him. He didn't care if he was heard by the others in the house, didn't care about anything at all. He sat up in a sudden fury and wrenched her around to face him. He spoke bitingly, trying to make every word sting like the stroke of a lash.

"Not on your life, my little prima donna. You invited me in here. Now you've got me. That was the game, Kristin. You knew it was going to go by my rules—"

"My God!" she cried, jerking away from his touch. "Have you no consideration, no—"

"Compassion? Not a whit. This is what you wanted, and now you've got it."

She was beautiful still, he thought. The moonlight was playing over her breasts, and they were damp and shimmering and very, very fine, the nipples still enlarged and hard. He felt a quickening inside him all over again, and with it felt the return of the pain. The pain of betrayal. It was all right with whores, with tavern girls. It was something else with this innocent young beauty.

He scowled fiercely and turned his back on her. "Go to sleep, Kristin."

She didn't move. She didn't answer him. Not for endless seconds.

"Go to sleep?" she repeated incredulously.

"Damn it, yes, go to sleep." He swung around again and pressed her down on the bed. She started to fight him, and he wasn't in the mood to take it. Dark anger was in him, dark, brooding anger, and though he didn't mean to be cruel to her, he didn't seem to be able to help himself. He caught her shoulders and shook them. "Good night, Kristin. Go to sleep."

"Leave," she said stubbornly.

"I'll be damned if I will."

"Then I'll leave."

"And I'll be damned if you'll leave, either. Now go to sleep!"

He turned around, offering her his back once again. He didn't know why he had started this bout, but now that he had begun it, he wasn't about to lose.

He felt it when she started to rise, and he turned with frightening speed, sweeping his arm around her waist and holding her still. He felt her heart beating like that of a doe.

"Go to sleep!"

He heard her teeth grating, but she didn't move, not again. He knew she was planning to wait until he fell asleep, then slip away.

He smiled. She had another think coming. He would feel her slightest movement. He would awaken.

When she did try to move, he kept his eyes closed and held her fast. He heard her swearing softly, and he heard the threat of sobs coming to her whispering voice.

But then it was she who fell into an exhausted sleep. And it was he who awoke first with the morning. He stood and stretched and padded naked to the window and looked out on a beautiful summer's day. It was a fine ranch, he thought. Then he sighed, and he knew that she would think she had sold herself dearly in the night.

He had sold himself dearly, too. He had sold his honor, and he would have to stay, and he would have to protect her.

He walked over to the bed. The evidence of their night together was painfully obvious in the twisted bedding.

Her face was covered by long, soft tendrils of hair that picked up gold from the sun. A hand seemed to tighten around his heart and squeeze. Cole stepped closer to the bed and covered Kristin with the top sheet and the comforter. Then he stepped to the door, glanced out and returned to the room across the hall to wash and dress.

Kristin knew it was late when she awoke. She opened her eyes and saw that the sun had risen high, then closed her eyes again and discovered that she was shaking.

She had almost believed that she had dreamed the entire episode.

But she hadn't. Cole Slater was gone, but he had definitely been there, and just thinking about everything that had happened made her shake again and burn crimson to the roots of her hair.

A knock sounded at her door. "Kristin?"

It was Shannon. Kristin sat bolt upright and looked at the bed. The comforter seemed to hide the sins of the night.

"Shannon, just a minute!" she cried out. Her gown was on the floor beside the bed. She made a dive for it, wincing at the soreness that plagued her thighs. Then she realized that the gown was torn and ragged, and she knew why it had seemed to melt away the night before. Bitterly she wound it into a ball, stuffed it into her dresser and dragged out an old flannel gown. Breathless, she told Shannon to come in.

Shannon came in with a pot of coffee and a cup and breakfast on a silver tray. Kristin stared at it blankly and arched a brow at her younger sister.

"Good morning, sleepyhead," Shannon told her.

"Breakfast? In bed?" The ranch was a place where they barely eked out their existence. Breakfast in bed was a luxury they never afforded themselves. "After I've slept all morning?"

"Delilah was going to wake you. Cole said that maybe things had been hard on you lately and that maybe you needed to sleep."

"Oh, Cole said that, did he?"

Shannon ignored the question. "I rode out to the north pasture with Cole and Pete, and everything's going fine for the day."

Kristin kissed her sister's cheek and plopped on the bed, wincing again. It even hurt a little to sit.

She felt her face flood with color again, and she lowered her head, trying to hide her blush behind her hair. She still didn't know if she hated him, or if her feeling had become something different, something softer.

A little flush of fever seemed to touch her. She was breathing too fast, and her heart was hammering. She couldn't forget the night. She couldn't forget how she had felt, and she didn't know whether to be amazed or grateful or awed—or ashamed. The future loomed before them. They had a deal. He had said he would stay. And he hadn't left her room, and she—

She couldn't help wondering what he intended for their personal future together. Did he mean to do it . . . again?

"My Lord, Kristin, but you're flushed!" Shannon said with alarm.

"I'm all right," Kristin said hastily. She sipped the coffee too quickly and burned her lip. She set the cup down. "This was really sweet. The breakfast."

"Oh," Shannon said nonchalantly, "this was Cole's idea, too. He seemed to think you might have a little trouble getting up this morning."

"Oh, he did, did he?" She bit so hard into a piece of bacon that her teeth snapped together. He was laughing at her again, it seemed, and he didn't even have the decency to do it to her face. She longed for the chance to give him a good hard slap just once.

She caught herself. He had warned her. They were playing by his rules. And there was only one thing she was gaining from it all. Safety. She had agreed to the rules. She had meant to seduce him, she had meant for it all to happen, she had wanted the deal. It was just that she wasn't at all sure who had seduced whom.

"Where is Cole now?" she asked Shannon. She was surprised to find that she had a ravenous appetite.

Shannon shrugged. "I'm not sure. But do you know what?" she asked excitedly.

"No. What?"

"He says he's going to stay around for a while. Isn't that wonderful, Kristin?"

Kristin swallowed and nodded. "Yes. It's wonderful."

"Samson says it's a miracle. He says God has looked down on us with mercy at long last."

"The Lord certainly does work in mysterious ways," Kristin murmured dryly.

Shannon, who had seated herself at the foot of the bed, leaped up and hugged Kristin. "We're going to make it," she whispered. "We're really going to make it."

She had underestimated Shannon, Kristin realized. She had felt their father's death every bit as keenly as Kristin had.

And because she felt it so strongly, she had learned to hate, just as Kristin had.

"I've got to get back downstairs. Delilah is baking bread and making preserves and I promised to help."

Kristin nodded. "I'll be right down, too."

When her sister had left, Kristin washed hastily. She couldn't help remembering every place he had touched her, everything he had done to her. And then, naturally, she started trembling again, thinking about the feeling that had come over her. In the midst of carnage, a brief, stolen moment of ecstasy.

Shameful ecstasy.

Ecstasy.

She wondered if it had ever really been, if it could ever come again.

She dressed, trying desperately to quit thinking. If she didn't, she would walk around all day as red as a beet.

She dressed for work. There was some fencing down on the north side, and she had told Pete she'd come out and look at it. The stash of gold hidden in the hayloft was dwindling, but they could afford to repair the fencing. And if she could just hang on to her stock a while longer, she could command fair prices from any number of buyers in the spring. She had to remember that she was fighting for the land. Nothing else mattered.

In breeches and boots, Kristin started for the doorway. Then she remembered her bedding, and the telltale sheets.

Delilah usually did the beds. She kept the house with Shannon's help. Samson kept it from falling apart. Pete and Kristin ran the ranch. That was just the way things had worked out.

But she didn't want Delilah doing her bed. Not today.

He liked his women hungry. *Women.* Plural.

Kristin let loose with a furious oath and ripped the sheets from the bed. She jumped up and down on them a few times for good measure, then realized how ridiculous she was being and scooped them up. She carried them down with her to the stables, stuffing them into the huge trash bin. She would burn them later, with some of the empty feed bags.

She headed for the stable, determined to saddle Debutante and ride out. She paused in the doorway, aware that Cole was there, brushing down his black thoroughbred stallion. It was a beautiful animal, Kristin thought.

Very like the man who owned him.

She wasn't ready to see Cole Slater yet. She almost turned around, ready to change her plans for the day to avoid facing him. But he had sensed her there, and he turned, and there seemed to be nothing for her to do but stand there and meet his stare.

It was long, and it was pensive, and it gave no quarter. She would never accuse the man of being overly sensitive or overly polite. His gray eyes were sharp and curious, and she still thought he must be amused by her, because he was smiling slightly. There were times when she thought he hated her, but then he would stare at her in a way that warmed her and offered her a fleeting tenderness.

Very much like the way he made love...

She shouldn't have thought it. The color that had so alarmed her rose to fill her face, and she had to lower her eyes to still the blush. She prayed fervently that she could appear sophisticated for just this one encounter. But it was impossible to stand here now, fully clothed, and not remember what had gone on the night before. Things could never be the same again. She could never see life the same way again. She could never see him the same way again, for she knew the power of the form beneath the shirt and jeans, and he knew all that made up the woman she was.

"Sleep well?" he asked her after a moment.

There was something grating in the question, something mocking, and that helped. She squared her shoulders and tried to walk by him, heading for Debutante's stall. He caught her arm and swung her around. His eyes were serious now.

"Where do you think you're going?"

"Out to the north pasture. I have to see the fencing. I should have gone yesterday, but..." She paused, her voice fading away.

He shook his head impatiently. "I'll meet Pete."

"But it's my ranch!"

"And it's my life, Miss McCahy." He dropped her arm and put his hands, the currycomb in one, on his hips. "You're taking up my time. We made some ridiculous deal—"

"Ridiculous deal!" She was choked with rage. She was going to slap him this time. Right across the face.

She didn't make it. He caught her wrist. "I'm sorry, Kristin. I didn't mean it that way."

"I'm so terribly sorry if I disappointed you."

She'd thought his eyes would drop with shame. They didn't. Hers did. He was still smiling.

"You didn't disappoint me. You surpassed my wildest expectations. I'm sorry. I didn't mean to insult you. I meant that you really should be the hell out of here."

"You're not reneging?" she asked crisply.

He smiled slowly, tilted back his plumed hat and shook his head. "No, Kristin," he said softly. His low, grating voice sent tremors up her spine. "I never renege on a deal. But I'll be damned if I'm going to stick around so you can run off and be swept away beneath my very nose."

"But I—"

"Forget it, Kristin. I warned you. We play by my rules. And you're not riding out anywhere."

"But—"

"You ride out, I ride out."

"But... but you've already been... paid!" Kristin exploded.

His brows shot up, and his lips curled mockingly. "Paid?"

"You know what I mean."

He shook his head. "I sure as hell don't! That was it? One night in your arms and I'm supposed to gladly lay down my life and die?"

"You are no Southern gentleman."

"Did I say I was?"

"You are no gentleman at all!"

"I never claimed to be one, Kristin. In fact, I haven't made any claims to you at all. Remember that."

"I find it difficult to forget."

"Are you trying to renege?" he queried softly.

She drew herself up stiffly, determined to counter-attack. "So you're not from the South?"

"Does it matter where I'm from?"

"Maybe it does!"

He caught her hand and held it. They stared at one another. Behind them, the massive black stallion snorted. Cole stared at her seriously for a long moment and then said,

"No, it doesn't, Kristin. Nothing about me matters at all. No questions. No involvement. Remember that."

She jerked her hand away. "I'll remember, Mr. Slater."

She started toward Debutante's stall. Maybe she couldn't go riding, but she had to get away. She would take a moment to stroke the mare's velvet nose, and then she would escape. She didn't know how she would be able to bear it, though. She would be like a caged animal with all the emotions that were playing havoc in her heart.

She patted Debutante's nose and promised the horse in a low whisper that she would come out and give her a good grooming as soon as *he* was out of the stable.

Then she turned around, determined to walk out of the stables with her head held high, determined to hang on to her few remaining shreds of dignity.

"By the way, Kristin..." he began.

She paused, her back to him. She straightened, stiffening her shoulders, and turned in a swift circle. He wasn't watching her. He was combing the stallion's shining flanks.

"Why don't you move your things into the larger bedroom? We'll have more space there."

"What?"

"You heard me."

"But—but everyone will know! And just how many times do you intend to...to..."

"Get paid?" he suggested politely. He didn't even seem to be paying attention to her. He stroked the stallion's ears, then stared directly at her. "You want blood, Kristin. That's an expensive commodity. And as far as everyone knowing is concerned, that's exactly what I want."

"But—"

"I make the rules, remember?"

"I can't! I can't go by this one—"

"Delilah will understand. So will Shannon and Sam and Pete and everyone else. And if Zeke Moreau hears anything about it, he'll get the message, too."

"But—"

"Do it, Kristin."

She spun around in a dead fury again. She didn't look back. She stormed into the house, wishing desperately that *she* were a man. She would run away and join the army in two seconds.

She wouldn't even give a damn whose army she joined. Just as long as it was someone who hated Quantrill and his animals.

"Kristin, that you?" Delilah came into the hallway, smiling. "Want to give us a hand with the wax? I could surely use some help stirring. I've got Shannon jarring and sealing while I've been kneading the bread."

"Er...of course," Kristin said. She'd much, much rather run away and join the army.

Shannon gave her a bright smile when she came into the kitchen. "Did you find Cole?"

"Yes. I found him."

Shannon nodded. It was obvious that she approved of it all. They were all mad, Kristin decided.

"He wants me to move into Pa's bedroom with him," she blurted out.

Shannon had been holding a jar of jam, sealing it with wax. The jar slipped from her fingers and shattered loudly on the floor.

Delilah sent the bread she was kneading into the air. It fell back on the block table.

Both of them stared at her. Then they glanced at one another. Neither of them said a word.

"Say something!" Kristin demanded. "Help me make some kind of a decision!"

"You can't!" Shannon gasped.

"Seems to me like you've already made your decision," Delilah said softly. "But it ain't right. It just ain't right. Still..."

"He's much, much better than Zeke Moreau," Shannon said. She stooped to pick up the broken glass and the jam that was seeping into the floorboards. "Yes, maybe you have to. And he *is* much better than Zeke."

"So that's why I'm sleeping with a stranger." Kristin sank into a chair before the fire. "I cannot believe I'm doing this," she murmured.

"These are different times," Shannon murmured, staring at the floor. She looked up at her sister. "Kristin, we can't be blind to the facts! We need him. We need him, or else we just have to give up and pull out."

"Shannon!" Kristin exploded. "You're shocked, and you know it. Pa must be turning in his grave. We don't even know where Cole Slater comes from!"

Shannon's beautiful blue eyes widened. "But of course we do, Kristin."

"What?"

Shannon smiled broadly. "He's from Missouri. He was originally from Virginia, but his family bought a big spread out here. I think he comes from tobacco money, a lot of it. He went to West Point. He was in the same class as Jeb Stuart!"

Kristin stared at her sister, who appeared about to swoon. Shannon thought that the Confederate general Jeb Stuart was the handsomest, most gallant gentleman in the whole world. Shannon's reaction to Stuart's name didn't surprise her, but the fact that she seemed to know so much about Cole stunned her.

"What?" she repeated numbly.

Shannon sighed with supreme patience, as if she were the elder, explaining things to a sullen child.

"He's a Virginian, Kristin, moved to Missouri. He went to West Point. Once upon a time he was in the army in Kansas. He and Stuart served together."

"Wonderful," Kristin murmured.

So he *was* a Southerner. And he wasn't in uniform. He was one of them, one of the breed that ran with Quantrill....

She was a Southerner herself, she thought dully. Not all Southerners were like Zeke Moreau.

But Cole . . .

Cole had talked freely to Shannon. But the questions hadn't all been answered yet.

He had gone to West Point. He had served in the Union Army before the war with the gallant Southern calvary officer, Jeb Stuart.

But he wasn't wearing a uniform now. Not the Union's, and not the Confederacy's. Why not?

Delilah stirred something over the fire. She wiped her hands on her apron. "Well, Kristin? What do we do? If you want, I'll go move your things."

Kristin swallowed. She wanted to protest. She wanted to refuse Cole Slater.

She looked at Delilah. Delilah wasn't making any judgments.

Kristin nodded. She could give up the place or she could hold tight to Cole Slater. She really had no choice. But she vowed to herself that she'd find out everything there was to know about the man.

5

Kristin spent the day worrying about the night ahead. She prowled around upstairs, trying to keep busy. Though she hated it, she did what Cole had told her to, taking a few of her dresses and nightshirts and putting them in the armoire in her parents' bedroom.

Shannon came upstairs while she was at it. There was something about her knowing glance that made Kristin feel terribly ashamed. "Cole—Mr. Slater—thinks that Zeke ought to think there's something...um, that he and I, that..."

"I understand," Shannon said softly. Even her innocence was dead, Kristin thought. There was an awkward silence, but then Shannon came into the room and hugged her. "I like him," she told Kristin. "I like him a whole lot."

"Only because he knows Jeb Stuart."

Shannon made a face. "That helps." She sat down on the bed. "What happened here?" she queried softly.

"What do you mean?" Kristin asked her.

"So many men are so fine. General Lee is such a gentleman, by all accounts. And Jeb Stuart is so dashing! And then out here..."

"We get the bushwhackers and the jayhawkers," Kristin finished for her. She sat down beside Shannon and hugged her. "And don't forget," she reminded her, "we have a brother fighting in Mr. Lincoln's army."

"I never forget!" Shannon said.

They sat there in silence for a long time. Then suddenly, there was a volley of shots from outside. Kristin leaped to her feet and raced to the window.

Cole was out back with Samson. He'd set a few rows of old liquor and tonic bottles on the back fence to serve as makeshift targets. He'd already shot up the first set.

Kristin watched as he reloaded, then twirled his six-shooter in his hand and shoved it back in its holster. He paused. Then, in the wink of an eye, he cleared away another row. Then he spoke to Samson, and Kristin realized that it was a lesson.

Then it was Samson's turn with the guns. Kristin strained to hear Cole's words.

"Quantrill's boys usually carry four or five Colts, a shotgun or a rifle or maybe both. That's why they keep licking the pants off the Union troops. They're well armed, and the boys in blue are still trying to fire off muzzle-loading carbines. Zeke will always be well armed. So we've always got to be prepared to outshoot him in return. You understand, Sam?"

"Yes, Mr. Slater, that I do."

"Let's try it again. Hold your hand steady, and squeeze the trigger, don't jerk it."

Cole took off his plumed hat, ran his fingers through his hair and set the hat back on his head, low over his eyes. Then he said, "Go!" and Samson drew. He shattered a fair number of the bottles, then laughed. Cole slapped him on the back, congratulating him. Then the men's voices grew low, and Kristin couldn't hear any more.

Suddenly Cole looked up at the window. It was too late. She couldn't draw away.

He smiled and waved. She almost waved back, but then she realized that Shannon had come up beside her and that it was her sister he was waving to, because she was waving down to him.

"We're moving Kristin in!" Shannon called down.

Kristin was mortified. She felt his eyes on her, she saw his slow, lazy smile. She wanted to hit Shannon over the head. She backed away from the window instead.

"You coming up?" Shannon called.

"Shannon!" Kristin hissed.

But Cole shook his head. He looked handsome then, as tall as Samson, and hard and lean in his long coat and his plumed hat. "Tell your sister I'm on my way out to find Pete. Might be gone awhile. If I can take care of some things today, I will."

Shannon turned to Kristin. "Cole said—"

"I heard what Cole said."

"Shannon!" Cole said.

"Yes, Cole?"

"Tell your sister I may be back late. Tell her she doesn't have to wait up."

Shannon turned to Kristin. "Cole said—"

"I heard what Cole said!"

Kristin spun around and stormed out of the room. She returned to her own room and slammed the door. She sat down on her own bed and pressed her hands against her temples. She had a staggering headache, and her nerves were as shattered as the bottles Cole had shot up.

Well, he had shattered her world, too.

She needed to get this over with quickly. She needed him to be around. She wanted him. She hated him.

She wished to God she knew him. She wished to God she could get to know him. But she didn't think he would let anyone get close to him. Anyone at all.

No involvement . . .

She didn't want any involvement. And he couldn't possibly make her as nervous as Zeke Moreau made her hateful.

Or could he?

If he came back at all that night, Kristin never knew it. She lay on her parents' bed until the wee hours of the morning, and then exhaustion claimed her. When she awoke, it was almost noon. No one came for her. When she dressed and went downstairs, Delilah was busy with a big pot of lye and Shannon was putting their last two-year-old colt through his paces. Kristin longed to do something, to ride somewhere, but Samson found her in the stable and warned her that Cole had said she should stay close to home. She bit her lip but did as she was told, and Samson proudly showed her something of what he had learned.

Kristin was impressed with his newfound skill with a gun, and she told him so, but then she rested her chin on the fence and sighed. "Is it enough, Samson? Is it enough against Zeke?"

"Maybe not me alone, Miss Kristin, but Mr. Slater had all the boys out here this morning, and he can teach a whole lot about gun play, as well as practice it."

"You sound like you like him a lot, Samson."

"Yep. Yes, miss, I do. He complimented me on my language this morning, and when I told him how big your pa was on learning he said that he thought fine men came in both black and white, and that he was mighty proud to know me."

Kristin smiled. "That's nice, Samson. That's mighty nice."

They were both silent for a moment. Then Kristin began to grow uncomfortable, wondering what he really thought of what was going on with Cole Slater.

"The world just ain't the same anymore, Miss Kristin," Samson said at last. "The world just ain't the same." He chewed on a long blade of grass and stared out at the pastureland. "No, the world just ain't the same, and we can only pray that it'll right itself when this awful war is over."

Kristin nodded. Then she turned to him and gave him a big hug. She didn't know what she'd do without him and Delilah.

She didn't see Cole again all that day and night. He was still out with Pete and the boys at dinnertime, and later, much later, she heard laughter and the strains of Pete's fiddle coming from the bunkhouse. That night she slept alone again in the big sleigh bed in her parents' room.

In the morning she didn't know if he had ever come to bed or not. For some reason, she didn't think he had, and she wondered why he was taunting her this way when he seemed to have so little real interest in her. Her temper rose, but then she remembered that she should be grateful to have him here. And then she was afraid he would leave.

And then she hated him. He was supposed to want her. They were supposed to have a deal. She was supposed to loathe him for taking advantage of her weakness. But she was the one left wondering and wanting. No, not wanting. Merely curious, she assured herself. But she couldn't deny that she had been in a fever ever since he had come. She simply couldn't deny her emotions.

Then he was there. He was there all day. He passed her in the hallway and tipped his hat to her, a smile of amusement tugging at his lips.

"Wait!" she cried. "Where are you going?"

"Rounding up strays."

"Let me come."

His smile faded. "No."

"But—"

"My rules, Kristin."

"But—"

"My rules."

She gritted her teeth and stiffened, watching him for a moment in simmering silence. He smiled again. "But I will be back for supper this evening. Steak and sweet potatoes and Delilah's black-eyed peas, and blueberry pie for dessert. And then . . ." He let his voice trail off. Then he lifted his hat again and turned and left.

And she didn't even know where he had spent the night.

It was another wretched day. She fed the chickens. She groomed her horse. She played with little Daniel, marveling in spite of herself at the way the child grew daily. She wandered around upstairs. Then she found herself sitting at the foot of the big sleigh bed.

His blanket lay on the floor next to the dresser. Kristin hesitated, staring at it for a long while. Then she got up and went over to it.

And then she unrolled it and went through his personal belongings.

There wasn't much. If he had a wallet, he had it with him. There was a shaving mug and a tin plate, a leather sack of tobacco, another sack of coffee and a roll of hard tack.

And there was a small silver Daguerreotype frame.

Kristin stared at it for a moment then found the little silver clasp and flicked it open.

There were two pictures in the double frame. The first was of a woman alone, a very beautiful woman, with enormous eyes and dark hair and a dazzling smile.

In the second picture the woman was with a man. Cole.

He was in a U.S. Cavalry uniform, so the picture must have been made before the war. The woman wore a beautiful, voluminous gown with majestic hoops, and a fine bonnet with a slew of feathers. They weren't looking at the camera. They were looking at one another.

There was such tenderness, such love in their eyes, that Kristin felt she was intruding on something sacred. She closed the frame with a firm snap and put it back inside the blanket, trying to put everything back together as if she hadn't touched it at all. It didn't make any difference, she told herself dully. He should expect people who didn't know a thing about him to check up on him. No, that didn't wash, not at all, not even with her.

The woman was dead, she thought.

She didn't know how she knew, but she knew. Cole Slater had loved her, and Kristin was certain that he wouldn't be here with her now if the woman in the picture were still alive.

There seemed to be an ominous silence all over the house as dinnertime approached. Delilah had been out to feed the hands, and the table was set for the family.

Set for three.

They weren't using the fine service that evening. Shannon had set out the pewter plates, and the atmosphere in the dining room seemed as muted and subdued as the dull color of the dishes.

Cole had stayed out all day. Kristin had done her best to be useful, but the day had been a waste. There was no way out of it. She couldn't forget Cole's promise that he would be there that night, and she couldn't forget the woman in the picture, and she couldn't forget the startling array of emotions that it had all raised within her.

Kristin had dressed for dinner.

She was a rancher, and this ranch on the border between Kansas and Missouri was a far cry from the fine parlors and plantations back east, but she was still a woman and she loved clothes.

It was a weakness with her, Pa had told her once, but he'd had a twinkle in his eyes when he'd said it. He'd always been determined that his daughters should be ladies. Capable women, but ladies for all that. He had always been pleased to indulge her whims, letting her study fabrics, and to pick up her *Lady Godoy's* the minute the fashion magazine reached the local mercantile. Her armoire was still filled with gowns, and her trunks and dressers held an endless assortment of petticoats and hoops, chemises and corsets, stockings and pantalets. They had all lent a certain grace to life once upon a time. Before the carnage had begun. By day they had worked for their dream, and the dust and the tumbleweed of the prairie had settled on them. At night they had washed away the dust and the dirt, and after dinner Pa had settled back in his chair with a cigar and she and Shannon had taken turns at the spinet. Her own voice was passable. Shannon's was like that of a nightingale.

And there had been nights when Adam had been there, too. Sometimes winter had raged beyond the windows, but they had been warm inside, warmed by the fire and by the love and laughter that had surrounded them.

That was what Zeke had hated so much, she thought. He had never understood that laughter and love could not be bought or stolen. He had called her a traitor to the Southern cause, but she had never betrayed the South. She had merely learned to despise him, and so she had lost her father, and then Adam, too.

Today she could remember Adam all too clearly. He had loved books. He had always looked so handsome, leaning against the fireplace, his features animated as he spoke about the works of Hawthorne and Sir Walter Scott.

No one had told her that Adam was riding out after Zeke. She'd never had the chance to try to stop him.

And now she wondered painfully if she had ever really loved him. Oh, she had cared for him dearly. He had been a fine man, good and decent and caring, and he had often made her laugh.

But she had never, never thought of Adam in the way that she had Cole Slater, had never even imagined doing with Adam the things she had actually done with Cole Slater.

And she didn't love Cole Slater. She couldn't love him. No, she couldn't love him, not even now. How could a woman love a man who had treated her the way he had?

But how could she forget him? How could she forget all she had felt since she'd first seen the man? How could she forget all that had passed between them? Kristin realized that it was difficult just to be in the same room with him now. Her breath shortened instantly, and she couldn't keep her gaze steady, and she wanted to run away every time he looked her way. She couldn't look at him without remembering their night together, and when she did she wanted to crawl into a hole in the ground and hide. She was ashamed, not so much because of what she had done but because she had been so fascinated by it. Because she still felt the little trickles of excitement stir within her whenever he entered the room, whenever she felt his presence.

She knew instinctively when he came into the house for dinner.

Fall was coming on, and the evening was cool. She had dressed in a soft white velvet gown with black cord trim. The bodice was low, and the half sleeves were trimmed in black cord, too. The skirt was sweeping, and she had chosen to wear a hoop and three petticoats.

She'd made Delilah tie her corset so tightly that she wasn't sure she'd be able to breathe all evening.

Her appearance had suddenly become very, very important to her. He hadn't been cruel to her, but he had been mocking, and he'd warned her again and again that this terribly intimate thing between them had nothing to do with involvement. Her pride was badly bruised, and all she had to cling to was her dream of leaving him panting in the dust. Someday. When she didn't need him anymore.

She'd braided her hair and curled it high atop her head, except for one long lock that swept around the column of her neck and the curve of her shoulder to rest on the mound of her cleavage.

She never used rouge—Pa hadn't allowed it in the house—but she pinched her cheeks and bit her lips, to bring some color to her features. Still, when she gazed at her reflection in the mirror over the dresser—she had refused to dress in the other room—she was terribly pale, and she looked more like a nervous girl than a sophisticated woman in charge of her life, owner of her property, mistress of her own destiny.

She tried to sweep elegantly down the stairs, but her knees were weak, so she gave up and came down as quickly as she could. Shannon was setting cups on the table. She stared at Kristin with wide blue eyes, but she didn't say anything. Nor did Kristin have to question her about Cole.

"He's in Pa's office," Shannon mouthed. Kristin nodded. Nervously, she started through the house. She passed through the parlor and came around, pausing in the doorway.

He was sitting at her father's desk, reading the newspaper, and his brows were drawn into such a dark and brooding frown that she nearly turned away. Then he looked up. She was certain that he started for a moment, but he hid it quickly and stood politely. His gaze never left her.

"Bad news?" she asked him, looking at the paper.

He shrugged. "Not much of anything today," he said.

"No great Southern victory? No wonderful Union rout?"

"You sound bitter."

"I am."

"You got kin in the army?"

"My brother."

"North or South?"

"North. He's with an Illinois troop." Kristin hesitated. She didn't want him to feel that they were traitors to the Southern cause. "Matthew was here when Pa was killed. He learned a whole lot about hatred."

"I understand."

She nodded. Then curiously she asked him. "And have you got kin in the army, Mr. Slater?"

"Yes."

"North or South?"

He hesitated. "Both."

"You were in the Union Army."

"Yes." Again he paused. Then he spoke softly. "Yes. And every time I see a list of the dead—either side—it hurts like hell. You've seen the worst of it, Kristin. There are men on both sides of this thing who are fine and gallant, the very best we've ever bred, no matter what state they've hailed from."

It was a curious moment. Kristin felt warm, almost felt cherished. She sensed depths to him that went very far beyond her understanding, and she was glad that he was here for her.

However briefly.

But then he turned, and she saw his profile. She saw its strengths, and she saw the marks that time had left upon it, and she remembered the woman in the picture, and that he didn't really love her at all. And she felt awkward, her nerves on edge again.

"Supper's about on the table," she said.

He nodded.

"Can I . . . can I get you a drink? Or something?"

Or something. She saw the slow smile seep into his lips at her words, and she blushed, feeling like a fool despite herself. He nodded again.

"Madeira?"

"A shot of whiskey would be fine."

Kristin nodded, wondering what had prompted her to say such a thing. He was closer to the whiskey than she was, and he knew it, but he didn't make a move to get it. He kept staring at her, his smile mocking again.

She swept into the room and took the whiskey from the drawer. They were very close to one another. He hadn't changed. He was still wearing tight breeches and a cotton shirt and his riding boots. She knew he had ridden out to meet with Pete, and she knew, too, that he seemed to know something about ranching. Well, he was from somewhere around here, according to Shannon.

She poured him out a double shot of the amber liquid, feeling him watching her every second. She started to hand him the glass, but he didn't seem to notice. His eyes were on hers, grown dark, like the sky before a tornado.

He reached out and touched the golden lock of hair that curled over the rise of her breasts. He curled it around his finger, his thumb grazing her bare flesh. She couldn't move. A soft sound came from her throat, and suddenly it was as if all the fires of hell had risen up to sweep through her, robbing her of all strength. She stared up at him, but his eyes were on her hair, and on her flesh where he touched her. She felt heat radiating from the length and breadth of his body, and yet she shivered, remembering the strength of his shoulders, the hardness of his belly, the power of his thighs.

And she remembered the speed of his draw. He was a gunslinger, she thought, bred to violence.

No. He had been to West Point. He had served as a captain in the U.S. cavalry. That was what he had told Shannon, at least.

Did any of it matter? He was here, and as long as he was here she felt safe from the Zeke Moreaus of the world. And yet, she thought, their's must surely be a bargain made in hell, for when he looked at her, when he touched her even as lightly as he did now, she felt the slow fires of sure damnation seize her.

"Do you always dress so for dinner?" he asked her, and the timbre of his voice sent new shivers skating down her spine.

"Always," she managed to murmur.

His knuckles hovered over her breasts. Then his eyes met hers, and he slowly relinquished the golden curl he held. Expectation swirled around them, and Kristin was afraid that her knees would give, that she would fall against him. The whiskey in the glass she held threatened to spill over. He took the glass from her and set it on the desk. She felt heat where his fingers had brushed hers, and it seemed that the air, the very space between them, hummed with a palpable tension.

"You are a very beautiful woman, Miss McCahy," he told her softly, and she felt his male voice, male and sensual, wash over her.

"Then, you're not . . . you're not too disappointed in our deal?"

He smiled again, and his silver-gray eyes brightened wickedly. "Did we need a deal?"

"I don't know what you mean," she told him, though she knew exactly what he meant.

The light went out of his eyes. He picked up the whiskey and swallowed it quickly. "I'm still damned if I know what the hell I'm doing here," he muttered.

"I thought—" she began, and her face flamed.

He touched her cheek. "You thought the payoff went well, is that it?"

She shoved his hand away. She didn't want him to touch her, not then. "You do have a talent for making a woman feel just like river slime," she said, as sweetly as she could. He arched a brow, and she saw fleeting amusement light his features. She could hold her own in any fight, she thought, but only for so long. She needed to escape him now.

"I didn't mean to make you feel like . . . river slime."

"Don't worry. You already did so. Last night." With a sweetly mocking smile, Kristin turned to leave.

Then she paused and turned toward him again, biting her lip. She kept forgetting how much she needed him. Her eyes must have widened with the realization, for he was smiling cynically again and pouring himself another shot of whiskey.

"Don't worry," he told her smoothly. "I'm not walking out on you. Not yet."

Kristin moistened her lips. "Not yet?" she whispered.

"Why, Miss McCahy! I really couldn't leave a lady in such distress, could I?"

"What do you mean by that?"

He raised the glass. "Take it as you will, ma'am."

Kristin swore under her breath and strode over to him again. She snatched the glass from his hand and thought seriously of pouring the contents over his head. His eyes narrowed, and she quickly reconsidered.

She swallowed the whiskey down so quickly that her head spun in an instant and her throat burned with the fury of a brush fire. A double shot, straight. But she steeled herself, and she still managed to smile sweetly. "You don't owe me anything."

"No, darlin'. You owe me." He smiled, took the glass from her and poured another double. "And I'm real anxious for the next installment."

Kristin snatched the glass again and swallowed the liquid down. She didn't know if she was alive with anger or with desire.

She slammed the glass down and tried to spin around. He caught her arm, pulling her back. She tossed her head back, staring into his eyes.

"Isn't it what you want?" he asked her.

"I want revenge, nothing more," she told him.

"Nothing more?"

"I want you to—I want you to stay. I want to hold on to the ranch. I just want to hold on to what is mine."

"The precious ranch," he muttered darkly.

Fear fluttered briefly in her heart. "Cole...Mr. Slater, you really wouldn't...you wouldn't go back on your word, would you?"

"Not so long as you follow the rules."

Her head was really spinning now. He had poured so much whiskey, and she'd swallowed it down so fast. He was so warm, and so damn vibrant, and so shockingly male. And she'd already been in bed with him.

Her mother would be spinning in her grave, Kristin thought.

He was using her. He was using her because he had loved another woman and now he just didn't give a damn.

"Your rules! Just don't forget that the place belongs to me!"

She wrenched free of him, and this time she walked out. She wasn't afraid of him leaving. He was having too fine a time torturing her to leave now.

When she reached the dining room, she was startled to discover that he was behind her. He had followed her, as silent as a wraith. It was disconcerting.

"Stop it!" she demanded.

Shannon came out of the kitchen. Delilah was behind her. Both women stopped, startled.

Cole ignored them both. "Stop what?" he demanded irritably.

"Sneaking up on me!"

"I wasn't sneaking up on you. You told me it was time for supper, so I followed you."

"Whoa!" Shannon murmured, looking at her sister. "Kristin, you've been drinking!"

"Yes!" she snapped, glaring at Cole. "And I'll probably do a whole lot more drinking before...before..."

"Oh, hell, will you just sit the hell down!" Cole growled. He caught her hand, pulled out a chair and directed her into it with little grace. Her wide skirts flew. He pressed them down and shoved her chair in.

Kristin wanted to be dignified. She wanted to be sophisticated and elegant, and most of all she wanted to be in control. "You arrogant scallywag!" she said quietly, her voice husky with emotion.

"Kristin, shut up."

That was it. She started to push herself away from the table, but his hand slammed down on hers, holding her fast. "Kristin, shut up."

"Bas—"

"Now, Kristin." He came closer to her, much closer, and spoke in a whisper. This was between the two of them. "Or else we can get up and settle this outside."

The whiskey seemed to hit her anew right then, hit her hard. She thought she was going to scream. She burst into laughter instead. "Outside? With pistols?"

"Hardly, but you can call it what you want, darlin'."

The buzz of the liquor was nice. If he stayed around too long, Kristin thought, she'd find herself turning into a regular old drunk.

"Shall we eat?" Cole asked politely.

There was silence in the room. Shannon was staring at him.

"Sit!" he told her.

Shannon sat hastily, then lowered her head before looking surreptitiously over at Kristin, who hiccuped loudly.

Cole groaned, then he looked up at Delilah. "Don't you and Samson usually eat?"

"Oh, no, sir!" Delilah protested. "Why, you know it just wouldn't be right for black folks—"

"Delilah, cut the . . . er—" He broke off, looking from Samson to Kristin. Shannon was about to laugh.

"Manure," Kristin supplied.

Shannon did burst into laughter. Even Delilah grinned. Cole said, "Get your husband, woman, and sit down and eat. I once had the opportunity to discover that a black man could save my hide as good as a white one. Let's just have supper and get it over with, shall we?"

"Yessir, yessir," Delilah said, chuckling. "My, my, my," she muttered, moving off toward the kitchen.

Kristin sat primly, her hands folded in her lap. Her dress felt ridiculously heavy, now that she was sitting. She felt as if she was about to fall over. She realized that Cole was looking at her, but it didn't matter very much, and that was a nice feeling.

Delilah walked back in from the kitchen.

Cole gazed at her expectantly. "You've never washed her mouth out with soap, huh?" He indicated Kristin.

Kristin decided that she could sit straight. She told Cole that he reminded her of the stuff that people needed to wipe off their boots before they came in from the barn.

Shannon gasped, and then she began to giggle. Delilah stood stock-still. Samson, coming in behind his wife, turned an ashen color.

Cole was dead still. Explosively still. And then explosively in motion.

He was up, and Kristin sobered enough to know a moment's panic as he came around behind her and purposely pulled her chair away from the table. He lifted her, and her petticoats and hoops and shirt went flying. Kristin swore at him and pounded on his back.

"Cole!" Kristin gasped.

What manner of man had she let loose in her home, she wondered.

He started for the stairs.

"What are you doing?" she shrieked.

"Putting you to bed."

"I don't want to go!"

"My rules, Miss McCahy."

They were all watching her, Shannon and Delilah and Samson, and they weren't doing a thing to save her. They were just staring. She raised her head and saw that Delilah was openly grinning and Samson was hiding a smile.

"You son of a bitch!" she yelled.

"We are going to have to do something about that mouth of yours," Cole vowed grimly.

"This is my house!"

"My rules!"

She told him what he could do with his rules, but it was too late. They were already up the stairs. He booted open the door to the room he had decreed they would share, and before she knew it she had landed on the bed. She wanted to get back up, but she groaned instead and clutched her temples.

His leering face was above her.

"Why, what's the matter, Miss McCahy? Why, I would have thought you could drink any man west of the Mississippi under the table."

"Madeira," she whispered. "Not whiskey."

He showed her no mercy. Suddenly his hand was on her leg and he was pulling off her shoe. She managed to pull herself up to a sitting position and pummel his back. "What are you doing?"

"Taking your shoes off." But her shoes were off, and his hands were still on her, slipping along her calf, then her thigh. When his fingers touched her thigh, she gasped and tried to stop him. "Damn you Cole Slater—"

Her words ended in a gasp, for he turned quickly, pulling hard on her ankle so that she was lying flat on her back again. Her silk stockings came free in his hands, and he tossed them carelessly on the floor. She tried to rise, and he came down beside her on the bed, his weight on her.

"Where the hell are the damn ties to these things?" he muttered, working on her hoop.

Kristin struggled to stop him, but he found the ties. She reached for his hands, but they had already moved, freeing her from her hoop and petticoats, and he pulled her up, working on the hooks of her gown. In seconds he had it free and she was down to her pantalets, chemise and corset.

"Come here!" he demanded roughly. Kristin cried out, trying to elude him, but he pulled her back by the corset ties. He lossened the ties, and she gasped, amazed by the air that rushed into her lungs. But then she was naked except for her sheer chemise and pantalets, and his presence was overwhelming.

She began to protest. He caught her shoulders and slammed her down on the bed.

"Calm down and sleep it off!" he commanded.

He was straddling her, and his eyes were like steel. She wanted to slap his superior face. She tried. She missed by a mile, and he caught her hand.

"My rules."

She told him again what he could do with his rules.

"Stay here alone, or I'll stay here with you."

She went still, trying to grasp the meaning of his words. The room was spinning madly.

Then she understood. He stared at her. Then he lowered his head toward her and kissed her, and somewhere, within her hazy mind and her bruised heart she knew that he did desire her. And she knew, too, that he didn't love her, not at all.

His kiss was hard and demanding and, in its way, punishing. But then it deepened, and it was rich, and it betrayed a growing passion and hunger. She felt her body respond. She felt his hands move over her, felt him grow warm and hard. She began to tremble and suddenly she wanted him, but she wanted him loving her, loving her tenderly, not just wanting her with the raw desire that had finally brought him to her.

His mouth opened and closed hungrily upon her flesh. His teeth grazed her throat, and the tip of his tongue teased the valley between her breasts. He was a flame setting on her, seeping into her, and she was stunned that he could so easily elicit this willingness...

This eagerness...

Within her. She stiffened, fighting the whiskey haze in her heart and in her mind. She had to stop him. He hadn't meant to do this, not now. He had stayed away from her on purpose, she was certain of it. He wanted no involvements.

And she could too easily fall in love with him.

She forced herself to feel nothing, to allow the bitterness of the last years to invade her, so that his searing warmth could not touch her. When he rose above her, she met his steely gaze and spoke to him in a quiet, toneless voice.

"Who was she? Your wife?"

She might have struck him. All the heat left him. It was as if he turned to ice. He stared at her, his jaw constricted, his features as harsh as a desert. He rolled away from her and sat on the side of the bed. His fingers threaded through his hair, and he pressed his hand against his temple as if he were trying to soothe some awful pain.

"Go to sleep," he told her. "And stay off the hard stuff from now on."

Kristin cast her arm over her eyes. "Your rules," she murmured.

"I don't like this kind of a fight, Kristin," he said dully, "but..."

"But?"

"You start it, and I'll end it. Every time."

She felt his weight lift from the bed, and she started to shiver. Suddenly she was warmed. He had laid a blanket over her, and he was close by her again.

"Go to sleep," he said softly, his voice almost tender again.

Almost.

He got up and walked away. She heard the door close quietly, and to her great dismay she closed her eyes and started to cry as she hadn't done since they had come to tell her that Adam was dead.

6

It was the liquor, Kristin thought. Lying in the darkness, feeling miserable, she put her arm over her eyes and felt her head spin, and she wondered what had made her drink so much so fast. She was humiliated, but it was her own fault, and she was in no mood to do anything about it, except to suffer in silence.

And, in a way, she wasn't sorry. She could dimly hear the sounds of dinner, and she wondered if Samson and Delilah had sat down to eat. Cole Slater was an unusual man. A very unusual man.

The darkness closed in and whirled around her. She knew she ought to be sorry she had let the liquor ignite her temper, but instead she was glad of it. She didn't feel the awful pain for once. She didn't remember what it had been like to see Pa die, to see Matthew turn his back on his own people and ride away with the Union forces.

She didn't even quite remember what it was like to be with Cole Slater. To be so nervous that she lost all the wisdom her harsh life had taught her. To be afraid in a way, and yet to want something, some intangible thing, so badly.

Curiously—bless the liquor—she felt at peace.

She closed her eyes, and she must have dozed. Then she must have awakened, or else she was dreaming, because when she opened her eyes, the room was bathed in moonlight. Her mind was still spinning, and she still felt at peace.

He was in the room with her.

He had come in quietly, and the door had closed softly behind him. He stood just inside of it, his hands on his hips, and watched her where she lay upon the bed. The moonlight fell on his features, and they were both harsh and curiously beautiful. For the longest time he stood there. The wind seemed to rise, not to a moan, but to a whisper. She imagined that outside tumbleweeds were being caught and tossed in the strange, sweet dance of the West, buffeted as she was being buffeted. Her heart rose and fell like that tumbleweed, tossed around heedlessly.

No...

He was a marvelous creature, sleek as a cougar, sharp as an eagle. He was still standing there, his hands on his hips, his head at an angle, as if he were waiting, as if he were listening to the curiously tender whispering of the wind.

Then he moved. He unbuttoned his cuffs. He took off his boots and stripped off his socks. He came to her in silence, barefoot, and he dropped his gun belt beside the bed. Then he looked down at her, and saw that her eyes were open. "You're still awake."

She nodded gravely, and then she smiled. "I'm sorry. I was out of line this evening. And I...I don't want to fight."

Unbuttoning his shirt, he sat beside her on the bed. His eyes remained on hers. He reached over and touched her cheek. "I don't want to fight, either, Kristin. You've had a hard time of it, and you've done well. Someone else might have shattered a long, long time ago."

The gentle whisper of the wind was in his voice, and there was an evocative tenderness in his fingertips as they brushed her cheek. She didn't reply, but kept her eyes on his, and then the whisper of the wind seemed to sweep into her, to permeate her flesh and fill her veins. She was warm, and achingly aware of herself, and of the man. Surely, she was still asleep. Surely it was all a dream. It was a spell cast by the moonlight. It lived in the clouds of imagination.

But it was real. Very real. He leaned over then and caught her lips in a curious kiss. It was light at first. He tasted her lips, teasing them with the tip of his tongue. Then he plunged his tongue deep into her mouth, and she wrapped her arms around his neck and felt the rugged, steel-muscled frame of his chest against her. She felt his hands on her, rough and tender. Then his hands were in her hair, threading through the tendrils, and he was stroking her arm as he moved his lips over her throat and down to the place where her breasts spilled provocatively from her lace chemise. His mouth fastened over her nipple through the sheer fabric, and she cried out softly. He shifted swiftly, taking her mouth again, taking her cry into him.

He stood, dropping his shirt and stripping away his pants. The moonlight fell on him. He was tall and rugged, lean and sinewed, his skin shining almost copper in that light, his shoulders shimmering with it. She stared at him. If this was a dream, she was grateful for it. She wanted him. She wanted him with her heart and with her mind, she wanted him with every fiber of her being. She wanted him desperately.

She was not to be denied.

He came down beside her and took her in his arms, and she strained to meet his kiss again. He unlaced her chemise, and her breast spilled from it. He lowered his head again, touching her nipple with his tongue, fondling the weight of her breast with a touch so achingly soft.... She was barely aware that she arched to him, that she dug her fingers into his hair and cried incoherently for him to come to her. But it was not to be. His hands brushed her flesh, and where they had been she yearned for them again. His kisses ranged over the length of her, a mere breath, a mere whisper, and then were gone. She writhed. She tried to hold him, to pin him down. And she felt something move in her, like lava rising to the surface of the earth. She felt the earth teeming and bubbling with heat and steam, and still he pressed her. She moved her hands against him, felt the tension in his taut muscles, and touching him inflamed her, bringing her to still greater heights. She no longer knew herself. She had become some strange wanton. She felt his hands on her hips, and on her belly and she moved toward the feel of them, the promise of them. He made her touch him, and the pulsing heat and size of him gave her pause. Then a curious elation filled her, and for a moment she was afraid she might faint.

Her remaining clothes were gone now. Like him, she lay naked in the moonlight, her skin shimmering like copper beneath its glow.

Time had lost all meaning. She lay upon clouds of moonlight, and all that was real was the hardness of this man, the demand in his eyes. The wind had become the ragged cry of his breath, and the storm was the near-savage urgency that drove him. He did not tease. He sucked hard on her breast until she thought she would explode. He did not shyly caress her thighs, but stroked within, to the heart of her, and as he touched her, he caught her cries again with his lips. He knelt before her, caught her eyes again, then watched her, before he caught the supple length of her legs and brought them around him. He stared at her as he lowered his head, and she opened her mouth to stop him, but she could not.

He touched her intimately, with a searing demand, and she tossed her head, savagely biting her own lip so as not to scream. She could not bear it, and despite her efforts she did cry out. She lunged forward, she convulsed and she heard the soft tenor of his laughter. She longed to strike him, to hide from him. But he was above her, and he had her hands, and suddenly he was within her, igniting a fierce burning, and it was all happening again, all beginning again. His hands roughly cupped her buttocks, and again he led her into a shattering rhythm.

The clouds danced around them. She closed her eyes and buried her face against his chest, and she tasted the salt on his body. There was nothing gentle in him then. He moved in a frenzy, violent, urgent, and though she feared she would lose herself in him, she clung to him and fought to meet his every move. Ecstasy burst through again, even stronger than before, and she dug her fingers into his flesh, convulsing against him. He shuddered strongly against her, and she was filled with their mutual heat. Then he fell from her, smoothing the wild tangle of her hair.

They didn't say anything. Not anything at all.

The wind had died down again. It was a mere whisper. It caught the tumbleweeds down below and tossed them around.

Her heart was still beating savagely,. He must have felt it when he put his arm around her and pulled her against him. It was a wonderful way to sleep, her back to his chest, his fingers just below the full curve of her breast. She didn't think about the wind, or the night. The moonlight was still shining down on them. Perhaps it had all been a dream. She didn't want to know. She closed her eyes, and at long last the spinning in her head stopped. She slept.

He slept, too, and it was his turn to dream. The nightmare of the past, the nightmare that haunted him whether he was awake or asleep, came back to him now.

The dream unfolded slowly, so slowly. It always came to him first with sound...a soft, continual thunder, like the beating of drums. It was the sound of hooves driving across the earth, driving hard. Then he heard the shouts. They made no sense at first, they meant nothing, nothing at all. Then he realized that the hooves were churning beneath him. He was the rider. He was riding hard, riding desperately, and all he wanted to do was get home before...

Smoke. He inhaled sharply and it filled his nostrils and mouth with an acrid taste. There was something about that smell... He could feel a trail of ice streak along his spine. He recognized the awful odor of burning flesh.

Then he saw the horror up ahead. The house was burning; the barn was burning.

And he saw Elizabeth.

She was running, trying to reach him. He screamed her name, his voice ragged and harsh, and still he felt the

movement beneath him, the endless thunder of the horse's hooves. He rode across the plain, across the scrub brush. And she kept coming. She was calling to him, but the sound of her voice could not reach him. She could not reach him.

She fell and disappeared from sight. He rode harder, and then he leaped from the horse, still shouting her name, over and over. He searched through the grass until he found her. Her hair, long and lustrous and ebony black, was spread over the earth in soft, silken waves.

"Elizabeth . . ."

He took her into his arms, and he looked down, and all that he saw was red. Red, spilling over him, filling his hands. Red, flowing in rivers, red . . . the color of blood.

He cast back his head, and he screamed, and the scream echoed and echoed across the plain. . . .

He awoke with a start.

He was covered in sweat, and he was trembling. He shook his head, trying to clear it, and gazed at the woman beside him. He saw her golden hair, and the easy rise and fall of her chest with her breath.

She hadn't awakened.

He rose and went to the window, where he stared out at the moon. He hadn't woken her; it was going to be all right. Maybe he was getting better; at least he wasn't screaming out loud anymore.

He walked over to the bed and stared down at her; and she seemed incredibly young and pure, and very lovely. His fingers itched, and he wanted to shake her, to tell her that she didn't understand how deadly the game she was playing could be.

His fingers eased. Maybe she knew.

He went back to the window and stared at the moon again. Slowly, the tension left him, and he sighed. He went back to bed, but he couldn't bear to touch her, even though he knew that someday soon he would. He needed to touch her, just as he needed air to breathe.

He didn't sleep. In time, dawn came. He rose and dressed, then went outside. He gazed out over the plain, and in his mind he saw Elizabeth again, running toward him. He closed his eyes, and she was gone, but the pain was still with him, filling him, gnawing at his insides. He straightened his shoulders, and the pain slowly began to ebb, but it never fully left him. It clutched his heart with icy fingers, and he wondered what the hell he was doing here, then reminded himself that he had agreed to a "deal," and he might as well get on with it. He turned around and stared at her window. She was sleeping just beyond it. He marched back to the house.

She'd never expected to be awakened so rudely. One second she was so deep in blissful sleep, and the next she felt his hand against her rump. Her *bare* rump. He'd pulled the covers away from her.

Protesting, she grabbed the covers and sat with them pulled up to her chin, her eyes blazing with fury and indignation. He was up and dressed, standing at the foot of the bed and surveying her with cold eyes.

"I want you in the office. Now. If you want my help, you'd better show me the books."

"I'll come down to the office when I'm ready," she snapped. She couldn't understand the man. She couldn't understand his strange, distant behavior after the things they had shared in the night. It hurt.

"Get up."

She narrowed her eyes at this new battle.

"You get out and then I'll get up. When I'm ready."

He grabbed the sheets again. She lunged for them but she was too late, and he stripped them away. He eyed her dispassionately, his steely gaze sweeping over her form. She jumped out of bed, swearing once again, and leaped toward him, her temper soaring. He caught her arms, and his smile was curiously grim and somehow self-satisfied. It was as if he had been trying to pick a fight. She tried to wrench free of his touch. She didn't like the daylight on her naked flesh, and she didn't like the disadvantage of being undressed while he was clad from his scarf to his boots. He pulled her close against him. She felt the bite of his belt buckle and the texture of his shirt, but most of all she felt a hot tempest of emotions within him, no matter how calm, cold and in control he looked.

"I told you," he said sharply, "I call the shots. And you can't laze in bed all morning. You're a rancher. You should know that. Or do you just play at this thing? When you feel like riding with the boys, you do. And when you feel like playing the Southern belle, then you do that, too."

She was furious, but she smiled to hide it. Tense and still against him and staring up into his eyes, she smiled. "I don't play at anything, Mr. Slater. I am a rancher, and probably better at it than you ever were or could be. I just don't have to be as ugly as a mule's rump to do it. You call the shots? Well, that's just fine. When you want me up from now on, you knock. One knock, Mr. Slater, and I promise I'll be right out in less than five minutes. But don't you ever, ever touch me like that again!"

His brow arched slowly, and she saw his smile deepen. He released her and put his hands on his hips. She felt his gaze sweep over her again like fire. For a moment she thought he was going to sweep her up in his arms, right there, right then, in broad daylight. For a moment she was certain he was going to carry her over to the bed and take her there and then, with the morning sun shining on them.

She'd have to protest, she'd have to scream....

For the life of her she didn't know if she was afraid or if she wished he'd take a step forward and sweep her up in his arms....

He tipped his hat to her.

"I call all the shots, Kristin. All of them."

He turned around then and left her. The door closed sharply behind him.

She washed and dressed, wondering again what kind of a monster she had brought into her home. She touched her cheeks, and it was as if they were on fire.

When she came down the stairs, he was just finishing his breakfast. He tossed his checkered napkin on the table and rose at the sight of her. Kristin went to her chair.

"Flapjacks, honey?" Delilah asked her.

Cole was around the table before she had a chance to sit. He took her arm.

"Give her a cup of coffee, Delilah. Nothing else for the moment. We've got work to do."

She could make a scene, as she had at dinner. Delilah was staring at her, and Samson was staring at her, and so was Shannon. Her sister's eyes were very wide. They were all waiting.

Bastard! she thought. He was at fault! But she had been at fault the night before, and she knew she would look like a spoiled fool again if she created a problem.

"That's right. This is a busy, busy day, isn't it?" she said sweetly. "Coffee, Delilah." She accepted a cup and smiled her gratitude, gritting her teeth. She freed her arm from Cole's grasp. "Do come, Mr. Slater. The day is wearing on."

He followed her into the office, then swept past her, taking a seat behind her father's desk. He'd already been in there that morning, she was certain. He had the ledgers out, and before she could even seat herself he was firing out a barrage of questions. Where did she buy her feed, how much, how often? Had she considered moving any of the herd to avoid soldiers, Union and Confederate? Had she thought of leaving more pasture time, had she thought of introducing new strains? And on and on.

She didn't falter once. She was a rancher. She was bright, determined and well schooled, and she wanted him to know it. It occurred to her that he was just some drifter, that he had no rights here at all. But then she remembered that she had asked him to stay, that she had been desperate for him to stay.

That she had been willing to do anything at all to make him stay. And he had stayed, and she wasn't the same person anymore, not in any way. But whoever she was now, he wasn't going to treat her this way.

Suddenly he slammed the ledger he was examining shut and stood up. He stared across the desk at her, and for a moment she thought he must hate her.

He had saved her from Zeke, she reminded herself. He had ridden in, all honor and chivalry, and he had saved her from Zeke. Now he looked as if he wanted to flay her alive himself.

He looked as if he were about to say something. He shook his head impatiently. "I'm going out," he said. He jammed his hat low on his head, and came around the desk.

Kristin rose quickly and, she hoped, with dignity. "If you'd let me come with you—"

"No. I don't want you with me."

"I could show you—"

"God damn you, can't you hear? Or are you just incapable of listening? I'll see things myself. I'll see what I want to see. And you'll stay here by the house. Roam too far and come across Zeke and you'll wind up on your own this time. I swear it."

It might be better! she longed to shout. But she didn't do it, because it wasn't true. Zeke had killed her father. No matter how outrageously bad Cole's manners were turning out to be, he didn't compare with Zeke.

She crossed her arms over her chest and leaned back. "Don't let me keep you," she said sarcastically.

He walked past her.

She didn't know where he went. She was pretty sure he was never far away, but he didn't come by the house.

He had left a newspaper on the table, and she sat down and stared at the articles. War. It was all about war. About the Union troops holding Kansas, about the measures they intended to take against Quantrill and his raiders.

War and more war. The Union held New Orleans, and Grant was swearing he'd have Vicksburg soon. But whether the Union held sway or not, there was something that couldn't be changed. In the East, Lee was leading them all a merry chase. He had fewer men, he had less ammunition, he had less food. But he was brilliant, and not even the fact that the paper had been published in a town filled with Yankees could change the tenor of the articles. The South was strong. They could beat her and beat her, but she had the genius of Lee and Stonewall Jackson, and she had the daring of Jeb Stuart and Morgan Hunt and others like them.

Kristin laid her face against the cool wood of her father's desk. The news didn't make her happy or proud. It filled her heart with dread. It meant the war was going to go on and on. Nobody was going to go out and whomp the pants off anybody else. It was just going to keep going.

And Quantrill's outlaws would keep raiding and raiding....

After a while, Kristin lifted her head. There was a knock at the door. Delilah was there. She stuck her head in hesitantly.

"How about something to eat? Flapjacks and bacon?"

Her stomach was rumbling. She was starving. She hadn't had any supper, and she hadn't had any breakfast. She stood up and slid her hands into her back pockets.

"Flapjacks sound great."

"Fine. Come along."

"Delilah, wait."

Delilah hesitated there in the doorway. She met Kristin's eyes.

"Delilah, am I doing the right thing?"

"Honey, you're doing the only thing."

Kristin shook her head. "He made a fool out of me last night, Delilah."

"You let that happen."

"Yes, I did. But—"

"We need him," Delilah said bluntly. Then she smiled and gazed at Kristin, and Kristin was sure she was blushing beneath the gold and mahogany of her coloring. "We need him, and I like him. I like him just fine. You did well."

Kristin blushed herself. "I didn't marry him, Delilah. I'm ... I'm his ... mistress, Delilah."

"You did well," Delilah repeated. "I like him. I don't care what he seems to be, he's a right honorable fellow." She was silent for a moment. "You come along now and have something to eat."

Kristin did.

Then she set to the housework with a vengeance, cleaning and sweeping. Later she went out to the barn and spent some time grooming the horses that weren't out with the hands. She came back in and bathed, and while she sat in the tub she decided that although her feelings about him were entirely different from her feelings about Zeke, she still hated Cole Slater. She couldn't even take a bath in peace anymore. She kept thinking about him the entire time. She wanted to be clean, and she wanted to smell sweet, because she could just imagine him ...

She promised herself she would be cool and aloof and dignified through dinner and all through the evening.

She promised herself she would be cool and aloof and wouldn't allow him to touch her.

But he didn't come back for dinner. He didn't come back at all. At midnight she gave up and went upstairs. She managed to stay awake for an hour, but then she fell asleep. She had taken care to dress in a high-necked nightgown, one with a multitude of delicate little buttons at the throat.

Cole stayed out for a long time that night, waiting for her to fall asleep. He smoked a cigar and sipped a brandy and wondered where Quantrill's boys might be.

Quantrill was no bargain, Cole thought, but he wasn't the worst of the lot. He rode with some frightening company. Bill Anderson was a blood-thirsty soul. Zeke was a horror.

Cole had heard that some of the men liked to fight the way the Indians did, taking scalps from their victims.

Quantrill for the South...

And the likes of Lane and Jennison for the North. Killing anyone and anything that stood in their way. Making a jest out of a war that was being fought desperately on both sides for different sets of ideals.

Smoke rose high above him, and he shivered suddenly. He hadn't been able to get Elizabeth's face out of his mind all day. But now, curiously, when he closed his eyes, he saw Kristin. Saw her fighting for all she was worth. Saw her fallen in the dirt.

He stood up and dusted off his hands on his pants.

Kristin was alive, and Elizabeth wasn't. Elizabeth had died because of Doc Jennison and his jayhawkers; Kristin had been attacked by the bushwhackers.

He was angry with her for being alive, he realized. She was alive and Elizabeth wasn't. And he knew he couldn't explain that to her.

He threw his cigar down in the dirt and snuffed it out with the heel of his boot. Then he turned around. He couldn't back down on any of the demands he had made of her. Not ever. It was just part of his nature, he supposed. And it was important that Quantrill know that he was living with her—intimately.

He looked up at the house and swore, then entered it quietly. For a moment he paused in the darkness of the entry. It was a good house. It had been built sturdy and strong, and it had been made into a home. It had grace.

He paused and inhaled deeply. Then he started for the stairway and climbed the steps silently. He reached his room and opened the door, thinking that she must have returned to her own room.

She hadn't. She was curled up on the bed. Her hair spilled over on his pillow.

He cast aside his clothes impatiently and approached the bed, but before he could pull back the covers, his hand brushed a tendril of hair that lay on his pillow, and its soft scent rose up to greet him. Heat immediately snaked through him. He didn't want it this way. But all he had to do was touch her hair and see her innocent form and he was tied into harsh knots of desire.

He didn't have to give in to it, he reminded himself.

He stretched out and stared at the ceiling, drumming his fingers on his chest. She was sound asleep, and even if she were not she would surely not be particularly fond of him at the moment.

A minute later he was on his side, just watching her. He throbbed, he ached, his desire thundering, clamoring for release.

He touched her hair again and reminded himself that it should be black. He didn't love this girl.

He slipped his hand beneath her gown and slowly, lightly stroked her flesh, following the line of her calf, the length of her thigh, the curve of her hip. He rounded her buttocks with a feathery touch, then gently tugged her around and pressed his lips against hers.

She responded, warmly and sweetly and instinctively, to his touch. Her arms swept around him and her body pressed against his. Her lips parted and he plundered the honey-warm depths of her mouth with his tongue. His body pressed against hers intimately. He pulled her gown up farther and wedged his hips between her bare thighs. Her eyes remained closed. She was barely awake.

Then she awoke fully. Her eyes widened, and she pressed furiously against his shoulders. He thought he saw tears sting her eyes as she pronounced him a son of a bitch.

"I know," he told her.

"If you know—"

"I'm sorry."

He tried to kiss her again, but she twisted her head, and his lips fell against her throat.

"You behave like a tyrant."

"I know. I'm sorry."

"You treat people like servants—"

"I know. I'm sorry."

"You behave—"

Her mouth was open, and he caught her lower lip between his teeth and bathed it with his tongue. Then he began to move against her. He caught her cheeks between his palms and stroked her hair, and when she stared up at him again, gasping for breath, he kissed her again quickly, speaking against her lips.

"I am sorry. So damned sorry, for so damned much."

She was silent then, staring at him in the darkness. She was very still, very aware of his sex throbbing against her, so close. If she fought him he would leave.

She didn't fight him. She continued to stare at him, and he met her eyes. Then he moved, thrusting deep inside her. She let out a garbled little sound, and her arms came around him and she buried her face against the hard dampness of his shoulder. Her long limbs came around him, and he sank deeper into her and then deeper still.

She was instinctively sensual, and she offered him greater solace than he could ever have imagined. When it was over he lay with her hair tangling over his naked chest and reminded himself again that it was blond and not ebony black. They were strangers who had stumbled together. They had answered one another's needs, and that was all.

If he closed his eyes he would see her, Elizabeth, racing toward him. Running, running, running...

But it was not Elizabeth's face he saw in his dreams. Sweet blond hair flowed behind the woman who ran to him in his dreams. Kristin raced to him in the night, and he wanted to reach for her, but he was afraid to. He was afraid he might fail.

He was afraid he would take her in his arms and find her blood on his hands. He was afraid he would see Kristin's exquisite blue eyes on his and see her blood running red onto his hands.

7

When Kristin awoke, she could hear gunfire. Looking out the window, she saw that Samson and Delilah were practicing with Cole's six-shooters. She dressed quickly in a cotton shirt and pants and boots and hurried downstairs and out to the pasture. Delilah stumbled from the recoil every time she fired, but she had a set and determined expression on her face. Samson laughed at her, and she gave him a good hard shove. Cole actually grinned. Then he looked at Kristin and saw that she wasn't happy at all. Perched on a fence, he nodded to her and arched a brow, and she flushed. The nights they shared were real, she thought. But the nights were one thing, and the harsh light of day was another. She wasn't going to act like a child again, and she wasn't going to try to pretend that he hadn't touched her in a way she would never forget, that he hadn't awakened her to something incredible. What if it was wrong according to all moral and social standards? Murder was wrong, too. The world wasn't run according to moral standards anymore. She didn't mind getting close to Cole. He knew how to treat a woman, knew when to be tender, knew when to let the wild winds rage. Even now, as his eyes flickered over her, she felt the warmth of their intimacy, and it wasn't an unpleasant feeling, despite her current impatience. Cole just didn't seem to understand what he was doing to her. He didn't speak. He watched her. Waiting.

"Miz Kristin, I am going to get this down pat!" Delilah swore.

Kristin tried to smile. "Delilah, you can master anything you set your mind to. I've see you." She set her thumbs in the pockets of her pants and said to Cole, "May I speak with you a moment?"

"Speak," Cole said flatly. He had said he was sorry about lots of things, but his manner toward her didn't seem to be much better today than it had been before. And he didn't come down from the fence.

"Alone," she said.

He shrugged, and started to climb down.

"Don't you bother, Mr. Slater," Samson said behind her. Kristin whirled around in surprise. Samson looked at her, his expression almost sorrowful, and gave her a rueful grin. "Meaning no disrespect, Miz Kristin, and you know it. But you're gonna tell him that you don't want him teaching us any more about gunfire. 'Cause of us being free blacks. She thinks that if we don't shoot they'll just put us on a block and not think to shoot us or string us up. Delilah and me talked about it a long, long time. We're in this together. If there's more trouble, we got to stick together. Delilah's got to shoot just like everybody else. You see, Miz Kristin, I been a free man now a long time. And it's mighty sweet."

"Samson..." Kristin swallowed and closed her eyes. "Samson, if you're alive, you can get free again. If you're dead—"

"I believe in the good Lord, Miz Kristin. And one day there's going to be a meetin' 'cross that river. And I ain't going to that meetin' being no coward, or a man who didn't live up to what I believe in. We're in this together, Mis Kristin."

She stared furiously at Cole. He shrugged.

"You fool!" she snapped at him. "Samson is a black man."

"Samson is a man," he replied. "A free man. Your daddy made him so. The way I see it, he's made his choice."

They were all staring at her. No one said anything, and no one moved. The sun streamed down on them all. Cole kept watching her. She couldn't begin to read the emotions in his eyes. I don't know this man, I don't know him at all, she thought in sudden panic. But did it matter? she asked herself. It couldn't matter. The die had been cast.

"I've got to get back to the house now," Delilah said. "I've got to get Daniel and let Shannon come on down here."

"Shannon?" Kristin whispered.

Cole hopped down from the fence at last. He took his gun from Delilah, and he slowly and deliberately reloaded it. His hat shaded his eyes from her when he spoke. "You want your little sister to be defenseless?" He looked straight at her.

Kristin smiled sweetly and took the gun from him. He had a row of bottles set up on the back fence. She took her time, aiming as slowly and deliberately as he had loaded. She remembered everything her father and Adam had ever taught her. Remember the recoil, and remember that it can be a hell of a lot for a small woman to handle. Squeeze the trigger gently. Don't jerk back on it....

She didn't miss once. Six shots, six bottles blown to bits, the glass tinkling and reflecting the sunlight as it scattered. With a very pleasant smile, she turned to Cole, daintily handing him the Colt.

He wasn't amazed; he didn't even seem surprised. He studied her. He slipped a second Colt from his gunbelt and handed it to her.

"What happens when the target moves?" he demanded.

"Try me."

Cole nodded to Samson. Samson grinned approvingly. He picked up a bottle and sent it flying high and fast into the air. Kristin caught the missile at its peak, just before it curved back downward to earth. Once again the sun shimmered on the exploding pieces, and they fell in a rainbow of color.

"Not bad," Cole murmured. He nudged back his hat and looked at her sharply. "And Shannon?"

Shannon was already on her way to the yard from the house. Delilah had gone inside. Shannon was dressed like a ranch hand today, too. She seemed all the more feminine for the way her budding curves filled out her shirt and breeches. She glanced slyly at Kristin, and Kristin knew that she was thinking of the fiasco at dinner the night before. She was tempted to give her a sharp slap, but that would be wrong, and she knew it. She decided to ignore her sister's amusement. "Shannon, Cole wants to see you shoot."

"I know." She smiled at Cole. Shannon liked him. A lot. Kristin wanted to spin her around and shake her. He'll be gone in a blink one day! she wanted to tell her sister. Don't care too much!

Then she wondered if Shannon needed the warning, or if Kristin did.

"Show him," Kristin suggested.

Shannon proceeded to do so. She was an even better shot than Kristin, and Cole told her so. He didn't seem to give anyone lavish praise, but he was always gentler with Shannon than with anyone else.

"Good. Damned good," Cole told her.

Shannon flushed, delighted by the compliment.

Kristin turned on her heel and headed for the house. He didn't want her riding away from the house, and he would insist that she stay. If she didn't, he would leave her to the mercy of the bushwhackers. She was going to be mature today, mature and dignified, and she wasn't going to get into any fights over the ranch.

"Kristin!" he called to her.

She turned to look at him.

"What are you doing?" His plumed hat was set at a cocky angle, his hands were on his hips, and his frock coat hung down the length of his back. There was something implacable about him as he stood there, implacable, unfathomable and hard. But that was why she had wanted him. He couldn't be beaten. Not by Quantrill's gang. Not by her.

That last thought made her tremble slightly. She clamped down hard on her jaw and wondered just how long the war could last, and wondered if maybe she shouldn't run after all.

"Paperwork," she told him calmly. "I wouldn't dream of going against your rules, Mr. Slater," she said, and walked away.

He rode out later. She knew when he rode out; she heard the sound of his horse's hooves as she sat in the office, trying hard to concentrate on numbers. She walked out front and watched him, and she was restless. This was hard. She had always been such an important part of things.

But they were playing for high stakes. Damned high stakes. She forced herself to sit down again. She weighed the prices she could receive for her beef against the distances she would have to take the herd to collect the money. Then her pencil stopped moving, and she paused and chewed the eraser, and she wondered what it would be like when he came home for dinner that night.

If he came home for dinner that night.

It didn't matter, she told herself. She was forgetting that this whole thing was business. She was certain Cole never forgot for a moment that it was a deal they had made and nothing more.

She had to learn to be aloof. Polite and courteous and mature, but aloof. She had to keep her distance from him. If she didn't, she would get hurt.

Maybe it was too late already. Maybe she had already come too close to the fire. Maybe no matter what happened she was doomed to be hurt. She wasn't so naive that she didn't know she pleased him, but neither was she so foolish as to imagine that it meant anything to him. There was a coldness about him that was like a deep winter frost. It wasn't that he didn't care at all—he did care. But not enough. And he never could care enough, she was certain.

She gave herself a mental shake and decided that she would have to remember herself that it was business—all business. But still she wondered what he would be like if he returned for dinner, and she swore to herself that her own behavior would be the very best the South had ever had to offer.

Cole did return.

And Kristin was charming. She dressed for dinner again, elegantly, in a soft blue brocade with underpanels and a massive, stylish skirt. She remembered her mother, and she was every bit as gracious as she had been. She was careful to refer to him as "Mr. Slater" all the way through the meal. He watched her and he replied in kind, perfectly courteous, as if he'd been trained for society in the finest drawing rooms back East.

When the meal was over, he disappeared outside. Kristin tried to stay up, but at last everyone else had gone to bed, and she walked up the stairs and to the window. She could see him out on the porch, smoking one of her father's fine cigars and drinking brandy from a snifter. He was leaning against one of the pillars and looking up at the night sky.

She wondered what he was thinking, where his heart really lay.

He turned and stared up at her, there in the window. Her face flamed, but he smiled at her.

"Evening," he said softly.

She couldn't reply to him. He watched her curiously for another moment, and his smile deepened, striking against his well-trimmed beard and mustache.

"I'll be right up."

Her heart hammered and slammed against her chest, and she nearly struck her head trying to bring it back in beneath the window frame. She clutched her heart and reminded herself that she had decided to be mature and dignified and not get as flustered as a schoolgirl.

But she was still trembling when he came up the steps. She heard his footsteps in the hallway, and then he opened the door and came into the room. She was still dressed in her blue brocade. He stared at her for a moment, watching the way her breasts rose and fell above the deep décolletage of her gown. He saw the pulse that vibrated against the long, smooth line of her throat. He smiled, and she sensed the curious tenderness that could come to his eyes. "Come here," he told her softly. He held out a hand to her, and she took it and found herself in this arms. And there was nothing awkward about it at all. He kissed her and touched her face, and then he turned her around, and the touch of his fingers against her bare back as he released her gown set her skin to glowing. Like her heart, her flesh seemed to pulse. It occurred to her that he disrobed her so expertly because he had done the same for many women, but it didn't really matter. All that mattered was that her clothing was strewn on the floor and that he was lifting her in his arms and that the soft glow of the moon was with them again. He carried her to the sleigh bed and set her down, and she saw the passion rise in his eyes and come into his touch. She wrapped her arms around him and sighed, savoring the exquisite feel of him against her, the masculine hardness of muscle and limb, the starkly demanding feel of his shaft against her. Somewhere the tumbleweeds tossed, and somewhere the wind blew harsh and wicked and cruel, but here a tempest rose sweet and exciting, wild and exhilarating.

Somewhere battles raged. Somewhere Northerner fought Southerner, and the nation ran with the blood shed by her youth. Blood washed over Kansas and Missouri as if some shared artery had been slashed, but for tonight, Kristin didn't care.

She was alive in his arms, feline and sensual. She was learning where to touch him, how to move with him and against him and how to leave the world behind when she was with him. No drug and no liquor could be so powerful as this elation, so sweet, so all-encompassing.

That night he slept. She stared at his features, and she longed to reach out and touch them, but she did not. She decided that even his nose was strong, long and straight, like a beak against his features. His cheekbones were high, his forehead was wide and his jaw was fine and square beneath the hair of his beard. She wondered at the fine scars that criss-crossed his shoulders and his chest, and then she remembered that he had been with the Union cavalry before the war, and she wondered what battles had done this to him. She longed to touch him so badly. . . .

She reached out, then withdrew her hand. He was an enigma, and he was fascinating. He drew her like the warmth of a fire, and she was afraid. There was so much she didn't know about him. But her fear went deeper than that, for she sensed that though he cared he would never stay. He liked her well enough. He could even be patient with her temper and her uncertainties. He could be careful, and he could be tender, and he seemed as immersed in this startling passion as she was.

But she sensed that he would not stay, could not stay. Not for long. Worse, she sensed that he could never love her, and that she could fall in love with him all too easily. Already, she thought, other men seemed to pale beside him.

Other men . . . if any remained when the carnage was over.

She walked to the window and looked out at the night. The moon was high, and the paddocks and the outbuildings looked so peaceful there, rising against the flatland. She sighed. For the rest of the country the war had begun when the first shots had been fired at Ford Sumter back in April of '61, but Kansas seemed to have been bleeding forever, and Missouri along with it. The Army of Northern Virginia had defeated the Army of the Potomac at Manassas twice, while along the Mississippi the Union troops were faring a bit better. The North had won the Battle of Shiloh, and just last April New Orleans had fallen to Union troops under Farragut.

It should matter, she thought. It should matter to her who lost and who won. She should care. At Sharpsburg, Maryland, by Antietam Creek, both sides had suffered horribly. She had been in town when the list of the dead had arrived, and it had been devastating. The papers had all cried that the single bloodiest battle of the war had been fought there, and that men had slipped in the blood, and that bodies had fallen on top of other bodies. All she had seen was the tears of the mothers, the sweethearts, the lovers—the families of boys who had left to join the Union Army and the families who had sons fighting with the Confederacy. She had looked for Matthew's name, and she had not seen it, and she had thanked God. But then she had felt the tears around her, felt the agony of the parents, the sisters, the brothers. And yet sometimes it felt as if the real war were remote here. Here the war had been reduced to sheer terrorism. Men did not battle men; they set out to commit murder.

Here it had become a question of survival. All she wanted to do was survive.

She shivered suddenly and realized that she had come naked from the bed and that the night air was cold. She turned and saw that Cole was awake. His eyes were caught by the moonlight as he watched her. They glimmered curiously, and again she wondered at his secret thoughts. Then his gaze fell slowly over the length of her and she realized again that she was naked, and that his very eyes could touch her like a caress.

"Are you all right?" he asked her.

She felt as if she were going to cry, and she didn't know why.

"I was just thinking about the war," she said quietly.

Something covered his eyes, some careful shield. "It seems far away right now, doesn't it? Then again, I don't think we're even fighting the same war as the rest of the country here." There was a harsh bitterness in his tone, and she suddenly felt cold, as if she had turned him against her, or as if she had even made him forget she was there. But then his eyes focused on her again, and they were rueful and surprisingly tender. "Don't think about it," he told her. "Don't think about the war. You can't change it."

She wanted to say something, but she couldn't find her voice, and so she nodded.

"Come back to bed. It's late," he said. Even when he whispered, his voice was so deep. It entered into her and became the wind again.

She forgot about the war. She forgot about the rest of the world. His voice, his beckoning, had that power over her. Her stomach fluttered and her nipples hardened, and she felt she had to cover herself quickly. She had become so bold, so brash. She was standing here naked as a jaybird, and they were talking, and she should have the decency to reach out for something and cover her nudity.

But she did not. She straightened and tossed back her head, and her hair, golden fire in the moonlight, tumbled down the length of her back. She walked toward him. If nothing else, perhaps they could have honesty between them. She honestly wanted him. She wanted these nights. She wanted the way she felt in his arms, wanted this ecstasy that seemed sweeter than life itself.

She came, he thought, very slowly, very sinuously. She allowed a natural sway to come into her walk, and she moved with a feline grace and purpose that set his blood aflame. He was glad that covers lay over his body, for his response to her was instant and instinctive. He clenched his fists at his sides and waited for her. Waited until she stood above him. Then he reached out, pulled her down to him and held her in his arms. He savaged her lips, groaning with the sweet, aching pleasure of it.

He had never thought it could happen, but he had found an oasis with her. He had known she was beautiful, like a sunrise, like the corn that had grown endlessly in the fields before they had run with blood. He had known that he wanted her.

He had not known how badly, how completely, he would come to need her.

Her eyes were a distant sea that claimed him, and the golden skeins of her hair were webs that entrapped him and brought him softly into a dream of paradise. He could not love her, but he could want her, and he did. He hungered for her, as if he could not be filled. She sated him completely, but then she touched him again, or she moved, or she whispered, and he wanted her again. He had taken her from innocence and he had set the woman within her free, and though she came to him with sensual grace, she held on to something of innocence too, and he wondered at that gift. He had to touch her, had to run his fingers over the fine, delicate beauty of her face, had to press his palms against the lush curve of her breast. He had to breathe in her scent.

It had to end, he knew. But he groaned aloud as her nails stroked against his back, as her hips thrust forward. It had to end, he reminded himself. . . .

But then he ceased to think and gave way to urgent need and fevered desire. He looked into her eyes, blue eyes that were soft, radiant and glazed with passion. He swept her beneath him, and he sank into her as he sank into the dream. She eased the pain. She gave him moments of ecstasy. He could not remember ever having needed a woman so badly. He could not remember so insistent a beat, so desperate, so thunderous a rhythm.

This was like nothing he had ever known. Beautiful, sleek, sensual, she moved beneath him. He became as taut as wire, then shook and shuddered, and spasms continued to rack him.

Later she slept. He cast an elbow behind his head and stared bleakly at the ceiling, shadowed in the moonlight.

It was wrong, he thought. When vengeance lay upon his soul and his heart was barren, it was wrong.

But he could not, would not, make himself cease. She had come to him with the deal. He had not wrung it from her.

That didn't excuse him.

But he needed her. . . .

That didn't excuse him, either. But it mattered. Somehow they had interwoven their lives, and that—as with so many other things—was simply the way it was.

That was simply the way it was.

But still he turned to her. He saw the beautiful curves of her body as she slept, and the tangle of her hair over her shoulders, falling to her flanks, wild and yet somehow virginal. He saw her features, her parted lips and the soft way she breathed. He saw her brow, and he touched it gently, trying to ease the frown line from it. She seemed so very young to have suffered so very much. But she was a fighter. No matter what they had done to her, she had come back up, kicking, fighting. Maybe that was why he couldn't leave her.

He had to leave her, he reminded himself. Soon.

This time it was he who rose. He walked to the window and looked out at the moon. He would have to leave soon, for a time, at least.

He watched the moon, and at last he shrugged. He'd get to the telegraph office tomorrow and hope he could get a message through. He didn't know how long he would have to be gone, but he didn't want her alone. Not now.

Just how long could he guard her?

And would he keep dreaming? He closed his eyes. Dreaming again and again, of one death, of another...

The question washed over his heart, cold as ice. He didn't know. No, he did know. Come hell or high water—or Yankees or Quantrill's raiders—he would find a way to guard her. He wasn't sure why. Maybe it was because this was a matter of honor, and there wasn't much honor left in his world.

And maybe it was because he wanted her so badly. Because she was the only antidote to pain. Because when he was with her he could almost forget...

He didn't want to forget.

Yes, he did. For those few moments.

Whatever the reason, he thought impatiently, he had struck a bargain. He would protect her. He would protect her if she grew hair all over her body and sprouted a full mustache, he swore to himself.

Then he smiled slowly. He was one hell of a liar, he thought, even to himself. She needed him, and he wanted her. That was the bargain.

No. He would protect her, damn it and he would do it so that he never had to hold her bleeding in his arms. He clenched his jaw to keep from crying out. He would protect her because he could not let it happen again.

He breathed slowly and tried to relax.

He would protect her. He had the power. They would help each other, and then he would ride away. The war had to end some day.

Please, God, he thought bleakly. It had to.

The days passed and things were very much the same. After a few days Cole let Kristin ride with him. It was necessary, because the men were busy with the cattle. Kristin showed Cole the length and breadth of her land. She showed him the water holes, and where the land was apt to flood when the rains came too heavily. They went out together searching for a calf that had strayed, and they went into town to buy a length of fencing for the north pasture.

But things felt strange even though they were together. They were polite workmates, cool, courteous acquaintances. Kristin and Shannon always dressed for dinner, because Kristin was determined to cling to what was left of civilization in her life, and the evening meal was her chance to do that. But the conversation there was stilted, too. Cole seldom had much to say to her that wasn't directly concerned with the ranch, with guns, with warnings about the future. She was never to wander around unarmed, and neither was Shannon. He didn't seem to need to warn Delilah or Samson.

He was always polite to Shannon. It seemed to Kristin that her little sister was growing up before her very eyes. Shannon would be eighteen soon, and she was beginning to look every inch the woman. Cole treated her like a child, not condescendingly but with a gentle patience that irritated

Kristin. She would have liked some of that patience for herself. Sometimes she asked him very blunt questions, but he invariably ignored her or turned the tables on her. When she demanded to know why he insisted on being such a mystery to her, he merely replied that she had no right to know anything about his past or his future and that she shouldn't be asking.

It didn't matter if she walked away from him, and it didn't matter if she made a sharp reply. He just let her go, or he let her say whatever she wanted and then walked away himself.

But the nights were always the same.

There were times when she couldn't believe she was the same girl who had first met him, innocent, frightened, naive. Even when she felt her temper soar she longed for the night. And even if she turned away from him he stroked her back slowly, moving his fingers down her spine to her buttocks, so lightly that she thought she had imagined it. But his touch was lightning, and it always instilled the same seeds of desire within her. If she really tried to ignore him and he let her be, she sometimes resorted to a soft sigh, feigning sleep, and rolled against him...until he touched her again. Then she sensed his smile, and knew that he knew that she wasn't asleep at all, and that he didn't mind pretending that he needed her more than she needed him.

It went on....

It went on until she woke up one morning, cold and alone. That wasn't so unusual. He was able to get by on much less sleep than she. But somehow she didn't think he had awakened and gone downstairs. She felt a growing sense of dread.

He was gone.

She heard sounds. A rider. Wrenching a sheet from the bed, she raced to the window and stared down at the paddock area. A man had just come riding in on a big bay horse.

She put her hand to her mouth, biting down hard to keep from crying out. He was dressed in gray. She studied the uniform and gold trim.

Cavalry. The man was a Southern cavalry officer.

She turned around and dressed quickly, finding pants and a shirt and her boots. She told herself that she was a Southerner, that she had been born a Southerner and that only Quantrill had made her fear and hate her own people. She tried to smile, reminding herself that Shannon's great hero was Jeb Stuart, a Southern cavalry officer.

It didn't help. Fear raced through her, and she wondered if the officer had been sent by Zeke or his men.

Cole had told her never to walk around unarmed. She had proven she could use a Colt six-shooter and use it well. She slid her narrow gun belt over her hips and nervously checked to see that her weapons were loaded. Then she started down the stairs.

The house was silent. Where was Shannon? she wondered. She couldn't help it. She had awful visions of her beautiful sister caught in the stables with the men all out on the ranch, caught and thrown down in the hay and viciously raped.

She swallowed and tried to tell herself that she was panicking for nothing. But the house was silent, and she still sensed that Cole was gone. Not just off on the ranch somewhere—gone. She couldn't have explained how she knew. It was an emptiness. It festered inside her, and it held her in an awful anguish.

But this...

This was more urgent. "Delilah?"

No one answered her. Delilah was not in the kitchen, and neither was Samson. She didn't hear the baby crying, and she had no idea where Shannon was.

And the cavalry officer hadn't come to knock at her door.

She crept out the back door, careful to keep it from slamming behind her. Walking as quickly and silently as she could, she came around the corner of the house. The man was gone, and the horse was gone.

Her heart was beating much too quickly. She dropped low and raced over the dry sand to the barn. She followed the line of the buildings, coming closer and closer to the corner.

She paused and inhaled sharply. Her blood raced, and she tried desperately to still her erratic breathing.

She rounded the corner and she came face-to-face with an Enfield rifle.

Behind it stood the man in the Confederate cavalry officer's uniform. It was worn and faded, the gold epaulets frayed.

"Drop it!" he warned her. His eyes were teal, a beautiful color. They were also sharp as razors.

She realized that she was aiming the Colt at him.

"You drop it!" she barked.

He smiled. She realized that he was young and very, very good-looking. And familiar in some way she couldn't quite put her finger on.

"This Enfield can blow a hole right through you."

"It's not a totally dependable weapon."

"At this range? Impossible to miss."

"A Colt will scalp you faster than an Indian would dare dream."

He was tall, masculine and elegant in the worn uniform. He didn't intend to harm her, she was certain. But she didn't lower the barrel of the gun. She had learned not to take any chances.

"Kristin McCahy?"

"Yes."

He laughed and lowered the rifle. "Why in God's name were you sneaking up on me like that?"

She jammed the Colt into her holster, instinct assuring her that she was in no danger. She shook her head ruefully.

"I'm sorry. This is my property. And you are a total stranger, you know. Slinking around on it. My property, that is. I mean . . . who the hell are you?"

"Slinking?" he inquired indignantly, but there was a twinkle in his eyes. He swept his hat from his head and bowed deeply, an elegant and manly cavalier. "Miss McCahy, I assure you that Slaters do not slink."

"Slater?" she demanded with a quick frown.

"Captain Malachi Slater, ma'am. Cole's brother. On leave—and on new duty, or so it seems. You mean to tell me that Cole didn't say anything?"

She felt as if her knees were going to crumble. Cole was gone. And he hadn't even said goodbye.

"Cole—"

"He had a few things to attend to. I'll be with you for a while. If you don't mind."

She did mind. She minded terribly. Not that Malachi was here, but that Cole was gone. She forced herself to smile and to extend her hand. "Why, Mr. Slater, I'm thrilled and grateful for your appearance. Completely thrilled and entirely grateful."

"Thank you, Miss McCahy." He took her hand and raised it to his lips. Then his blue eyes met hers again and she was certain that he knew everything. And there was something in his gaze that suggested that he understood her feelings.

She withdrew her hand suddenly. "Oh, my God!"

"What?"

"You're a Confederate officer."

He stiffened, and his jaw took on a stubborn set that reminded her of his brother. "Miss, last I heard, Missourians were still considering themselves Southerners—for the most part, that is."

Kristin nodded vaguely. "Well, yes, Mr. Slater. But this is a border country. Half the land around here is occupied by Federal forces."

"Don't worry about me. I'll change into civilian clothing quickly, and I'll avoid the Federals."

She shook her head again. "It's just that, well, I have a brother who is a—"

"A Yankee?"

"Ah . . . yes, a Yankee."

He looked a lot like Cole. A whole lot. He was very tall and very broad-shouldered in his dress shirt and cape, and at the moment he looked very severe, as if he were about to explode.

But he didn't explode. He suddenly started laughing. "Well, it's one hell of a war, isn't it, Miss McCahy? One hell of a war."

Suddenly the wall behind them exploded. Wood chips went flying from the solid impact of a bullet.

"What the hell?" Malachi shouted. He dragged her to the ground, shielding her with his body. Once again there was the sound of gunfire, and another bullet tore into the walls, sending more wood chips cascading down on them.

"Damn it, what the hell!" Malachi repeated.

What the hell indeed? Kristin had no idea who was firing at them.

8

Kristin lay facedown on the ground, dirt in her mouth, with Malachi on top of her, protecting her. Finally the firing stopped and she heard soft footsteps.

"Get off her, Reb!" Kristin almost laughed out loud with relief. It was Shannon.

"Watch it with that thing, little girl," Malachi said slowly, easing himself away from Kristin. He had angry narrowed eyes leveled on her sister. Kristin sprang to her feet and stepped between them. Shannon's temper was flaring, and her eyes were sparkling dangerously.

"I'm not a little girl, Reb, and I swear I'm damned accurate with this Colt," Shannon replied.

"Why, you little—" Malachi began.

"Stop, stop!" Kristin begged, reaching for the gun. She couldn't imagine trying to explain to Cole Slater why they had murdered his brother. "Shannon—"

"He's a Reb, Kristin. He's probably one of Quantrill's—"

"Don't you know a regular cavalry uniform when you see one, girl?"

Kristin lost patience and swung around. "Mr. Slater, please, just for a minute, shut up. Shannon, this is Cole's brother."

"Brother?"

Her eyes wide, she looked at Malachi, then at Kristin again. "Are you sure? They don't look much alike!"

"We have identical big toes," Malachi snapped sarcastically. Shannon stiffened.

Then, suddenly, there was the sound of another explosion. The three of them stared at one another blankly. Wood chips flew as a second bullet struck the barn wall above their heads.

"Get down—" Malachi began.

"Drop that gun!" The order was spoken in a commanding, masculine tone.

Shannon wasn't about to obey. She spun around, aiming. Malachi swore and slammed his fist down on her wrists. The Colt fell to the ground, and Shannon turned on Malachi, swearing and flailing at him with her fists. Malachi swore in return, and Kristin wondered how the two of them could be going at one another this way when someone else was firing at all three of them. They were warning shots, she realized. She stared blankly across the yard and saw that another man had come out of the shadows of the porch. He was younger than Cole and Malachi and dressed like a rancher in high boots, a long railway frock coat and a slouch hat that sat low on his forehead. Malachi paid no attention to him. As he came forward, the stranger tipped his hat to Kristin.

"They've got a set of rotten tempers between them, huh?"

"Do they?" Kristin crossed her arms over her chest and stared at the young man who had been doing the shooting. Shannon was still shrieking, fighting the hold Malachi had on her. Kristin ignored them both and kept staring at the newcomer. "Why were you shooting at us?"

"I thought she meant to poke a hole right through old Malachi there," he said solemnly. He had cloudlike bluegray eyes and tawny hair. He smiled again. It was an engaging smile, and Kristin almost smiled, too, in spite of herself.

"I take it you're another Slater? Or are you a friend of the family?"

He stuck out his hand. "Jamie, ma'am."

Malachi let out something that sounded like a growl. "Damned brat bit me!" he thundered.

"Shannon!" Kristin implored.

She might have bitten Malachi, but the bite didn't keep him from maintaining his hold upon her, his arms around her waist. Her toes were barely touching the ground.

"Ah, Malachi." Jamie shook his head sorrowfully and said to Kristin, "He met Grant at Shiloh but he can't handle a little wisp of a girl."

"I'm not—" Shannon began.

"You are a foolish little brat!" Malachi said, releasing her at last and shoving her towards Kristin. She would have swung at him again, but Kristin caught her sister's arms. "Shannon, please!"

But Shannon was still staring at Malachi, seething. "I am not a brat, Reb. You attacked my sister—"

"And you attacked my brother," Jamie said pleasantly. "We're all even. And if Cole were here he'd say the entire lot of us were a pack of fools playing around with firearms. But then, Cole isn't here, and that's why Malachi and I are. Maybe we ought to try and start over."

"Cole sent you, too?" Kristin asked Jamie.

"Yes, ma'am, he did."

"I see," Kristin said stiffly.

Jamie grinned broadly. "No, ma'am, I doubt if you see at all. He had some business to attend to."

"I told her," Malachi said.

"My brother is a cavalry officer," Shannon snapped at Malachi, ignoring everything else. "And if he knew you were on his property he'd skewer you right through!"

He shook his head, looking as if he were about to explode. Then he exhaled in an exaggerated display of patience. "I thought I was supposed to be looking out for Quantrill, not a two-bit piece of baggage!" He shoved his hat down hard over his forehead and started walking toward the house. Kristin, amused, stared after him. Shannon, amazed, placed her hands on her hips.

"Where do you think you're going?" she called.

Malachi stopped and swung around. "In. For coffee and breakfast. And if you don't like it, little girl, that's just too damned bad. You take it up with Cole the next time you see him. He asked me to be here, and I'm here, and I won't be leaving, not until he gets back. Until that time, you do us both a favor. You stay clear of me. Way clear." He paused, then swore softly again. "Hell, I could still be out there with the Yankees. It'd be a hell of a lot less nerve-racking than a morning here!" Once again he turned. Kristin saw that Delilah was on the steps, watching them. She was grinning broadly.

"You must be Mr. Malachi."

Delilah's voice floated down to Kristin, and Kristin arched a brow at her. She and Shannon hadn't known that Cole's brothers were coming, but Delilah had. Cole had told Delilah what he was up to, and he hadn't said a word to them.

She gritted her teeth, damning Cole a thousand times over. What was this business he had to attend to? They had made a deal. Zeke was still out there somewhere. She didn't need a pair of baby-sitters. She needed to have Zeke taken care of.

And she needed to have Cole talk to her, to tell her about his life, not just walk away from her when the sun came up.

"You come on in," Delilah was saying to Malachi. "Breakfast's on the table, boys. Breakfast's on the table."

Kristin felt Jamie watching her. She turned to him, and she flushed, surprised by the knowing assessment she saw in his eyes. He had been reading her mind, or else he had been wondering about her relationship with his brother. No, he seemed to know what their relationship was already. She could read that in the look he was giving her.

Then he smiled, as if he had already decided that he liked her, and so she smiled, too. She liked Jamie. And she liked

Malachi. She even liked the war he was waging with Shannon. She had felt like laughing as she'd watched them and she hadn't felt like laughing in a long time.

"I'm awful hungry, too," Jamie said. He offered her his arm. "Shall we go in for breakfast?"

Kristin hesitated, then took his arm, and they started toward the house. She paused, turning back to her sister. "Shannon?"

"I'll skip breakfast," Shannon said heatedly, her bright blue eyes still on Malachi's retreating back. "I don't rightly feel like sitting down with—" She paused when she saw that Jamie was studying her intently. "I'm not hungry." She spun around and stomped off to the barn. Kristin looked at Jamie again.

"Just where is Cole? I don't need looking after like this, you know. Cole and I had a—an agreement."

She studied his eyes, trying hard not to flush.

"You talk to Cole about his whereabouts later," Jamie said flatly. Neither of the Slaters was going to say a thing about Cole's absence, she realized. "And we're here 'cause of your agreement. We know Quantrill and his boys. We're just here to see that you're safe. Do you really mind? Terribly?"

"No, I, uh... of course not. You're both very welcome," she said, forcing herself to smile. They were welcome, they really were. It was just that...

It was just that she wondered where the hell Cole had gone. She wondered if it had to do with another woman, and she wondered if she could bear it if it did.

Don't fall in love with him! she warned herself again. But he was gone, and she was aching, and it was too late. He wasn't involved and she was, and it was gnawing away at her. She forced her smile to remain in place. "Jamie, you are very welcome. Come on. Delilah makes an incredible breakfast."

* * *

He rode southeast the first day. The farther east he went in Missouri, the more closemouthed and careful people were about Quantrill and his gang.

It was natural, he supposed. It had all turned into such a hideous, ugly thing. The ugliness had taken hold way back in the 1850s when John Brown had come into Missouri with his followers and killed slaveholders. Cole didn't really know what to think of John Brown. He had seen the man at his trial, and he had thought then that old John Brown spoke like a fanatic. But he had also thought that he spoke from conviction, too, when he said that only a bloodbath could cleanse the country of the sin of slavery.

John Brown and his followers had gone on to raid the arsenal at Harper's Ferry. Robert E. Lee—then an officer of the United States Army—had been sent in to capture John Brown. Jeb Stuart had been with the forces sent to Harper's Ferry, too.

Cole had been with them himself, riding right alongside Jeb. They had captured John Brown and taken him to Charlestown to stand trial. There hadn't been any Confederacy then. And Cole hadn't known what was to come.

In the North they had quickly begun to sing, "John Brown's body lies a-molderin' in the grave," conveniently forgetting that even if the man had been a God-fearing murderer, he had still been a murderer.

And in Missouri men had learned to retaliate.

Quantrill and his raiders were worshipped by the people here, people who had known nothing but death and destruction from the Kansas jayhawkers. Cole had to be careful. When he stopped at a farmhouse, he quickly made his presence known. He asked for a sip of water from a well, then asked if anyone knew where he might find Quantrill or any of his boys. He was polite, and he smiled, and he used his best country accent, and he kept it filled with respect.

In return he was pointed more and more toward the south. Finally, in a small town almost fifty miles south of Osceola, he heard that Quantrill was at the local saloon.

No one was afraid there. Quantrill's boys were in charge. The South had a good grip on its own here. At a farmhouse outside the town, Cole was invited in for a meal, and the farmer assured him that he could find Quantrill at the saloon at about six that evening.

Cole rode in carefully. If he saw Quantrill first, or Anderson, he'd be all right, but he didn't want to run into Zeke, not now. In case he did, though, he rode in with his six-shooters and two shotguns loaded and ready.

Things were quiet enough as he rode into town. It was almost as if there were no war. Nicely dressed women with stylish hats stood outside the mercantile. As he rode slowly along the dusty main street, they stared at him, and he tipped his hat. They blushed and whispered to one another.

That was when Cole realized that the quiet little town was pulsing with an inner excitement and that things weren't really quiet at all. He could hear the sound of laughter and piano music up ahead and saw a sign that read Red Door Saloon. There were at least eight horses tethered out front.

Quantrill and company do reign here, he thought. He reined in his horse and dismounted, dropping the reins over the post in front of the saloon and dusting off his hands. Then he headed for the red door that had given the saloon its name.

He opened the door and stood there, blinking in the dim light. Then he swiftly cast his gaze over the Red Door's patrons.

Zeke wasn't there.

But William Clarke Quantrill was, playing cards at a round table, leaning back with a thin cigar in his mouth. He was a pale, ashen man with dark hair and a neat brown mustache. He saw Cole just as Cole saw him, and he smiled. He tossed his cards down and stood. He was of average height, about five foot nine. There was nothing about the man to label him the scourge of the West. Nothing except his eyes. They were pale blue and as cold as death.

"Cole. Cole Slater. Well, I'll be damned. To what do I owe this honor?"

Cole didn't answer him. He'd already looked around the room, and looked hard. Zeke wasn't there, but Cole was certain that Quantrill wasn't alone. He wasn't. Cole recognized the other four around the table as young recruits. The two James boys, Jesse and Frank, were there, along with Bill Anderson and little Archie Clements. Cole was sure, too, that Quantrill had more men in the saloon. It wasn't that he had anything to fear here. He was a hero in these parts. It didn't matter that he made out lists of men to be executed. It didn't matter that his men were rapists, murderers and thieves. All that mattered was that what had been done to the Missourians by the jayhawkers was being returned to the Kansans twice over by the bushwhackers.

Cole hadn't come here to do battle, anyway. He strode into the saloon, toward the poker table. The piano player had stopped playing. Everyone in the room was watching him.

He reached Quantrill. Quantrill had his hand extended. Cole took it. "Quantrill," he acknowledged quietly, nodding to the other men at the table. "Jesse. Frank. Archie. Bill. You all look fit. War seems to agree with you."

"Bushwhacking agrees with me," Archie Clements admitted freely. He was dark and had a mean streak a yard wide. "Hell, Cole, I couldn't make it in no ordinary unit. Besides, I'm fighting Yanks for Missouri, and that's it. 'Course, now, you aren't so much regular army, either, are you, Cole? What do they call you? A spy? A scout? Or are you still just a raider?"

"I'm a major, Archie, and that's what they call me," Cole said flatly.

Quantrill was watching the two of them. He turned to the piano player and said, "Hey, what's the problem there, Judah? Let's have something light and fancy here, shall we?

Archie, you and Bill take the James boys over to the bar for a whiskey. Seems to me that Cole must have made this trip 'cause he's got something to say. I want to hear it."

Archie stood, but he looked at Cole suspiciously.

"You alone, Cole?"

"That's right, Archie. I'm alone."

Archie nodded at last. Young Jesse James kept staring at Cole. "It was good to see you again, Major Slater. We miss you when we ride. You were damned good."

Damned good with his guns, that was what the boy meant. What the hell was going to be in store for these men when the war was over? If they survived the war.

"You take care, Jesse. You, too, Frank," Cole said. He drew up a chair next to Quantrill. Quantrill started to deal out the cards. "You still a gambling man, Cole?"

"Always," Cole told him, picking up his cards. A buxom brunette with a headful of rich curls, black fishnet stockings and a blood-red dress came over. She nudged up against Quantrill's back but flashed Cole a deep, welcoming smile.

"Want some whiskey for your friend there, Willy?"

"Sure. Bring over the best. We've got a genuine Confederate scout in our midst. But he used to be one of mine, Jennifer. Yep, for a while there he was one of my best."

"He'd be one of anybody's best, I'm sure," Jennifer drawled, fluttering her dark lashes.

Cole flashed her an easy smile, surprised to discover that he felt nothing when he looked at her. She was a pretty thing, very sexual, but she didn't arouse him in the least. You're too satisfied, he warned himself. He found himself frowning and wondering if he shouldn't be interested. At least then he'd know he could be. He shrugged. He was committed—for the moment. And he'd be taking a long ride away soon enough. There'd be plenty of time to prove things to himself then if he had to. That bothered him, too. He shouldn't have to feel the need to prove things to himself.

He shouldn't feel any of these things. Not when his wife lay dead.

"Get the man a whiskey," Quantrill said sharply. Jennifer pouted, then spun around. "What's this all about?" he demanded of Cole.

"The McCahy girls," Cole said flatly.

Quantrill frowned. He didn't seem to recognize the name, and Cole felt sure he wasn't acting. "I don't know them."

Jennifer returned with a new bottle of good Irish whiskey and a pair of shot glasses. She was going to pour out the amber liquid, but Quantrill shooed her away and poured out the shots himself.

"Your man Zeke has been after them."

Quantrill met his frown. "Zeke? Zeke Moreau? I didn't even know the two of you had met. Zeke came in after you were gone."

"Not quite. We met. But I don't think he remembered me when we met again."

Comprehension dawned in Quantrill's cold eyes. "The farmhouse? Near the border? That was you, Cole?"

"Yeah, that was me." Cole leaned forward. He picked up his glass and swallowed down its contents. It was good. Smooth. The kind of stuff that was becoming rare in the South as the war went on and on. He poured himself another shot. He could feel Quantrill's eyes on him. He sensed that Quantrill wasn't angry. He seemed amused more than anything else.

"So you came back to beat my boys up, huh?"

Quantrill poured himself another glass of whiskey, then sat back, swirling the liquid, studying its amber color. Cole looked at him. "No, I just happened by your boys at work, and I'll admit I was kind of sick to my stomach at the war they were waging. They dragged out an old man and killed him. Then they came back after his daughter. Seems the lady had the bad luck to dislike Zeke."

Quantrill shrugged. His amusement was fading. "You don't like my methods?"

"You've become a cold-blooded killer, Quantrill."

"I didn't know anything about the McCahy place."

"I believe you," Cole said.

Quantrill watched him for a moment, a sly smile creeping onto his lips again. "Hell, Cole, you're starting to sound like some damned Yankee."

"I'm not a Yankee."

"Yankee lover, then."

"I don't want the girl touched, Quantrill."

"My, my..." Quantrill leaned back, idly running a finger around the rim of his glass. "Seems to me that you weren't so finicky back in February of '61, Mr. Slater. Who was heading up the jayhawkers back then? Was it Jim Lane, or was Doc Jennison calling the shots by then? Don't make no real matter, does it? They came riding down into Missouri like a twister." He came forward, resting his elbows on the table. "Yessir, just like a twister. They burned down your place, but that wasn't enough. They had to have their fun with Mrs. Slater. Course, she was a beauty, wasn't she, Cole?"

Cole felt his face constrict. He felt his pulse hammering against his throat. He longed to jump forward and throttle the life out of Quantrill, to close those pale, calculating eyes forever.

"Nope, you weren't so finicky about methods when I met you first, Cole Slater. You had revenge on your mind, and nothing more."

Cole forced his lips to curl into a humorless smile. "You're wrong, Quantrill. Yeah, I wanted vengeance. But I could never see murder done in cold blood. I could never draw up a list of men to be gunned down. I could never see dragging terrified, innocent women out of their beds to be raped and abused. Or shooting down children."

"Hell, Cole. Children fight in this war."

"And that's the hell of it, Quantrill. That's the whole bloody hell of it. The war is hell enough. The savagery is too much."

"We fight like we've been attacked, and that's the plain truth of it. You go see the likes of Lane or Jennison. Tell them about innocents. You can't change the war, Cole. Not you, and not anybody else. Not anybody."

"I didn't come here today to end the war, Quantrill," Cole said calmly.

"You just want me to rein in on Zeke, is that it?"

"Well," Cole told him casually, "you can rein in on him or I can kill him."

Quantrill grinned and shrugged. "You're overestimating my power, Slater. You want me to call Zeke in when this girl isn't anything to you. Not anything at all. She's not your sister and she's not your wife. Hell, from what I understand, Zeke saw her first. So what do you think I can do?"

"You can stop him."

Quantrill sat back again, perplexed. He lifted a hand idly, then let it fall to his lap. "What are you so worried about? You can outdraw Zeke. You can outdraw any ten men I know."

"I don't perform executions, Quantrill."

"Ah...and you're not going to be around for the winter, huh? Well, neither are we. We'll be moving south soon enough—"

"I want a guarantee, Quantrill."

Quantrill was silent. He lifted his glass, tossed back his head and swallowed the whiskey down in a gulp, then wiped his mouth with his sleeve. His eyes remained on Cole. He set the glass down.

"Marry her."

"What?" Cole said sharply.

"You want me to give the girl a guarantee of safety. A girl Zeke saw first. A girl he wants—badly, I'd say. So you give me something. Give me a reason to keep him away from her. Let me be able to tell the men that she's your wife. That's why they have to stay clear. She'll be the wife of a good loyal Confederate. They'll understand that."

Cole shook his head. "I'm not marrying again, Quantrill. Not ever."

"Then what is this McCahy girl to you?"

What indeed, he wondered. "I just don't want her hurt anymore, that's all."

Quantrill shook his head slowly, and there was a flash of something that might have been compassion in his pale eyes. "There's nothing that I can do, Slater. Nothing. Not unless you can give me something to go on."

The damnedest thing about it, Cole thought, was that Quantrill seemed to want to help him. He wasn't trying to be difficult and he wasn't looking for a fight. He was just telling it the way it was.

"We will be gone pretty soon," Quantrill said. "Another month of raids, maybe. Then the winter will come crashing down. I intend to be farther south by then. Kansas winter ain't no time to be foraging and fighting. Maybe she'll be safe. From us, at least. The jayhawkers might come down on the ranch, but Quantrill and company will be seeking some warmth."

"Another month," Cole muttered.

Quantrill shrugged.

The two men sat staring at one another for several moments. Then Quantrill poured more whiskey.

He couldn't marry her. She couldn't be his wife. He'd had a wife. His wife was dead.

He picked up the whiskey and drank it down in one swallow. It burned. It tore a path of fire straight down his throat and into his gut.

"You going east?" Quantrill asked.

Cole nodded. Maybe he shouldn't have, but Quantrill knew he would have to get to Richmond sooner or later, and probably sooner.

Cole let out a snarl and slammed his glass down on the table. The piano player stopped playing again. Silence filled the saloon, like something living and breathing. All eyes turned toward Cole and Quantrill.

Cole stood. "I'm going to marry her," he told Quantrill. Then he looked around at the sea of faces. "I'm going to marry Kristin McCahy, and I don't want her touched. Not her, and not her sister. The McCahy ranch is going to be my ranch, and I'm promising a slow, painful death to any man who thinks about molesting any of my property.''

Quantrill stood slowly and looked around at his men. "Hell, Cole, we're all on the same side here, aren't we, boys?''

There was silence, and then a murmur of assent. Quantrill lifted the whiskey bottle. "Let's drink! Let's drink to Cole Slater's bride, Miss McCahy! Why, Slater, not a man jack here would think to molest your property, or your woman. She's under our protection. You've got my word on it.''

Quantrill spoke loudly, in a clear voice. He meant what he said. Kristin would be safe.

Quantrill offered Cole his hand, and Cole took it. They held fast for a moment, their eyes locked. Quantrill smiled. Cole stepped back, looked around the room and turned to leave. He had his back to the room, but he had probably never been safer in his life. Quantrill had guaranteed his safety.

He walked through the red door, his shoulders squared. Outside, he felt the sun on his face, but the breeze was cool. Fall was fading, and winter was on its way.

He had just said he would marry her.

Hell.

The sun was bright, the air was cool, and the sky was cloudless and blue. He stared at the sun, and he felt cold. He felt a coldness that seeped right into him, that swept right around his heart. It was a bitter cold, so deep that it hurt.

He found his horse's reins and pushed the huge animal back from the others almost savagely so that he could mount. Then he turned and started at a trot down the street.

It couldn't be helped. He had said he would do it, and he had to carry it through.

He had to marry her.

It wouldn't be real, though. It wouldn't mean anything at all. It would just be the way it had to be, and that would be that.

The cold seeped into him again. It encompassed and encircled his heart, and he felt the numbness there again, and then the pain.

He couldn't do it. He couldn't marry another woman. He couldn't call her his wife.

He would marry her. But he never would call her his wife.

Malachi was the more serious of Cole's two brothers, Kristin quickly discovered. Like Cole, he had gone to West Point. He had studied warfare, from the campaigns of Alexander the Great to the American Revolution to Napoléon's grand attempts to take over Europe and Russia. He understood the South's situation in the present struggle for independence, and perhaps that understanding was the cause of gravity. He was on leave for no more than three weeks, so he would have to be returning soon to his unit. Kristin wondered if that meant Cole would return soon. Malachi was courteous to her. He seemed to be the last of the great Southern gentleman, perhaps the last cavalier. Shannon retained her hostility toward him, though. Since Malachi's arrival, she had become a Unionist. She loved to warn both Malachi and Jamie that her brother would come back and make them into nothing more than dust in the wind. Jamie was amused by Shannon. Malachi considered her a dangerous annoyance. Since Kristin had her own problems with Cole, she decided that Shannon was on her own.

Kristin didn't think Matthew would make it home. The last letter she had received from him had stated that his company had been sent East and that he was fighting with the Army of the Potomac.

Malachi didn't wear his cavalry butternut and gray while he was with them at the ranch. He fit into Matthew's breeches fine, and since Federal patrols had been known to wander over the border, it seemed best for him to dress in civilian clothing. Two weeks after his arrival, Kristin heard hoofbeats outside and hurried to the porch. To her vast astonishment, Jamie sat whittling on the steps while Malachi held Shannon in a deep engrossing embrace, kissing her as hotly as a newlywed. Stunned, Kristin stared at Jamie. Jamie pointed to two men in Union blue who were riding away.

"She started to mention that things might not be all they seemed," Jamie drawled. "Malachi didn't take kindly to the notion of spending the rest of the war in a Yankee prison camp."

There was a sharp crack. Kristin spun around to see that Shannon had just slapped Malachi.

Her sister's language was colorful, to say the least. She compared Malachi Slater to a milk rat, a rattlesnake and a Texas scorpion. Malachi, her fingerprints staining his face, didn't appreciate her words. Kristin gasped when he dragged her onto his lap and prepared to bruise her derriere.

Shannon screamed. Jamie shrugged. Kristin decided she had to step in at last. Kristin pleaded with him, but he ignored her at first. She hadn't the strength to come to physical blows with him, so all she could do was appeal to his valor. "Malachi, I'm sure she didn't mean—"

"She damned well did mean!" Malachi shouted. "And I may fall to a Yankee bullet, but I'll be damned if I'll rot in a hellhole because this little piece of baggage has a vicious heart!"

His palm cracked just once against Shannon's flesh.

"Rodent!" Shannon screeched.

"Please—" Kristin began.

Malachi shifted Shannon into his arms, ready to lecture here.

Then Jamie suddenly stood up, dropped his knife and the wood he'd been whittling and reached for his Colt.

"Horses!" he hissed.

A sudden silence settled over them. Malachi didn't release Shannon, but she froze, too, neither sniffling in indignation nor screaming out her hatred.

Kristin glanced at Jamie. She could tell he was afraid that the Union patrol was on its way back. That Malachi's act just hadn't been good enough. That Shannon had exposed them all to danger.

They all saw the riders. Two of them.

Kristin saw Jamie's tension ease, and then Malachi, too, seemed to relax. Even his desire for vengeance against Shannon seemed to have ebbed. He suddenly set her down on the wooden step, not brutally but absently. Still, Shannon gasped out, startled. Malachi ignored her. Even Kristin ignored her. Kristin still couldn't see the riders clearly, but apparently Malachi and Jamie knew something.

Then she realized it was Cole's horse. It was Cole, returning.

Instantly she felt hot and then cold. Her heart seemed to flutter in her breast. Then butterfly wings seemed to soar within her, and she was hot and then cold all over again.

Cole...

No matter what she wanted to think or believe, she had thought of nothing but him since he had gone away. Waking or sleeping, he had filled her heart and her mind. She had touched the bedding where he had lain and remembered how he had stood, naked, by the window. She had remembered him with the length of her, remembered the feel of his fingers on her flesh, the staggering heat of his body against hers, the tempest of his movement. She had burned with the thoughts and she had railed against herself for them, but they had remained. And in her dreams she had seen him naked and agile and silent and sleek and coming to her again. And he would take her so tenderly into his arms...

And in her dreams it would be more than the fire. He would smile, and he would smile with an encompassing tenderness that meant everything. He would whisper to her,

and the whispers would never be clear, but she would know
what they meant.

He loved her....

He did not love her.

He rode closer, a plump, middle-aged man at his side. She
barely noticed the other man. Her eyes were for Cole, and
his rested upon her.

And her heart ran cold then, for he was staring at her with
a startling dark hatred.

Her fingers went to her throat, and she backed away
slightly, wondering what had happened, why he should look
at her so.

"Cole's back," Jamie said unnecessarily.

"Cole!"

It was Shannon who called out his name, Shannon who
went running out to him as if he were a long-lost hero. Kristin couldn't move.

Cole's horse came to a prancing halt, and Shannon stood
there, staring up at him in adoration, reaching for him. To
his credit, Kristin admitted bitterly, he was good to Shannon. His eyes gentled when they fell upon her, and if there
was a certain impatience about him, he hid it from her well.
He dismounted from his horse in front of the house. Both
Jamie and Malachi stood there watching him in silence,
waiting for him to speak. He stepped forward and greeted
both of his brothers.

"Malachi, Jamie."

He grasped both their hands, and Jamie smiled crook-
edly while Malachi continued to observe him gravely. Then
Cole's eyes came to her again, and she would have backed
up again if she hadn't already been flush against the door.
His gaze came over her, as cold as the wind of a twister, and
perhaps, for just a second, with the same blinding torment.
Then the emotion was gone, and all that remained was the
staggering chill.

Her mouth was dry, her throat was dry, and she couldn't
speak. She was grateful then for Shannon, who told Cole

how glad she was to see him, how grateful she was that he was back.

Then she was suddenly still, and Kristin realized that the pudgy middle-aged man was still sitting atop his horse, looking at them all. She was the hostess here. She should be asking him in and offering him something cool to his throat from the dust and dirt of his ride. She should be doing something for Cole, too. If she could only move. Cole should be doing something, too, she thought, not leaving the little man just sitting there.

She forced her eyes away from Cole's to meet those of the man. She even made her lips curl into a semblance of a welcoming smile. "Hello, sir. Won't you come in?"

Jamie smiled. "Welcome, stranger. Cole, you're forgetting your manners. Who is this man?"

Cole turned to the man on the horse. "Sorry, Reverend. Please, come down."

"Much obliged," the man said, dismounting from his horse. Jamie stepped forward to tether the horses. The wind picked up and blew a handful of dirt around.

"This is the Reverend Samuel Cotter," Cole said. "Reverend, my brothers, Malachi and Jamie. And Miss Kristin McCahy in the doorway there, and Miss Shannon McCahy here by my side."

The reverend tipped his hat. "A pleasure, ladies. Gentlemen."

Then they were all just standing there again. The reverend turned his hat awkwardly in his hands. He had a nice face, Kristin thought. Heavy-jowled, with a nice, full smile and bright little eyes. She wished she could be more neighborly, but she was still having difficulty moving.

"Maybe we should all move into the house," Jamie suggested.

"Perhaps the reverend would like a sherry," Shannon murmured.

"The reverend would just love a whiskey!" the little man said, his eyes lighting up.

Malachi laughed. Cole came forward, his hands on his hips. He stood right in front of Kristin, and his eyes were just like the steel of Malachi's cavalry sword. His hands fell on her shoulders, and she almost screamed.

"You're blocking the door, Kristin," he said.

"Oh!" She moved quickly, jumping away from his touch. Her face flushed with color. She looked at the little man. "Forgive me my lack of manners, sir. Please, please, do come in." She paused, looking at Cole's hard, dispassionate features, then back at the reverend. "Um ... just what are you doing here, sir?"

The little man's brows shot up. "Why, I've come to marry you, miss."

"Marry me?"

"Why, not myself!" He laughed hard, enjoying his own joke. "I've come to marry you to Mr. Slater here."

"What!" Kristin gasped. She turned to stare at Cole again. She saw the ice, and the hatred in his eyes, and she thought it must be some horrible joke.

"Oh, no! I can't marry Mr. Slater." She said it flatly and with grim determination.

His hands were on her shoulders once again. His eyes bored into hers, ruthless, demanding. His fingers bit into her flesh, brutal and challenging.

"You will marry me, Kristin. Now. While we have the nice reverend here. It took me four days to find him, and I don't intend to have trouble now."

She gritted her teeth against the pain of his touch, against the force of his will. She wanted to cry, but she couldn't do that, and she couldn't explain that she couldn't possibly marry him, not when the mere idea made him look at her with such hatred.

"I will not—"

"You will!"

He turned around and shoved her through the door to the house. His touch stayed upon her, the warmth and strength of his body radiated along her spine, and his whisper touched her ear like the wind.

"Damn it, Kristin, stop it! You will do this!"

Suddenly tears glistened in her eyes. She'd dreamed about just such an occasion, but it hadn't been like this. He hadn't looked at her this way.

"Why?" she managed to whisper.

"We have to."

"But..." She had to salvage some pride. "I don't love you."

"I don't love you."

"Then—"

"Kristin, you've got your choices."

"I see. This is another threat. If I don't go through with this, you'll ride away."

"I have to ride away, Kristin. No matter what. And this is the only safeguard I could find for you."

"I can't do it—"

"Then plan on entertaining Zeke Moreau, Kristin. And if you can't think about yourself, think about Shannon."

"This is a travesty!"

His eyes burned with silver emotion for a moment. He was a stranger again as he stood there, touching her yet somehow distant from her.

"War is a travesty, Kristin. Cheer up. If it ever ends, you can divorce me. I'm sure you'll have plenty of cause. But for the moment, Miss McCahy, get into the parlor, stand sweetly and smile for the nice reverend, please."

PART 3

Her Husband

9

It was not what she had expected her wedding day to be like, and it was certainly not what she had dreamed it would be like.

Cole and the reverend were still covered with dust from their ride. She wore a simple cotton day dress with a single petticoat, since Cole had sworn impatiently when she had murmured something about changing. Shannon was wearing a shirt and trousers. The only concession to the fact that it was a wedding was the little bouquet she held, hurriedly put together by Delilah from ferns and late-blooming daisies.

They stood stiffly in the parlor. Cole was brusque, and the reverend tried to be kind. Malachi stood up for Cole, and Shannon acted as bridesmaid. Jamie, Delilah and Samson looked on. The reverend kept clearing his throat. He wanted to say more, wanted to speak about the sanctity of marriage and the commitment made thereby between a man and a woman. Cole kept shifting his weight from foot to foot. Then he snapped at the man, "Get on with it!"

Hastily the reverend went on.

Kristin listened to the droning voice and found herself looking around her mother's beautiful parlor and wondering what it had been like for her parents. Not like this. They had loved one another, she knew. She could remember her father's eyes, and the way they had misted over when her mother's name had been spoken. They had built their lives on a dream, and the dream had been a good one.

But they weren't living in a world of dreams, and Cole didn't love her. He didn't even pretend to love her.

"Kristin?"

"What?"

Startled, she looked up at him. She realized that they were standing side by side, she in simple cotton, he in denim and Missouri dust. His hand was around hers, and his flesh felt dry and hot. He squeezed her hand, and she gasped at the pressure, her eyes widening.

"Kristin!" His eyes were sizzling silver and dangerous. "The reverend just asked you a question."

She looked at the reverend. He was flushed and obviously uncomfortable, but he tried to smile again.

"Kristin . . . do you take this man for your lawful wedded husband, to have and to hold, from this day forward, to love, to cherish and to obey in all the things of this earth?"

She stared at him blankly. It wasn't right. He didn't love her. And she was falling in love with him.

"I, er . . ."

"Kristin!" The pressure of his fingers around hers was becoming painful.

"Cole . . ." She turned to him, trying to free her hand from his grasp. "Cole, this is marvelously noble of you, honestly. But I'm sorry, I don't think—"

"Kristin!" Shannon gasped.

"Kristin . . ." Cole began, and there was a definite threat in his tone, like a low rumble of thunder. What could he do to her, here, with all these people, she wondered recklessly.

He caught her shoulders and jerked her against him. The revered was sucking air in and out out of his cheeks very quickly. "Mr. Slater, if the young lady isn't prepared to take this step, if she isn't completely enamored of you—"

"She's enamored, she's enamored!" Cole snapped. He wound his fingers into Kristin's hair and kissed her hotly. He kissed her with such conviction and passion that she felt herself color from the roots of her hair to her toes. His lips molded around hers, and his tongue plunged deep into her mouth. She couldn't breathe, and she could barely stand, and her knees were beginning to shake.

"Really, now—" the reverend protested.

"They really *are* in love!" Jamie assured him cheerfully.

"Cole—" Malachi tapped his brother on the shoulder, "I—er...think you've made your point."

Cole lifted his lips from Kristin's by just a whisper. His eyes burned into hers. "Say 'I do,' Kristin. Say it."

She inhaled. Her ribs felt as if they had been crushed. She tried to shake her head, but it wouldn't move. "Say 'I do,'" he insisted.

She felt as if the trembling in her heart were an earthquake beneath her feet. She parted her lips, and they felt damp and swollen.

"For God's sake, do it!" Shannon whispered. "We need him. Don't be so naive!"

She nodded, but she couldn't speak. Cole caught her fingers and brought their hands together and squeezed. "'I do,' Kristin! Say it!"

She formed the words at last. I do.

"Go on!" Cole roared at the reverend.

The reverend asked Cole the same question he'd asked Kristin.

He almost spat out the answer. "I do!" His lips twisted bitterly, as if, having forced her to do what he wanted, he had found a new contempt for her. She tried to wrench her hand away from him, but he held her firm and slipped a ring on her finger. It was a wide gold band, and it was too big for her.

She heard Delilah saying that if they twined some string around it it would fit fine.

Then the reverend announced that they were man and wife, and Cole released her. No one said anything, not a single word. The silence went on and on, but Delilah finally broke it.

"This calls for some of that fine white wine in the cellar, I think. Samson, you go fetch it up here, please."

"Yessir, a wedding sure calls for wine," Samson agreed.

The room seemed very still, and Kristin was still unable to move. She was hot and cold by turns. She had never felt more alone in her life. Cole had moved away from her, far away, as if he couldn't bear to touch her now that the words had been spoken. He thanked the reverend and paid him. Then he seemed to notice Kristin again. She had to sign the marriage certificate.

She balked again. He grabbed her hand and guided it to the paper, and she managed to scratch our her name. Nothing seemed real. Delilah said she would set out a cold supper, and Shannon promised to help. Somehow Kristin wound up in one of the big plush wing chairs in the parlor. Jamie stood beside her, resting a hand on her shoulder.

"He's really not as bad as he seems, you know," he whispered.

She clenched her teeth together to keep them from chattering. "No, he's worse." Jamie laughed, but there was an edge to his laughter. He sat down on the sofa across from her and took her hands in his. His eyes were serious. "Kristin, you have to try to understand Cole."

"He doesn't want to be understood," she replied softly.

"You're not afraid of him, are you?" he asked.

She thought for a moment, then shook her head, smiling ruefully. "Afraid of Cole? Never. He saved my life. No, Jamie, I'm not afraid of him. I just wish that—"

"That what?" Jamie murmured.

They could both see Cole. He was rubbing the back of his neck as he talked to Malachi. He looked tired, Kristin thought. She bit her lower lip, and wished for a moment that the marriage was real. She wanted to tiptoe up behind him and touch his shoulders with soothing fingers. She wanted to press her face against the coolness of his back and pretend there was no war, no Zeke, no chaos.

"I wish I understood him," she said at last, staring straight at Jamie. "Want to help?"

He straightened and released her hands. "I'm sorry, Kristin. I can't." He stood and smiled down at her. "Look at that, will you? Delilah is a gem. A cold supper, indeed. She's got biscuits and gravy, turnip greens and a shank of ham over there. Come on!" He took her hands in his again and pulled her to her feet. Suddenly, impulsively, he gave her a kiss on the cheek. "Hey, welcome, sister," he whispered.

Some instinct caused her to look behind him. Cole was watching them. He scowled darkly and turned his attention to Malachi again.

"I'm not very hungry, Jamie," Kristin said. It was true. She wasn't hungry at all. She smiled at him, though and whispered, "Thank you, Jamie!" She felt like crying again, and she shook herself impatiently. It was absurd. She had stood tall in the face of tragedy. Now there was only confusion, but it was tearing her apart.

Cole didn't seem to be very hungry, either. He waited with barely concealed impatience for his brothers to finish their meal. When they had, he started toward the door with long strides, and they followed. He paused in the doorway and said to Kristin, "We're going to ride out and take a look at things. I want to tell the ranch hands."

He was going to announce their wedding the way he might have spread the news of a battle. She nodded, wondering again at the fever that touched his eyes. He couldn't wait to be away from her, she thought. Then why, she thought angrily, had he done it at all? Surely his obligation to her wasn't as great as that.

She didn't say anything. He looked at the reverend, thanking him again for making the trip and urging him to make himself at home. Then he paused again. Malachi and Jamie shifted uncomfortably, exchanging worried glances.

"Write to your brother," Cole told Kristin. "Write to him immediately. There's a good possibility I may stop a Yankee bullet before this is all over, but I don't intend it to be because of a stupid mistake."

Then the three of them were gone. Kristin stood up, watching as the door closed, listening as their booted feet fell against the floorboards of the front porch.

Then, ridiculously, she felt her knees wobbling. She heard a humming in the air, and it was as if wind were rising again, bringing with it a dark mist.

"Kristin!"

She heard Shannon calling her name, and then she heard nothing. She sank to the floor in a dead faint.

Several hours later the Slater brothers rode back from their inspection of the ranch. They'd told all the ranch hands about the marriage. Old Pete had spit on the ground and told Cole he was damned glad. He seemed to understand that with Cole and Kristin married, they were all safer from Zeke Moreau. He didn't seem to care much whether the marriage was real. He seemed to think it was none of his business.

The brothers had gone on to ride around the perimeters of the McCahy ranch. It was a quiet day. By the time they headed back for the house, night was coming and coming fast. Still, when they were within sight of the place, Cole suddenly decided he wanted to stop and set up camp.

Jamie built a fire, and Malachi unsaddled the horses. Cole produced a bottle of whiskey and the dried beef and hard tack. By then the stars had risen, bright against the endless black velvet of the night sky.

Malachi watched Cole, and he noticed the nervous tension that refused to ease from his features. There was a hardness about him today. Malachi understood it. He just didn't know how to ease it.

Let it rest! Malachi thought. Let it go. Kristin McCahy— no, Slater now—was young, beautiful and intelligent, and if he wasn't mistaken, she was in love with Cole. Cole was too caught up in his memories of tragedy to see it. Even if he did see it, it might not change anything. Malachi knew his brother had acted out of a sense of chivalry. He also knew

Kristin would have preferred he hadn't. Malachi sighed. Their personal lives were none of his business. He had to leave. He was a regular soldier in a regular army, and his leave was about up.

"This is kind of dumb, ain't it?" Jamie demanded, swallowing some of the whiskey.

"Dumb?" Cole asked.

"Hell, yes. You've got yourself a gorgeous bride, young and shapely—"

"And what the hell do you know about her shape?" Cole demanded heatedly.

"Come on, you can't miss it," Malachi protested dryly. He was determined to have a peaceful evening. He sent Jamie a warning scowl. They both knew what was bothering Cole. "Jamie . . . stop it."

"Why? Does Cole think he's the only one who's been hurt by this war?"

"Damned brat—" Cole began angrily.

"But the damned brat came running when you asked, Cole, so sit back. Hell, come on, both of you stop it."

"I just think he should appreciate the woman, that's all. And if he didn't mean to, damn it, he shouldn't have tied her up in chains like that."

Cole, exasperated, stared at Malachi. "Will you shut him up, or should I?"

"There's a war on, boys!" Malachi reminded them both.

"He should be decent to her—" Jamie began.

"Damn it, I am decent to her!" Cole roared.

"Leaving her alone on her wedding night—"

"Leaving her alone was the most decent damned thing I could do!" Cole said. He wrenched the whiskey bottle from his brother's hands. "You're too young for this stuff."

"Hell, I'm too old," Jamie said softly. He grinned ruefully at his brother, and all the tension between them seemed to dissipate. "I'm twenty, Cole. By some standards, that's real old. Seventeen-year-old boys are dying all over the place."

"Quantrill is running a bunch of boys," Cole said. He lifted his hand in a vague gesture. "The James boys. The Youngers. And that butcher Bill Anderson. He's just a kid."

He swallowed the liquor, then swallowed again. He felt like being drunk. Really drunk.

Malachi reached for the bottle. The firelight played over his hair, and he arched his golden brows at Cole. "You think that Quantrill can really control his men? That marrying Kristin can keep her safe?"

Cole looked out at the Missouri plain before him, gnawing on a blade of grass. He spit out the grass and looked over at his brothers, who were both looking at him anxiously. If he hadn't been knotted up inside he might have smiled. They were both concerned. There was something about the McCahy place that got to a man. He could understand how even the great struggle between North and South had ceased to matter here, had ceased to matter to Kristin. The brutality here was too much. It left the mind numbed.

"I know Quantrill is about to head south for the winter. He doesn't like the cold. He'll make one more raid, I'm certain. Then he'll head on somewhere south—maybe Arkansas, maybe Texas. I'll stick around until he moves on. Then I'll go on over to Richmond. If I can just find some train tracks that are still holding together, I should make it in time."

"If Jefferson Davis is still in the Cabinet," Jamie said glumly.

Cole looked at him sharply. "Why? What have you heard?"

"Nothing. It's just that the battle of Sharpsburg left a lot of dead men. A whole lot of dead men."

"Watch your step around here," Malachi warned Cole. "There's Federal patrols wandering all around the McCahy place."

"Yeah, I know."

"That little witch just about got me hauled in today."

"Witch?" Cole asked.

"Shannon," Jamie supplied.

Malachi grunted. "I envy you your wife, Cole, but not your in-laws."

"And he doesn't mean the Yankee brother." Jamie laughed. "It's a good thing Malachi has to ride out soon. I don't think she's too fond of him, either."

Malachi looked as if he wanted to kill somebody, Jamie thought, but at least Cole laughed, and Cole needed it the most. "What have I missed?" Cole asked.

"The antics of a child," Malachi replied, waving a dismissing hand in the air. He reached for the liquor bottle. It was going down quickly.

"Some child!" Jamie said. "Why, she's coming along just as nicely as that wife of yours, Cole."

Malachi and Cole looked at one another. "We could end this war if we just sent this boy to Washington to heckle the Union commanders," Malachi said.

Cole grunted his agreement. Jamie grinned and lay back against his saddle, staring up at the stars. "You know, Cole," he said suddenly, "I am sorry about the past. I sure am."

There was a long silence. The fire snapped and crackled. Malachi held his breath and held his peace.

"But if I were you," Jamie went on, "I wouldn't be out here with my brothers. Not when I had a woman like that waiting. A woman with beautiful blond hair and eyes like sapphires. And the way she walks, her hips swinging and all . . . Why, I can just imagine what it'd be like—"

"Son of a bitch!" Cole roared suddenly. He stood up, slamming the nearly empty whiskey bottle into the fire. The liquor hissed and sizzled. Jamie leaped to his feet, startled by the deadly dark danger in his brother's eyes. Malachi, too, leaped to his feet. He couldn't believe that Cole would really go for Jamie, but then he had never seen Cole in a torment like this. Nor had he ever seen Jamie so determined to irk him.

"Cole—" Malachi reached for his brother's arm, and they stared at one another in the golden firelight.

"No!" Jamie told Malachi, his eyes on Cole. "If he wants to beat me up, let him. If he thinks he can strike out at me and feel better, fine. Let him hurt me instead of that poor girl waiting for him at the house. At least I understand why he strikes out. Hell, she doesn't even know why he's so damned hateful."

"What the hell difference does it make?" Cole thundered. "All she wanted from me was protection!"

"She deserves some damned decency from you!"

"I told you—"

"Yeah, yeah, you came up with some puny excuse. You are a bastard."

"You don't know—"

"I know that it wasn't my wife killed by the jayhawkers, but we loved her, too, Cole. And she loved you, and she wouldn't want you making your whole life nothing but ugly vengeance."

"Why, I ought to—"

"Cole!" Malachi shouted. Between the three of them, they'd consumed almost an entire bottle of liquor. This wasn't a good time for Jamie to be goading Cole, but Jamie didn't seem to care. And now Cole was losing control. He shook off Malachi's arm and lunged at Jamie with a sudden fury. Then the two of them were rolling in the dust.

"Jesus in heaven!" Malachi breathed. "Will the two of you—"

"You don't know! You don't know anything!" Cole raged at Jamie. "You didn't find her, you didn't feel the blood pouring out all over you! You didn't see her eyes close, you didn't see the love as it died. You didn't watch her eyes close and feel her flesh grow cold!"

"Cole!"

His hands were around Jamie's neck, and Jamie wasn't doing anything at all. He was letting Cole throttle him. Malachi tried to pull him off, and Cole suddenly realized what he was doing. Horrified, he released his brother. Then he stood and walked away, his back to his brothers.

"I need to stay away from Kristin," he said softly.

Jamie looked at Malachi and rubbed his throat. Malachi spoke to Cole.

"No. You don't need to stay away from her. You need to go to her."

Cole turned around. He came over to Jamie and planted his hands on his brother's shoulders. "You all right?"

Jamie nodded and grinned. "I'm all right."

Cole walked over to his horse. He untied the reins which were tethered to a tree, and walked the horse into the open. Then he leaped up on the animal's back without bothering to saddle it.

"You going back?" Malachi asked.

"Just for another bottle of whiskey."

Malachi and Jamie nodded. They watched as Cole started back toward the house, the horse's hooves suddenly taking flight in the darkness.

"He's just going back for another whiskey bottle," Jamie said.

Malachi laughed. "We betting on when he's going to make it back?"

Jamie grinned. "You get to bring his saddle in the morning." He lay down again and stretched out, feeling his throat. "Too bad I wasn't blessed with sisters!" He groaned.

Malachi grunted, pulled his hat low over his face and closed his eyes. The fire crackled and burned low, and at last the two of them slept.

Cole heard one of Pete's hounds barking as he approached the house. Then Pete himself, shirtless, the top of his long johns showing above his hastily donned trousers, came out to challenge him.

"Just me, Pete," Cole assured him.

"Evening, boss," Pete said agreeably, and headed back to the bunkhouse.

Cole dismounted from his horse, sliding from the animal's back without his accustomed grace. He gave his head a shake to clear it. The whiskey had gotten to him more than he would have cared to admit, but not enough to really knock him out the way he wanted, not enough to take away the last of his pain. He was determined to be quiet, but it seemed to him that his boots made an ungodly noise on the floorboards of the porch.

The house was dark. He stumbled through the hall and the parlor and into what had been Gabriel McCahy's office. He fumbled around for a match and lit the oil lamp on the desk, then came around and sat in the chair, putting his feet up on the desk and digging in the lower right hand drawer for a bottle of liquor—any kind of liquor.

Then he heard a click, and the hair on the back of his neck stood straight up. His whiskey-dulled reflexes came to life, and he slammed his feet to the floor, reaching for his revolver.

He pointed it at the doorway—and right at Kristin, who stood there with a double-barreled shotgun aimed at his head. He swore irritably, returning his gun to his holster and sinking back into his chair.

"What the hell are you doing?" he growled.

"What am I doing? You son of a bitch—" She lowered the shotgun and moved into the room. She stopped in front of the desk, caught in the soft glow of the lamplight. Her hair was loose, a soft storm of sunshine falling over her shoulders. She was dressed chastely enough, in a nightgown that buttoned to her throat, but the lamplight went through the fabric and caressed her body. He could see all too clearly the sway of her hips, which Jamie had so admired. He could see the curve of her breasts, the flow and shape of her limbs, and suddenly the sight of her hurt him. It was as if some mighty hand reached down and took hold of him, squeezing the life from him. He felt his heart pounding, felt his shuddering pulse enter his groin and take root there. His fingers itched to reach out to her, to touch her. She was staring at him, her blue eyes a raging sea of fury, and not even that deterred him. It only made the pulse within him beat all the harder.

He didn't love her. To love her would be disloyal. But he had married her. What the hell else could she want?

"What are you doing in here?" she snapped.

"Kristin, put the gun down. Go to bed."

"You scared me to death! And *you* taught *me* not to go wandering around unarmed!"

"Kristin, put the gun down." He hesitated. Then he smiled suddenly. "Come on. We'll go to bed. Together."

Her eyes widened. "You're out of your mind, Cole Slater."

"Am I?" He came around the desk, slowly, lazily, yet purposefully. Kristin raised the shotgun again.

"Yes! You are out of your mind."

"You're my wife."

"And you walked out of here this afternoon and didn't come back until three in the morning—after treating me with the manners of a rabid squirrel. I promise you, Mr. Slater, if you think you're going to touch me, you're out of your mind."

He *was* out of his mind, and he knew it. He swallowed raggedly. He had forgotten so much. He had tried to forget. He had forgotten that she could hold her head with such incredible pride. He had forgotten her eyes could snap this way, and he had forgotten that her mouth was wide and generous and beautifully shaped. He had forgotten that she was beautiful and sensuous, and that her touch was more potent than whiskey or wine or the finest brandy. He had forgotten so much....

But now he remembered. The revealing lamplight glowed on the lush curves of her body, and the thunder inside him became almost unbearable. He took a step forward, and she cocked the shotgun. His smile deepened.

"Fire it, Kristin."

"I will, damn you!"

He laughed triumphantly, stepped toward her again and took the shotgun from her hands. He pulled her hard against him, and he lowered his head and seized her lips in a kiss. It was not at all brutal, but it was filled with a shocking need and a shocking thirst. For an instant she thought to twist from him, but his kiss filled her with a searing, liquid heat, and she felt as if she were bursting with the desire to touch him, to be touched by him.

He broke away from her, and his eyes sought hers. "No!" she told him angrily, but he smiled and swept her up into his arms. Her eyes were still angry but she locked her arms around his neck. He carried her effortlessly through the darkened parlor, up the stairs and into the bedroom. He closed the door with his foot and set her down by the window. The moonlight found her there, dancing over her fine, delicate features and her rich, feminine curves.

"You're horrid," she told him.

He smiled tenderly. "You're beautiful."

"You're filthy."

He kissed her forehead, and he kissed her cheeks, and he rimmed her lips with the tip of his tongue, teasing them, dampening them. His fingers went to the tiny buttons of her gown, and he tried to undo them but they wouldn't give, and he finally ripped the gown open impatiently. The moonlight fell on her naked flesh. He groaned and kissed her shoulder and her throat, feeling the urgent quickening of her heart.

"Does it matter so terribly much?" he whispered.

She didn't answer. He stroked her breast. Then he lowered his head and touched his lips to the nipple. He teased it with his teeth, then sucked it hard into his mouth and finally gentled it with his tongue. Rivers of pleasure streaked through her, and she threaded her fingers roughly into his hair, and he savored the little tug of pain. He lowered himself slowly to his knees, holding her hips, then her buttocks.

"Does it matter so terribly much?" he repeated, looking up into her dazed eyes. He teased her navel with the tip of his tongue.

"Yes!" she whispered. He started to move away from her, but she wouldn't let him. He bathed her belly with kisses, cupping her buttocks hard and pressing close to her, sliding his tongue along the apex of her thighs and into the golden triangle there. She shuddered and cried out, but he held her firmly, and when it seemed she was about to fall he lowered her carefully to the floor. He touched her gently and tenderly, and then he brought his mouth over hers again. "Does it really matter so terribly much?" he demanded.

She closed her eyes and wrapped her arms around his neck. "No," she whispered, and she released him to tug at his buttons and then at his belt buckle. She groaned in frustration, and he helped her, stripping quickly. She was so very beautiful, there in the full flood of the moonlight. All of him quickened, and desire spread through him like a raging wind, and he cried out in a ragged voice. She was there, there to take him, there to close around him, a sweet and secret haven. Nothing on earth was like this.

He sank into her, swept into her, again and again. She rose to meet his every thrust, and the pulse raged between them. She was liquid fire when she moved. She was made to have him, made to love him, made to take him. The culmination burst upon them swiftly. She gasped and shuddered, and he thrust heatedly, again and felt his climax spew from him. He held her tight. He felt the sweat, slick between them. He felt the rise and fall of her breath and the clamor of her heart, slowing at last.

He stroked her hair, and he marveled at the ecstasy of it.

Then he remembered that he had made her his wife, and suddenly he hated himself again.

He should have said something. He should have whispered something to her. Anything. Anything that was tender, anything that was kind.

He couldn't bring himself to do it.

Instead, he rose, his skin glistening in the moonlight. Then he bent down and took her naked form in his arms. She was silent, her eyes lowered, her hair a tangle around them.

He laid her down upon the bed. Her eyes met his at last, and he saw in them a torment that seemed to match that within his heart. She was so very beautiful. Naked, she was a goddess, her breasts firm and full and perfect, her limbs shapely and slim, her belly a fascinating plane between her hips. He pulled the covers over her. Her sapphire eyes still studied him.

"I'm . . . I'm sorry," he muttered at last.

She let out a strangled oath and turned away from him.

He hesitated, then slipped in beside her. He crossed his arms behind his head and stared up at the ceiling, wishing he were drunker, wishing fervently he could go to sleep.

But he lay awake a long, long time. And he knew she didn't sleep, either.

At dawn he rose and left.

And at dawn Kristin finally slept. She had the right to stay in bed all day, she told herself bitterly. She was a bride, and this was the morning after her wedding day.

Cole wasn't in the house when she finally did get up. Shannon told her he had gone out with Malachi.

Jamie was there, though. He told her that they were low on salt and that they needed a couple of blocks for the cattle to lick through the winter. Cole had said that she and Pete were to go into town and buy them.

The Union had control of most of the border area—despite Quantrill's sporadic raids—and the town had managed to remain quieter than the McCahy ranch. Kristin was glad to take the buckboard and ride into town with Pete. She was glad to be away from the house.

It was a three-hour ride. The town of Little Ford was small, but it did have two saloons, one reputable hotel, two doctors old enough to be exempted from military service and three mercantile stores. In Jaffe's Mercantile she saw Tommy Norley, a newspaperman and and old friend of Adam's from over the Kansas border.

"Kristin!"

He was limping when he came over to her. He tipped his hat quickly, then took both her hands in his. "Kristin, how are you doing out there? Is everything all right? You and Shannon should have moved on, I think. Or maybe into town. Or maybe out to California!"

She smiled. He was a slim man, pale-faced, with a pencil-thin mustache and dark, soulful eyes.

"I'm doing well, Tommy, thank you." She searched his eyes. She had last seen him when they had buried her father. He had written a scathing article about guerrilla attacks.

"You should move, Kristin."

She chose to ignore his words. "Tommy, you're limping."

He smiled grimly. "I just got caught by Quantrill."

Her heart skipped a beat. "What do you mean? What happened?"

"The bastard attacked Shawneetown last week. I was with the Federal supply train he and his maniacs caught up with on their way in." He paused and looked at her, wondering how much he should say to a lady.

"Tommy, tell me! What happened?"

He took a deep breath. "Kristin, it was awful. Quantrill and his men came after us like a pack of Indians, howling, shouting. They gunned down fifteen men, drivers and escorts. I rolled off the side of the road, into the foliage. I took a bullet in the calf, but I lived to tell the tale. Kristin, they went on into town and murdered ten more men there. Then they burned the village to the ground.''

"Oh, God! How horrible!'' Kristin gasped.

"Kristin, come to Kansas. I'm opening an office in Lawrence, and I'm sure you'll be safe.''

She smiled. ''Tommy, my home is in Missouri.''

"But you're in danger.''

"I can't leave the ranch, Tommy.'' She wondered if she should tell him that she had married to save her ranch and that she would probably be in real danger from her new husband if she deserted him and ran off to Kansas.

"You should have seen them,'' Tommy murmured. "Kristin, they were savages. You should have seen them.''

She held on to the counter in the mercantile, suddenly feeling ill. He kept talking, and she answered him as politely as she could. She cared about Tommy. He had been a good friend to Adam. It was just that Adam had begun to fade from her life. It was not that she hadn't loved him. She had. But Cole was a stronger force in her life.

Kristin hesitated, then asked him if he thought he could get a message to Matthew for her. He promised to try, and she bought some stationery from Mr. Jaffe and quickly wrote a letter to Matthew. It wasn't easy to explain her marriage. She did it as carefully and as cheerfully as she could, then turned the letter over to Tommy, hoping she had done well.

She kissed Tommy and left him. Pete had gotten the salt licks, and he had stacked the remaining space in the buckboard with alfalfa to help get them through the coming winter.

She told him about Shawneetown, then fell silent. The news bothered her all the way home.

When they arrived at the ranch, she still felt ill. She went out back and stood over her parents' graves. Cold and chilled, she tried to pray, but no thoughts came to her mind.

A while later she felt a presence behind her, and she knew that it was Cole. She was angry, and she didn't know why, unless it was because she knew he didn't love her, and because she knew she was falling in love with him. He was attracted to her, certainly. Maybe he even needed her. But he didn't love her.

She spun around, ready to do battle.

"Quantrill and his animals attacked Shawneetown last week. They killed the men escorting a supply train, and then they went into the village and killed some more, and then they burned the whole place down."

His eyes narrowed, and he stared at her warily, but he didn't say anything. She walked up to him and slammed her fists against his chest. "He's a captain! The Confederates made him a captain!"

He grabbed her wrists hard. "I don't condone Quantrill, and you know it. The Missouri governor considers him and his raiders like an elephant won at a raffle."

"Let go of me!" she hissed furiously.

"No. You listen to me for a minute, lady. Quantrill has no monopoly on brutality! Quantrill came *after* the likes of Lane and Jennison. Unionists, Kristin! Jayhawkers! You want to know some of the things they've done? They've ridden up to farmhouses and dragged men out and killed them—men *and* women! They've murdered and they've raped and they've tortured, exactly the same way Quantrill has! You remember that, Kristin! You bear that in mind real well!"

He pushed her away from him and turned, his long, angry strides taking him toward the house. The rear door opened and then slammed shut, and he disappeared inside.

She waited a moment, and then she followed him. She didn't know if she wanted to continue the fight or try to make up with him somehow.

It didn't matter. He wasn't in the house anymore.

And that night he didn't come back at all.

10

Cole might have slept somewhere else during the night, but he appeared at the breakfast table in the morning. Kristin was angry and wondered what everyone must think. He came and went like the breeze, with no regard for her feelings. Kristin was sharp when he spoke to her. When he asked her to pass him the milk, she seriously considered splashing it in his face or pouring it in his lap. He caught her hand and the pitcher before she could do either. He stared at her hard, and she looked away.

She didn't like Cole's ability to stay away from her. She wanted to fight with him. She wanted to do anything just to bring him close to her again. It was an effort to turn away from him, to find some trivial thing to discuss with Jamie and Shannon.

Cole remained in a foul temper all day. With winter coming on, there was a lot to do. Cole was anxious to have it all done before he left for the East and before Malachi and Jamie had to leave to rejoin their units. They spent the day gathering up as much of the herd as they could for Pete to drive to market. Kristin had been surprised that Cole was willing to let her sell the beef on the Union side of the line, but he had reminded her that the ranch belonged to her brother, Matthew, and that Matthew was fighting for the Union. Cole couldn't go north himself, but Pete could handle the cattle drive, and Malachi and Jamie would be around until he got back at the end of the week.

By dinnertime, Cole seemed to be in a somewhat better mood, and Kristin maintained a polite distance from him. Cole, Jamie and Malachi all sat down to dinner with Kristin and Shannon that night. Delilah refused to sit and made a big fuss over everyone. Jamie made the meal a pleasant affair. He told the two girls about a pair of hammers his mother had bought for Cole and Malachi when they were boys and about how the two of them had used their hammers on one another. Even Shannon laughed and refrained from engaging in verbal warfare with Malachi. Cole listened to the story with a smile on his face, and at one point his eyes met Kristin's and he gave her an entrancing grin and a sheepish shrug.

After dinner, Kristin played the spinet and Shannon sang. She sang a few light tunes, then gave a haunting rendition of "Lorena", a ballad about a soldier who returns from the wars to find that his love is gone. When it was over, they were all silent. Then Cole stood up and told Shannon in a strangled voice that her singing was very beautiful. He excused himself and left them.

Kristin bit her lip as she watched him leave the room. Jamie gave her an encouraging pat on the knee, and Malachi practically shoved Shannon out of the way and began a rousing chorus of "Dixie."

When he had finished, Shannon regained her place and sang "John Brown's Body."

"Shannon McCahy, you are a brat," Malachi told her.

"And you're a rodent," Shannon replied sweetly.

"Children, children!" Jamie protested with a sigh.

But Shannon said something, and though Kristin could see that Malachi was striving for patience, he replied sharply, and the battle was on once again.

Kristin rose and left them bickering. She went upstairs and was surprised to find that Cole was already in bed. She thought he was asleep, but when she crawled in beside him, trying not to disturb him, he turned over and took her in his arms. She tried to study his eyes in the darkness, but she could see only their silver glow. She tried to speak, but he silenced her with a kiss. Tenderly at first, and then with a growing passion, he made love to her. When it was over, he held her close, his bearded chin resting against the top of her head. He didn't speak, and neither did she. She knew he lay there awake for a long time, and she wished she could reach out to him, wished she knew what to say to him. She could not apologize, for she had done nothing wrong. She kept silent.

Eventually Kristin fell asleep.

Sometime later, something woke her. She didn't know what it was at first. She heard something, some hoarse, whispered words that she didn't understand. Struggling to free herself from the web of sleep, she opened her eyes, just as Cole's arm came flying out and slammed against her shoulder.

She sat up in bed, calling out his name. He didn't answer her, and she fumbled for a match to light the oil lamp on the bedside table. The glow filled the room and fell on Cole.

The bare flesh of his shoulders and chest was gleaming with sweat. The muscles there were tense and rigid and knotted. His fingers plucked at the sheet that lay over him.

His features contorted, his head tossing from side to side, he screamed, "No!" His entire body was stiff and hard.

"Cole!" Kristin pleaded, shaking him. "Cole—"

"No!" he screamed again.

She straddled him, took him by the shoulders and shook him hard, determined to wake him.

His eyes flew open, but he didn't see her. He called out again, and then he struck out at her, and the force sent her flying to the floor. He jerked upright as she fell. Stunned, Kristin sat on the hard floor, rubbing her bruised behind.

"Kristin?"

He whispered her name slowly, fearfully. There was something in his voice that she had never heard before, a frightened tone, and it touched her deeply.

"I'm here," she whispered ruefully.

He looked over the side of the bed and swore. He leaped swiftly from the bed, and took her in his arms. She felt the pounding of his heart, felt the tremors that still racked him as he laid her down on the bed again.

"I hurt you. I'm so sorry."

His voice was deep, husky. She felt her own throat constrict, and she shook her head, burrowing more deeply against his naked chest. "No. You didn't hurt me. I'm all right, really."

He didn't say anything. He didn't even move. He just held her.

She wanted to stay there, where she was, forever. She had never felt so cherished before. Desired, admired, even needed. But never so cherished.

"You had a nightmare," she told him tentatively.

"Yes," he said.

"I wish you would tell me—"

"No."

It wasn't that he spoke so harshly, but that he spoke with absolute finality. Kristin stiffened, and she knew he felt it. He set her from him and rose. She watched as he walked over to the window, and as he stood there in the moonlight a dark web of pain seemed to encircle her heart. He walked with a pride that was uniquely his. He stood there for a long time, naked and sinewed and gleaming in the moonlight, and stared out at the night. Kristin watched as his muscles slowly, slowly eased, losing some of their awful rigor.

"Cole—" she whispered.

He turned back to her at last. He walked across the room, and she was glad when he lifted the covers and lay beside her again, drawing his arm around her and bringing her head to his chest. He stroked her hair.

"Cole, please—"

"Kristin, please. Don't."

She fell silent. His touch remained gentle.

"I have to leave tomorrow," he said at last.

"Where are you going?"

"East."

"Why?"

He hesitated for a long time. "Kristin, there are things that you probably don't want to hear, and there's no good reason for me to tell you."

"No questions, no involvement," she murmured. He didn't answer her, but she felt him tighten beneath her.

"It's late," he said at last. "You should—"

She rose up and touched his lips with her own, cutting off his words. She wondered if she should be angry, or at least cool and distant. Nothing had changed. He had married her, but he still didn't want any involvement.

That didn't matter to her. Not at that moment. She only knew that he was leaving, and that in these times any man's future was uncertain at best. She ceased the flow of his words with the soft play of her tongue and leaned the length of her body over his, undulating her hips against his groin and the hardened peaks of her breasts against his chest. She savored the sharp intake of his breath and the quick, heady pressure of his hands upon her back and her buttocks.

Now it was her turn to inflame him. She nuzzled her face against his beard, and she teased his throat and the hard contours of his shoulders and chest. She tempted him with her tongue and with her fingertips and with the entire length of her body. She moved against him, crying out again and again at the sweet feel of their flesh touching. She teased him with her teeth, moving lower and lower against him. He tore his fingers into her hair and hoarsely gasped out her name. She barely knew herself. She was at once serene and excited, and she was certain of her power. She took all of him without hesitation. She loved him until he dragged her back to him and kissed her feverishly on the lips, then drew her beneath him. There was a new tension etched into his features, and a new blaze in his eyes. Taut as wire, he hovered above her. Then he came to her, fierce and savage and yet uniquely tender.

She thought she died just a little when it was over. The world was radiant, painted with shocking strips of sunlight and starlight, and then it was black and she was drifting again.

He held her still. He didn't speak, but his fingers stroked her hair, and for the moment it was enough. His hand lay over her abdomen. Tentatively she placed her fingers over his. He laced them through his own, and they slept.

But in the morning when she awoke, he was gone.

Three days later, Kristin was pumping water into the trough when she looked up to see a lone rider on the horizon, coming toward the house. For a moment her heart fluttered and she wondered if it might be Cole returning. Then she realized it couldn't be him. It wasn't his horse, and the rider wasn't sitting the horse the way he did.

"Malachi!" she called. He and Jamie would be with her for another few days. She frowned and bit her lip as she watched the approaching rider. It wasn't Zeke, she knew. Zeke never rode alone. Besides, there was no reason for her to be afraid of Quantrill's boys. Cole had gone through with the wedding to protect her, and anyway, Quantrill was supposed to be moving south for the winter. There was no reason to be afraid.

She was afraid anyway.

"Malachi—" she began again.

"Kristin?" He appeared at the door to the barn, his thumbs hooked in his belt, his golden brows knit into a furrow. He hurried over to her and watched the rider come. His eyes narrowed.

"Anderson," he murmured.

"Who?"

"It's a boy named Bill Anderson. He's . . . he's one of Quantrill's. One of his young recruits."

"What does he want? He is alone, isn't he?" Kristin asked anxiously.

"Yes, he's alone," Malachi assured her.

Jamie appeared then, coming out of the barn, his sleeves rolled up, his jacket off. He looked at Malachi. "I thought Quantrill was already on his way south. That's Bill Anderson."

Malachi nodded. "He seems to be alone."

The rider came closer and closer. He was young, very young, with a broad smile. He had dark, curly hair and a dark mustache and beard, but he still had an absurdly innocent face. Kristin shivered, thinking that he was far too young to be going around committing murder.

He drew his horse up in front of them. He was well armed, Kristin saw, with Colts at his waist and a rifle on either side of his saddle.

"Howdy, Malachi, Jamie."

"Bill," Malachi said amiably enough. Jamie nodded an acknowledgment.

"Cole's headed east, huh?" Anderson asked. He smiled at Kristin, waiting for an introduction. "You his new wife, ma'am? It's a pleasure to meet you."

He stuck out his hand. Kristin thought about all the blood that was probably on that hand, but she took it anyway and forced herself to smile.

"I'm his new wife," Kristin said. She couldn't bring herself to say that it was a pleasure to meet him, too. She could barely stand there.

"Kristin Slater, this is Bill Anderson. Bill, what the hell are you doing here? There's a lot of Union soldiers around these parts, you know," Malachi said.

"Yep," Jamie agreed cheerfully. "Lots and lots of Federals in these parts. And you know what they've been saying about you boys? No mercy. If they get their hands on you they intend to hang you high and dry."

"Yeah. I've heard what the Union has to say. But you've been safe enough here, huh, Malachi? And you, too, Jamie."

"Hell, we're regular army," Jamie said.

Anderson shrugged. "They have to catch us before they can hang us. And I'm not staying. I just had . . . well, I had some business hereabouts. I've got to join Quantrill in Arkansas. I just thought maybe I could come by here for a nice home-cooked meal."

Malachi answered before Kristin could. "Sure, Bill. Jamie, why don't you go on in and ask Delilah to cook up something special. Tell her we've got one of Quantrill's boys here."

Jamie turned around and hurried to the house. Delilah was already standing in the doorway. As Kristin watched, Shannon's blond head appeared. There was a squeal of outrage, and then the door slammed. Jamie came hurrying back to them.

"Malachi, Delilah says she needs you. There's a bit of a problem to be dealt with."

Malachi lifted an eyebrow, then hurried to the house. Kristin stood there staring foolishly at Bill Anderson with a grin plastered to her face. She wanted to shriek, and rip his baby face to shreds. Didn't he understand? Didn't he know she didn't want him here?

Men using Quantrill's name had come here and murdered her father. Men just like this one. She wanted to spit in his face.

But he had evidently come for a reason, and Malachi seemed to think it was necessary that he be convinced that Kristin was Cole's wife and that this was Cole's place now.

Kristin heard an outraged scream from the house. She bit her lip. Shannon obviously realized that one of Quantrill's men was here, and she didn't intend to keep quiet. She certainly didn't intend to sit down to a meal with him.

Anderson looked toward the house, hiking a brow.

"My sister," Kristin said sweetly.

"Her baby sister," Jamie said. He smiled at Kristin, but there was a warning in his eyes. They had to make Bill Anderson think Shannon was just a little girl.

And they had to keep her away from him.

Apparently that was what Malachi was doing, because the screams became muffled, and then they were silenced.

Malachi—the marks of Shannon's fingernails on his cheek—reappeared on the front porch. "Come on in, Bill. We'll have a brandy, and then Delilah will have lunch all set."

Bill looked from Malachi to Kristin and grinned. "That came from your, uh... baby sister, Mrs. Slater?"

"She can be wild when she wants," Kristin said sweetly. She stared hard at Malachi. He touched his cheek and shrugged. Kristin walked by him. "Too bad they can't send her up to take on the Army of the Potomac. We'd win this war in a matter of hours. Old Abe Lincoln himself would think that secession was a fine thing just as long as Shannon McCahy went with the Confederacy."

"Malachi!" Kristin whispered harshly. "You're talking about my sister!"

"I ought to turn her over to Bill Anderson!" he muttered.

"Malachi!"

Anderson turned around, looking at them curiously. "Where is your sister?" he asked.

"The baby is tucked in for her nap," Malachi said with a grin. "We don't let her dine with adults when we have company in the house. She spits her peas out sometimes. You know how young 'uns are."

Kristin gazed at him, and he looked innocently back at her. She swept by him. "Mr. Anderson, can we get you a drink? A shot of whiskey?"

"Yes, ma'am, you can."

Kristin took him into her father's study and poured him a drink. As he looked around the room, admiring the furnishings, Malachi came in and whispered in her ear.

"Shannon's in the cellar."

"And she's just staying there?" Kristin asked, her eyes wide.

"Sure she's just staying there," Malachi said.

Soon they sat down to eat. Sizzling steaks from the ranch's own fresh beef, fried potatoes, fall squash and apple pie. Bill Anderson did have one big appetite. Kristin reminded herself dryly that he was a growing boy.

He was polite, every inch the Southern cavalier, all through the meal. Only when coffee was served with the pie did he sit back and give them an indication of why he had come.

"Saw your husband the other day, ma'am."

Kristin paused just a second in scooping him out a second slice of pie. "Did you?" she said sweetly.

"Sure, when he came to see Quantrill. He was mighty worried about you. It was a touching scene."

She set the pie down. "Was it?" She glanced at Malachi. His eyes were narrowed, and he was very still.

"He used to be one of us, you know."

"What?"

Despite herself, Kristin sat. She sank right into her chair. "What?" she repeated.

Jamie cleared his throat. Malachi still hadn't moved.

Bill Anderson wiped his face with his napkin and smiled pleasantly. "Cole is one of the finest marksmen I ever did see. Hell, he's a one-man army, he's so damned good. It was nice when he was riding with us."

Kristin didn't say anything. She knew all the blood had fled from her face.

Bill Anderson forked up a piece of pie. "Yep, Cole Slater was just the same as Zeke Moreau. Just the same."

Malachi was on his feet in a second, his knife at Anderson's throat. "My brother was never anything like Zeke Moreau!"

Jamie jumped up behind him. He was so tense that Jamie couldn't pull him away. Kristin rushed around and tugged at his arm. "Malachi!"

He backed away. Bill Anderson stood and straightened his jacket. He gazed at Malachi, murder in his eyes. "You'll die for that, Slater."

"Maybe I'll die, but not for that, Anderson!" Malachi said.

"Gentlemen, gentlemen!" Kristin breathed, using her softest voice. "Please, aren't we forgetting ourselves here?"

It worked. Like most young men in the South, they had both been taught to be courteous to females, that a lack of manners was a horrible fault. They stepped away from each other, but their tempers were still hot.

"You came here just to do that, didn't you?" Malachi said quietly. "Just to upset my sister-in-law. I'm willing to bet Zeke Moreau asked you to do it."

"Maybe, and maybe not," Anderson said. He reached over to the sideboard for his hat. "Maybe she's just got the right to know that Cole Slater was a bushwhacker. You want to deny that, Malachi?"

Kristin looked at Malachi. His face was white, but he said nothing.

Anderson slammed his hat on his head. He turned to Kristin. "Mighty obliged for the meal, ma'am. Mighty obliged. Cap'n Quantrill wants you to know that you should feel safe, and he's sorry about any harm that's been done to you or yours. If he had understood that your loyalties lay with the Confederacy, none of it would have come about."

It was a lie, a bald-faced lie, but Kristin didn't say anything. Anderson turned around, and she heard the door slam shut as he left the house.

Delilah came in from the kitchen. The old grandfather clock in the parlor struck the hour. They all stood there, just stood there, dead still, until they heard Bill Anderson mount his horse, until they heard the hoofbeats disappear across the Missouri dust.

Then Kristin spun around, gripping the back of a chair and staring hard at Malachi. "Is it true?"

"Kristin—" he began unhappily.

"Is it true?" she screeched. "Is Cole one of them?"

"No!" Jamie protested, stepping forward. "He isn't one of them, not now."

She whirled around again, looking at Jamie. "But he was! That's the truth, isn't it?"

"Yes, damn it, all right, he was. But there was a damned good reason for it."

"Jamie!" Malachi snapped.

"Oh, God!" Kristin breathed. She came around and fell into the chair. Malachi tried to take her hand. She wrenched it away and jumped to her feet. "Don't, please don't! Can't you understand? They are murderers! They dragged my father out and they killed him!"

"There are a lot of murderers in this war, Kristin," Malachi said. "Quantrill isn't the only one."

"It was Quantrill's men who killed my father," she said dully. "It was Quantrill's men who came after me."

Malachi didn't come near her again. He stood at the end of the table, his face pinched. "Kristin, Cole's business is Cole's business, and when he chooses, maybe he'll explain things to you. He's asked us to mind our own concerns. Maybe he knew you'd react just like this if you heard something. I don't know. But you remember this while you're busy hating him. He stumbled into this situation. He didn't come here to hurt you." He turned and walked to the door.

"He rode with Quantrill!" she whispered desperately.

"He's done the best he knows how for you," Malachi said quietly. He paused and looked back at her. "You might want to let your sister go when you get the chance. I tied her up downstairs so she wouldn't take a trip up here to meet Bill Anderson. He might not have liked what she had to say very much... and he might have liked the way that she looked too much."

He went out. The clock suddenly seemed to be ticking very loudly. Kristin looked miserably at Jamie.

He tried to smile, but the attempt fell flat. "I guess I can't tell you too much of anything, Kristin. But I love my brother, and I think he's a fine man. There are things that maybe you can't understand just yet, and they are his business to discuss." He paused, watching her awkwardly. Then he shrugged and he, too, left her.

It wasn't a good day. She sat there for a long time. She even forgot about Shannon, and it was almost an hour before she went downstairs to release her. When she did, it was as if she had let loose a wounded tigress. Shannon cursed and ranted and raved and swore that someday, somehow if the war didn't kill Malachi, she would see to it that he was laid out herself.

She would probably have gone out and torn Malachi to shreds right then and there, but fortunately he had ridden out to take a look at some fencing.

Shannon was even furious with Kristin. "How could you? How could you? You let that man into our house, into Pa's house! After everything that has been done—"

"I did it so that Quantrill would leave us alone from now on! Maybe you've forgotten Zeke. I haven't!"

"Wait until Matthew comes back!" Shannon cried. "He'll take care of the Quantrill murderers and Malachi and—"

"Shannon," Kristin said wearily, "I thought you were going to take care of Malachi yourself?" She was hurt, and she was tired, and she couldn't keep the anger from her voice. "If you want to kill one of the Slater brothers, why don't you go after the right one?"

"What do you mean?" Shannon demanded.

"Cole," Kristin said softly. She stared ruefully at her sister. "Cole Slater. The man I married. He rode with Quantrill, Shannon. He was one of them."

"Cole?" Shannon's beautiful eyes were fierce. "I don't believe you!"

"It's the truth. That's why Bill Anderson came here. He wanted me to know that I had married a man every bit as bad as Zeke Moreau."

"He's lying."

"He wasn't lying. Malachi admitted it."

"Then Malachi was lying."

"No, Shannon. You two have your differences, but Malachi wouldn't lie to me."

Shannon was silent for several seconds. Then she turned on Kristin. "They are Missourians, Kristin. They can't help being Confederates. We were Confederates, I guess, until . . . until they came for Pa. Until Matthew joined up with the Union. And if Cole did ride with Quantrill, well, I'm sure he had his reasons. Cole is nothing like Zeke. You know that, and I know that."

Kristin smiled. Shannon was right, and so was Malachi. Cole was nothing like Zeke, and she knew it. But she was still hurt, and she was still angry. She was angry because she was frightened.

And because she loved him.

"Maybe you're right, Shannon," she said softly.

"Cole would never do anything dishonorable! He wouldn't!" Shannon said savagely. "And—"

"And what?"

"He's your husband, Kristin. You have to remember that. You married him. He's your husband now."

"I'll give him a chance to explain," was all that Kristin said. She would give him a chance. But when? He was gone, and winter was coming, and she didn't know when she would see him again.

Two days later Pete and the hands returned from the cattle drive, and Jamie and Malachi prepared to ride back to the war. Kristin was sorry she had argued with Malachi, and she hugged him tightly, promising to pray for him. She kissed Jamie, and he assured her that since his unit was stationed not far away he would be back now and then to see how she and Shannon were doing.

Shannon kissed Jamie—and then Malachi, too. He held her for a moment, smiling ruefully.

Then the two of them rode away.

Kristin stood with Shannon at her side, and they watched until they could no longer see the horses. A cool breeze came up, lifting Kristin's hair from her shoulders and swirling around her skirts. Winter was on its way. She was very cold, she realized. She was very cold, and she was very much alone.

11

Winter was long, hard and bitterly cold. In December Shannon turned eighteen and in January Kristin quietly celebrated her nineteenth birthday. They awaited news from the front, but there was none. The winter was not only cold, it was also quiet, ominously quiet.

Late in February, a Union company came by and took Kristin's plow mules. The young captain leading the company compensated her in Yankee dollars which, she reflected, would help her little when she went out to buy seed for the spring planting. The captain did, however, bring her a letter from Matthew, a letter that had passed from soldier to soldier until it had come to her.

Matthew had apparently not received the letter she had written him. He made no mention of her marriage in his letter to her. Nor did he seem to know anything about Zeke Moreau's attack on the ranch after their father's murder.

It was a sad letter to read. Matthew first wrote that he prayed she and Shannon were well. Then he went into a long missive on the rigors of war—up at five in the morning, sleeping in tents, drilling endlessly, in the rain and even in the snow. Then there was an account of the first major battle in which he had been involved—the dread of waiting, the roar of the cannons, the blast of the guns, the screams of the dying. Nightfall was often the worst of all, when the pickets were close enough to call out to one another. He wrote:

We warn them, Kristin. "Reb! You're in the moon-light!" we call out, lest our sharpshooters take an un-wary lad. We were camped on the river last month; fought by day, traded by night. We were low on to-bacco, well supplied with coffee, and the Mississippi boys were heavy on tobacco, low on coffee, so we rem-edied that situation. By the end of it all we skirmished. I came face-to-face with Henry, with whom I had been trading. I could not pull the trigger of my rifle, nor lift my cavalry sword. Henry was shot from behind, and he toppled over my horse, and he looked up at me before he died and said please, would I get rid of his tobacco, his ma didn't know that he was smoking. But what if you fall? he asks me next, and I try to laugh, and I tell him that my Ma is dead, and my Pa is dead, and that my sisters are very understanding, so it is all right if I die with tobacco and cards and all. He tried to smile. He closed his eyes then, and he died, and my dear sis-ters, I tell you that I was shaken. Sometimes they egg me on both sides—what is a Missouri boy doing in blue? I can only tell them that they do not understand. The worst of it is this—war is pure horror, but it is bet-ter than being at home. It is better than Quantrill and Jim lane and Doc Jennison. We kill people here, but we do not murder in cold blood. We do not rob, and we do not steal, nor engage in any raping or slaughter. Some-times it is hard to remember that I was once a border rancher and that I did not want war at all, nor did I have sympathy for either side. Only Jake Armstrong from Kansas understands. If the jayhawkers robbed and stole and murdered against you, then you find yourself a Confederate. If the bushwhackers burnt down your place, then you ride for the Union, and the place of your birth doesn't mean a whit.

Well, sisters, I do not mean to depress you. Again, I pray that my letter finds you well. Kristin, again I urge you to take Shannon and leave if you should feel the

slightest threat of danger again. They have murdered
Pa, and that is what they wanted, but I still worry for
you both, and I pray that I will get leave to come and
see you soon. I assure you that I am well, as of this
writing, which nears Christmas, 1862. I send you all my
love. Your brother, Matthew.

He had also sent her his Union pay. Kristin fingered the
money, then went out to the barn and dug up the strongbox
where she kept the gold from the cattle sales and the Yankee dollars from the captain. She added the money from
Matthew. She had been feeling dark and depressed and
worried, but now, despite the contents of Matthew's letter,
she felt her strength renewed. She had to keep fighting. One
day Matthew would come home. One day the war would be
over and her brother would return. Until then she would
maintain his ranch.

By April she still hadn't been able to buy any mules, so
she and Samson and Shannon went out to till the fields. It
was hard, backbreaking labor, but she knew that food was
growing scarcer and scarcer, and that it was imperative that
they grow their own vegetables. Shannon and she took turns
behind the plow while Samson used his great bulk to pull it
forward. The herd was small, though there would be new
calves soon enough. By morning Kristin planned the day
with Pete, by day she worked near the house, and supper did
not come until the last of the daylight was gone. Kristin went
to bed each night so exhausted that she thought very little
about the war.

She didn't let herself think about Cole, though sometimes he stole into her dreams uninvited. Sometimes, no
matter how exhausted she was when she went to bed, she
imagined that he was with her. She forgot then that he had
been one of Quantrill's raiders. She remembered only that
he was the man who had touched her, the man who had

awakened her. She lay in the moonlight and remembered him, remembered his sleek-muscled form walking silent and naked to her by night, remembered the way the moonlight had played over them both...

Sometimes she would awaken and she would be shaking, and she would remind herself that he had ridden with Quantrill, just like Zeke Moreau. She might be married to him now, but she could never, never lie with him again as she had before. He was another of Quantrill's killers, just like Zeke. Riding, burning, pillaging, murdering—raping, perhaps. She didn't know. He had come to her like a savior, but Quantrill's men had never obeyed laws of morality or decency. She wanted him to come back to her because she could not imagine him dead. She wanted him to come back to her and deny it all.

But he could not deny it, because it was the truth. Malachi had said so. Malachi had known how the truth would hurt, but hadn't been able to lie. There was no way for Cole to come and deny it. There was just no way at all.

Spring wore on. In May, while she was out in the south field with Samson, Pete suddenly came riding in from the north pasture. He ignored the newly sown field, riding over it to stop in front of Kristin.

"He's back, Miz Slater, he's back. They say that Quantrill is back, and that Quantrill and company do reign here again!"

The house was still a long way off when Cole reined in his horse and looked across the plain at it. Things looked peaceful, mighty peaceful. Daisies were growing by the porch, and someone—Kristin? Shannon?—had hung little flowerpots from the handsome gingerbread on the front of the house.

It looked peaceful, mighty peaceful.

His heart hammered uncomfortably, and Cole realized that it had taken him a long time to come back. He didn't know quite why, but it had taken him longer than necessary. He hadn't been worried at all, at least not until he had heard that Quantrill was back. He didn't understand it. All through the winter, all through the early spring, he'd had dreams about her. He had wanted her. Wanted her with a longing that burned and ached and kept him staring at the ceiling or the night sky. Sometimes it had been as if he could reach out and touch her. And then everything had come back to him. The silky feel of her flesh and the velvety feel of her hair falling over his shoulders. The startling blue of her eyes, the sun gold of her hair, the fullness of her breasts in his hands . . .

Then, if he was sound asleep, he would remember the smell of smoke, and he would hear the sound of the shot, and he would see his wife, his first wife, his real wife. . . . Running, running . . . And the smoke would be acrid on the air, and the hair that spilled over him would be a sable brown, and it would be blood that filled his hands.

It hurt to stay away. He needed her. He wanted her, wanted her with a raw, blinding, burning hunger. But the nightmares would never stay away. Never. Not while his wife's killer lived. Not while the war raged on.

He picked up the reins again and nudged his mount and started the slow trek toward the house. His breath had quickened. His blood had quickened. It coursed through him, raced through him, and it made him hot, and it made him nervous. Suddenly it seemed a long, long time since he had seen her last. It had been a long time. Almost half a year.

But she was his wife.

He swallowed harshly and wondered what his homecoming would be like. He remembered the night before he had left, and his groin went tight as wire and the excitement seemed to sweep like fire into his limbs, into his fingertips, into his heart and into his lungs.

They hadn't done so badly, he thought. Folks had surely done worse under the best of circumstances.

When the war ended . . .

Cole paused again, wondering if the war would ever end. Those in Kansas and Missouri had been living with the skirmishing since 1855, and hell, the first shots at Fort Sumter had only been fired in April of '61. Back then, Cole thought grimly, the rebels had thought they could whomp the Yankees in two weeks, and the Yankees had thought, before the first battle at Manassas, it would be easy to whip the Confederacy. But the North had been more determined than the South had ever imagined, and the South had been more resolute than the North had ever believed possible. And the war had dragged on and on. It had been more than two years now, and there was no end in sight.

So many battles. An Eastern front, a Western front. A Union navy, a Confederate navy, a battle of ironclads. New Orleans fallen, and now Vicksburg under seige. And men were still talking about the battle at Antietam Creek, where the bodies had piled high and the corn had been mown down by bullets and the stream had run red with blood.

He lifted his hands and looked at his threadbare gloves. He was wearing his full dress uniform, but his gold gloves were threadbare. His gray wool tunic and coat carried the gold epaulets of the cavalry, for though he was officially classified a scout he'd been assigned to the cavalry and was therefore no longer considered a spy. It was a fine distinction, Cole thought. And it was damned peculiar that as a scout he should spend so much of his time spying on both sides of the Missouri-Kansas border. He wondered bleakly what it was all worth. In January he'd appeared before the Confederate Cabinet, and he'd reported honestly, as honestly as he could, on the jayhawkers' activities. Jim Lane and Doc Jennison, who had led the jayhawkers—the red-legs as they were sometimes known because of their uniforms—were animals. Jim Lane might be a U.S. senator, but he was still a fanatic and a murderer, every bit as bad as Quantrill. But the Union had gotten control of most of the jayhawkers. Most of them had been conscripted into the Union army and sent far away from the border. As the Seventh Kansas, a number of jayhawkers had still been able to carry out raids on the Missouri side of the border, plundering and burning town after town, but then Major General Henry Halleck had ordered the company so far into the center of Kansas that it had been virtually impossible for the boys to jayhawk.

As long as he lived, Cole would hate the jayhawkers. As long as he lived, he would seek revenge. But his hatred had cooled enough that he could see that there was a real war being fought, a war in which men in blue and men in gray fought with a certain decency, a certain humanity. There were powerful Union politicians and military men who knew their own jayhawkers for the savages they were, and there were men like Halleck who were learning to control them.

No one had control of Quantrill.

By that spring, General Robert E. Lee had been given command of the entire Confederate Army. When he had met with that tall, dignified, soft-spoken man, Cole had felt as if the place he had left behind could not be real. War was ugly, blood and death were ugly, and screaming soldiers maimed and dying on torn-up earth were ugly, too. But nothing was so ugly as the total disregard for humanity that reigned on the border between Kansas and Missouri. Lee had listened to Cole, and Jefferson Davis, the Confederate president, had listened long and carefully to him, too. Judah P. Benjamin, secretary of war, had taken his advice and when Quantrill had demanded a promotion and recognition, his request had been denied.

Cole wondered briefly if the violence would ever stop. He wondered if he would ever be able to cleanse his own heart of hatred.

Suddenly he forgot the war, forgot everything.

He could see the well to the left of the house, near the trough, and he could see Kristin standing there. She had just pulled up a pail of water.

Her hair was in braids, but a few golden strands had escaped from her hairpins and curled over her shoulders. She was dressed in simple gingham—no petticoats today—and she had opened the top buttons of her blouse. She dipped a handkerchief into the bucket and doused herself with the cool water, her face, her throat, her collarbone, then flesh bared by the open flaps of her blouse. Hot and dusty, she lifted the dipper from the pail and drank from it. Then she leaned back slightly and allowed the cool water to spill over her face and throat.

Cole's stomach tightened, and he felt his heartbeat in his throat, and he wondered what it was about the way she was standing, savoring the water, that was so provocative, so beguiling, so sensual. He nudged his horse again, eager to greet her.

He came in at a gallop. She spun around, startled. The water spilled over her blouse, and the wet fabric outlined her young breasts. Her eyes widened at the sight of him, first with panic, he thought, then with startled recognition. He drew up in front of her and dismounted in a leap. Her blouse was soaked, and her face was damp. Her lips were parted, and her face was streaked with dust. She was beautiful.

"Cole . . ." she murmured.

He pulled her hard against him. He found her lips, and he kissed her deeply, and she tasted even sweeter than he remembered. She was vibrant and feminine. He choked out something and touched her breast, feeling her nipple hard as a pebble beneath his palm. She melted against him. She gasped, and she trembled beneath his touch. Her lips parted more fully, and his tongue swept into the hot dampness of her mouth.

Then, suddenly, she twisted away from him with another choking sound. Startled, he released her. She shoved hard against his chest, backing away from him, wiping her mouth with her hands as if she had taken poison. Her eyes remained very wide and very blue. "Bastard!" she hissed at him. She looked him up and down. "Stupid bastard! In a Confederate uniform, no less! Don't you know this whole area is crawling with Yankees?"

"I'll take my clothes right off," he offered dryly.

She shook her head stubbornly. She was still trembling, he saw. Her fingers worked into the fabric of her skirt, released it, then clenched the material again. Her breasts were still outlined by her wet blouse, the nipples clearly delineated. He took a step toward her. "For God's sake, Kristin, what the hell is the matter with you? You're my wife, remember—"

"Don't touch me!"

"Why the hell not?"

"You're a bushwhacker!" she spat out. "You're his—you belong to Quantrill, just like Zeke."

That stopped him dead in his tracks. He wondered how she had found out. A haze fell over his eyes, a cool haze of distance. It didn't really matter. He'd had his reasons. And though he wasn't with Quantrill anymore, if he'd found the right man when he had been with him, he would have been as savage as any of them.

"A friend of yours stopped by here right after you left in the fall," Kristin informed him. "Bill Anderson. You remember him? He remembered you!"

"Kristin, I'm not with Quantrill any longer."

"Oh, I can see that. You got yourself a real Reb uniform. It's a nice one, Cole. You wear it well. But it doesn't cover what you really are! Who did you steal it from? Some poor dead boy?"

His hand slashed out and he almost struck her. He stopped himself just in time.

"The uniform is mine, Kristin," he said through clenched teeth. "Just as you're my wife."

He didn't touch her. Her face was white, and she was as stiff as a board. He started to walk past her, heading straight for the house. Then he spun around. She cringed, but he reached for her shoulders anyway.

"Kristin—" he began. But he was interrupted by a man's voice.

"You leave her alone, Johnny Reb!"

Cole spun around, reaching for his Colt. He was fast, but not fast enough.

"No!" he heard Kristin scream. "Matthew, no, you can't! Cole, no—" She threw herself against his hand, and he lost his chance to fire. She tore her eyes from his and looked over at the tall man in the Union blue coming toward them with a sharpshooter's rifle raised. Kristin screamed again and threw herself against Cole. He staggered and fell, and he was falling when the bullet hit him. It grazed the side of his head. He felt the impact, felt the spurt of blood. He felt a sheet of blackness descend over him, and wondered if he was dying. As he railed against himself in black silence for being so involved with Kristin that he never heard or saw the danger, Cole heard the next words spoken as the man who had called to him, the man who had shot him, came forward.

"Oh, no! Oh, my God—"

"Kristin! What's the matter with you? I'm trying to save you from this jackal—"

"Matthew, this jackal is my husband!"

As he slowly regained consciousness, Cole realized he wasn't dead. He wasn't dead, but he'd probably lost a lot of blood, and it seemed as if he had been out for hours, for it was no longer daylight. Night had fallen. An oil lamp glowed softly at his side.

He was in the bedroom they had shared, the bedroom with the sleigh bed. Everything was blurred. He blinked, and the room began to come into focus. He could see the windows and a trickle of moonlight. He touched his head and discovered that it had been bandaged. He drew his fingers away. At least he couldn't feel any blood. Someone had stripped off his uniform and bathed the dust of the road from him and tucked him between cool, clean sheets.

Someone. His wife. No, not his wife. Kristin. Yes, his wife. He had married her. She was his wife now.

She had stopped him from killing the man.

But she had stopped the man from killing him, too.

A sudden pain streaked through him. He was going to have one terrible headache, he realized. But he was alive, and he was certain that the bullet wasn't embedded in his skull. It had just grazed him.

He heard footsteps on the stairs, and then on the floor outside his door. He closed his eyes quickly as someone came into the room. It was Delilah. She spoke in a whisper. "Dat boy is still out cold." She touched his throat, then his chest. "But he's living, all right. He's still living, and he don't seem to have no fever."

"Thank God!" came in a whisper. Kristin. Cole could smell the faint scent of her subtle perfume. He felt her fingers, cool and gentle, against his face. Then he heard the man's voice again. Matthew. She had called him Matthew. Of course. The brother. The one he had told her to write to just so that this wouldn't happen.

"A Reb, Kristin? After everything that happened—"

"Yes, damn you! After everything that happened!" Kristin whispered harshly. "Matthew, don't you dare preach to me! You left, you got to go off and join up with the army! Shannon and I didn't have that luxury. And Zeke came back—"

"Moreau came back?" Matthew roared.

"Shut up, will you, Matthew?" Kristin said wearily. She sounded so tired. So worn, so weary. Cole wanted to open his eyes, wanted to take her into his arms, wanted to soothe away all the terrible things that the war had done to her. He could not, and he knew it.

She probably didn't want him to, anyway. She would probably never forgive him for his time with Quantrill. Well, he didn't owe anyone any apologies for it, and he'd be damned if he'd explain himself to her. And yet...

"Kristin," Matthew was saying huskily, "what happened?"

"Nothing happened, Matthew. Oh, it almost did. Zeke was going to rape me, and let every man with him rape me, and then he was probably going to shoot me. He was going to sell Samson and Delilah. But nothing happened because of this man. He's a better shot than Shannon or me. He's even a better shot than you. He happened by and it was all over for Zeke.''

"Zeke is dead?''

"No. Zeke rode away." A curious note came into her voice. "You see, Matthew, he won't murder a man in cold blood. I wanted him to, but he wouldn't. And after that, well, it's a long story. But since he's married me, none of them will harm me, or this place. They're—they're afraid of him.''

"Damn, Kristin—" He broke off. Cole heard a strangled sound, and then he knew that brother and sister were in one another's arms. Kristin was crying softly, and Matthew was comforting her. Cole gritted his teeth, for the sound of her weeping was more painful to him than his wound. I will never be able to touch her like that, he thought. He opened his eyes a fraction and took a good look at Matthew McCahy. He was a tall man with tawny hair and blue eyes like his sisters. He was lean, too, and probably very strong, Cole thought. He was probably a young man to be reckoned with.

He shifted and opened his eyes wider. Sister and brother broke apart. Kristin bent down by him and touched his forehead. Her hair was loose, and it teased the bare flesh of his chest. "Cole?''

He didn't speak. He nodded, and he saw that her brow was furrowed with worry, and he was glad of that. She hated him for his past, but at least she didn't want him dead.

"Cole, this is Matthew. My brother. I wrote him, but the letter never reached him. He didn't know that—he didn't know that we were married.''

Cole nodded again and looked over at Matthew. He was still in full-dress uniform—navy-blue full-dress uniform. As his gaze swept over Matthew, Cole couldn't help noticing that Matthew McCahy's uniform was in far better shape than his own, and in much better condition than that of the majority of the uniforms worn by the men of the South. The blockade was tightening. The South was running short of everything—medicine, clothing, ammunition, food. Everything. He smiled bitterly. The South had brilliance. Lee was brilliant, Jackson was brilliant, Stuart was brilliant. But when a Southerner fell in battle, he could not be replaced. Men were the most precious commodity in war, and the Confederacy did not have nearly enough.

The Union, however, seemed to have an inexhaustible supply of soldiers, volunteers and mercenaries.

Cole knew a sudden, bleak flash of insight. The South could not win the war.

"Reb—Sorry, your name is Cole, right? Cole Slater." Matthew came around and sat at the foot of the bed. He swallowed uncomfortably. "You saved my sisters' lives, and I'm grateful to you. I wouldn't have shot you if I'd known. It was the uniform. I'm with the North." He said it defensively. It was not easy for a Missourian to fight for the North.

"You had just cause," Cole said. His voice was raspy, his throat dry. His mouth tasted of blood.

Matthew nodded. "Yes. I had just cause." He hesitated. "Well, I'm home on leave, and I guess that you are, too."

"Something like that," Cole said. Kristin made a little sound of distress, but she quickly swallowed it down. Cole didn't glance her way. He smiled at Matthew and reached for her hand. She was playing the loving wife for her brother, he knew, and he wondered how far she would go. She let him take her hand, let him pull her down beside him.

"We'll have to manage while we're both here," Matthew said. He stretched out a hand to Cole, and Cole released Kristin's long enough to take it. "Does that sound fair to you, Reb?"

"It sounds fine to me, Yankee."

Matthew flushed suddenly. "Well, maybe I'd best leave the two of you alone." He rose quickly.

Kristin was on her feet instantly. "No! I'm coming with you!"

Matthew's brow furrowed suspiciously. "Kristin—"

"Sweetheart . . ." Cole murmured plaintively.

"Darling!" Kristin replied sweetly, syrup dripping from her tone, "I wouldn't dream of disturbing you now. You must rest!"

She gave him a peck on the forehead, and then she was gone, practically running out of the room.

Matthew smiled at Cole. "Too bad there's a war on, ain't it?"

"Yeah. It's too damn bad," Cole agreed.

"She's stubborn," Matthew said.

"Yeah. I've noticed."

"Just like a mule."

"Well, I guess I agree with you there, Yankee."

Matthew laughed, then left and closed the door behind him.

Three days later, Cole was feeling damned good, and damned frustrated. Kristin had managed to elude him ever since his return, sweetly pleading his weakened condition. She had spent her nights in her own room, leaving him to lie there alone. But as night fell on his third day back, Cole jerked awake from a doze to realize that Kristin had come into the room.

He heard her breathing in the darkness, each breath coming in a little pant. Her back was against the door, and she seemed to be listening. She thought he was sleeping, he realized.

Cole rose silently and moved toward her in the dark. He clamped a hand over her mouth and pulled her against the length of his naked body. She gave a muffled gasp and stiffened then began to struggle to free herself.

"Shush!" he warned her.

She bit his hand, and he swore softly.

"Let me go!" she whispered.

"Not on your life, Mrs. Slater."

"Bushwhacker!"

His mouth tightened grimly. "You're still my wife, Kristin."

"Try to rape me and I'll scream. Matthew will kill you. You don't even have a gun up here!"

"If I touch you, Kristin, it wouldn't be rape," Cole assured her.

"Let go—"

He did not let go. He kissed her, plunging his tongue deep into her mouth, holding her so firmly that she could not deny him. He caught her wrists and held them fast behind her back, pressing his naked body still closer to hers. She wore a thin white cotton nightgown buttoned to the throat. It was so thin that he could feel all the sweet secrets her body had to offer.

He raised his lips from hers at last, and she gasped for breath. He pressed his lips to her breast and took the nipple into his mouth through the fabric, savoring it with his tongue.

"I'll scream!" she whispered.

"Scream, then," he told her. He lifted her into his arms and carried her to the bed, searching feverishly for the hem of the gown. He found it and pulled it up, and then they were together, bare flesh touching bare flesh. He seared the length of her with his lips, and she raged against him with husky words and whispers. But then she rose against him. She wrapped her arms around him and pulled his head down to hers and kissed him again. And then she told him he was a bastard, but she gasped when he caressed her thighs, and she buried her face against him when his touch grew intimate and demanding.

"Scream," he whispered to her. "Scream, if you feel you must . . ."

He thrust deep into her. She cried out, but his mouth muffled the cry, and then his tongue filled her mouth.

It had been so very long, and she had dreamed of him so many times.

He stroked and caressed her insides until she was in a frenzy. Then he drove into her with all the force he possessed, and she felt the familiar sweetness invade her once, and then again and again. Then, suddenly, he was gone from her. She was cold, and she was lost, but then he was kissing her again, her forehead, her cheeks, her breasts, her thighs.... He turned her over gently, and his lips trailed a path of fire down her spine. Then she was on her back again, and his silver-gray eyes were upon her and she swallowed back a shriek of pleasure as he came to her again....

The night was swept away.

Later, as she lay awake in the ravaged bed, Kristin berated herself furiously for her lack of principles. She reminded herself again that he had been with Quantrill, and she fought back tears of fury.

She slept with her back to him, and he did not try to touch her again. In the morning, she avoided him. At dinner she was polite, though she wanted to scream. She was disturbed to see that her brother and Cole talked about the cattle and the ranch easily, like two old friends. Shannon had talked to Matthew, and Shannon thought Cole was a hero, no matter what.

He's a bushwhacker! she wanted to shriek to her brother, but of course she could not. Matthew would want to kill Cole, if he knew. And Kristin had never seen anyone as talented with a gun as Cole. No one. If Matthew tried to kill him, Matthew would be the one who died.

Later that evening, when it was time for bed, Matthew walked upstairs with them, and Kristin had no choice but to follow Cole into her parents' bedroom. When the door closed behind them, Kristin stared at it. Cole was behind her, so close that she could feel his warm breath on the back of her neck.

"I hate you," she told him.

He was silent for a long time. She longed to turn around, but she did not.

"I don't think you do, Kristin," he said at last. "But have it however you want it."

He stripped off his clothes and let them lay where they fell, and he crawled into bed. She stayed where she was for a long time. She heard him move to blow out the lamp, and still she stood by the door. Then, finally, she stripped down to her chemise and climbed gingerly into the bed. She knew he was still awake, but he did not try to touch her. She lay awake for hours, and then she drifted off to sleep. While she slept, she rolled against him, and cast her leg over his. Their arms became entwined, and her hair fell over him like a soft blanket.

They awoke that way. Her chemise was up to her waist, her shoulders were bare, and her breast was peeking out. She gazed over at Cole and saw that he was awake and that he was watching her. Then she felt him, felt him like a pulsing rod against her flesh. He moved toward her, very, very slowly, giving her every chance to escape. She couldn't move. Her flesh was alive, her every nerve awake to shimmering sensation, and when he came inside her she shuddered at the pleasure of it, of having him with her, of touching him again, of savoring the subtle movement of his muscles, of feeling the hardness of him as he moved inside her.

And yet, when it was over, she could still find nothing to say to him. She rose quickly and dressed, aware all the while of his brooding eyes upon her.

"Where have you been?" she demanded at last.

"In Richmond."

"Not with—"

"You know I wasn't with Quantrill. You saw my uniform."

Kristin shrugged. "Some of them wear Confederate uniforms."

"I wasn't with Quantrill."

Kristin hesitated, struggling with her buttons. Cole rose and came up behind her, and she swallowed down a protest as he took over the task. "How long are you staying?"

"I've got another week."

"The same as Matthew," she murmured.

"The same as Matthew."

"And where are you going now?"

"Malachi's unit."

She hesitated. Liar! she longed to shout. Tears stung her eyes. She didn't know if he was lying or not.

He swung her around to face him. "I'm a special attaché to General Lee, Kristin. Officially, I'm cavalry. A major, but the only man I have to answer to is the grand old man himself. I do my best to tell him what's going on back here."

Kristin lifted her chin. "And what do you tell him?"

"The truth."

"The truth?"

"The truth as I see it, Kristin."

They stared at one another for a moment, enemies again. Hostility glistened in her eyes and narrowed his sharply.

"I'm sorry, Cole," Kristin said at last. "I can't forgive you."

"Damn you, Kristin, when did I ever ask you to forgive me?" he replied. He turned around. He had dismissed her, she realized. Biting her lip, she fled the room.

She avoided him all that day. She was tense at dinner as she listened to the conversation that flowed around her. Matthew, puzzled by her silence, asked if she was unwell, and she told him she was just tired. She went up to bed early.

She went to bed naked, and she lay awake, and she waited.

When Cole came to bed, she rolled into his arms, and he thought she made love more sweetly than ever before, more sweetly and with a greater desperation.

It went on that way, day after day, night after night, until the time came for Matthew to ride away again.

And for Cole to ride away again.

And then they were standing in front of the house, ready to mount up, one man she loved dressed in blue, one man she loved dressed in gray. Both handsome, both young, both carrying her heart with them, though she could not admit that to the man in gray.

Kristin was silent. Shannon cried and hugged them both again and again.

Kristin kissed and hugged her brother, and then, because there was an audience, she had to kiss Cole.

Then, suddenly, the audience didn't matter. May was over. They had heard that Vicksburg had fallen, and Kristin thought of all the men who would die in the days to come, and she didn't want to let either of them go.

She didn't want to let Cole go. She couldn't explain anything to him, couldn't tell him that she didn't hate him, that she loved him, but she didn't want to let him go.

She hugged him fiercely, and she kissed him passionately, until they were both breathless and they both had to step away. His eyes searched hers, and then he mounted up.

Shannon and Kristin stood together and watched as the two men clasped hands.

Then one rode west, the other east. Cole to Kansas, Matthew deeper into Missouri.

Shannon let out a long, gasping sob.

"They're gone again!" she said, and pulled her sister closer to her. "Come on. We'll weed out the garden. It's hot, and it'll be a miserable task, and we won't think about the men at all."

"We'll think about them," Shannon said. She was close to tears again, Kristin thought. Shannon, who was always so fierce, so feisty. And Kristin knew that if Shannon cried again, she would sob all day, too.

"Let's get to work."

They had barely set to work when they heard the sounds of hooves again. Kristin spun around hopefully, thinking that either her brother or her husband had returned.

Shannon called out a warning.

It was Zeke, Kristin thought instantly.

But it was not. It was a company of Union soldiers. At its head was a captain. His uniform was just like Matthew's. They stopped in front of the house, but they did not dismount.

"Kristin Slater!" the captain called out.

He was about Matthew's age, too, Kristin thought.

"Yes?" she said, stepping forward.

He swallowed uncomfortably. "You're under arrest."

"What?" she said, astonished.

His Adam's apple bobbed. "Yes, ma'am. I'm sorry. You and your sister are under arrest, by order of General Halleck. I'm right sorry, but we're rounding up all the womenfolk giving aid and succor to Quantrill and his boys."

"Aid and succor!" Kristin shrieked.

She might have been all right if she hadn't begun to laugh. But she did begin to laugh, and before she knew it, she was hysterical.

"Take her, boys."

"Now, you just wait!" Delilah cried from the porch.

The captain shook his head. "Take Mrs. Slater, and the young one, too."

One of the soldiers got down from his horse and tugged at Kristin's arm. She tore it fiercely from his grasp.

The young man ruefully addressed his captain. "Sir..."

"My brother is in the Union army!" Kristin raged. "My father was killed by bushwhackers, and now you're arresting me... for helping Quantrill? No!"

The soldier reached for her again, and she hit him in the stomach. Shannon started to scream, and Delilah came running down the steps with her rolling pin.

"God help us, if the Rebs ain't enough, Halleck has to pit us against the womenfolk!" the young captain complained. He dismounted and walked over to Kristin. "Hold her, men."

Two of them caught her arms. She stared at him.

"Sorry, ma'am," he said sincerely.

Then he struck her hard across the chin, and she fell meekly into his arms.

12

"**Y**'all have just the blondest hair! And I do mean the blondest!" Josephine Anderson said as she pulled Shannon's locks into a set of high curls on top of her head. She was a pretty young woman herself, with plump cheeks and a flashing smile and a tendency to blush easily. She never smiled when their Yankee captors were around, though. Josephine was a hard-core Confederate. She and her sister Mary had been brought in a week after Kristin and Shannon, and they all shared a corner of a big room on the second floor of a building in Kansas City. Josephine and Mary were both very sweet, and Kristin liked them well enough, despite their fanaticism. They had both wanted her and Shannon to meet their brother Billy—who turned out to be none other than Bill Anderson, the Bill Anderson who had stopped by the house to make sure that Kristin knew about Cole's position with Quantrill's raiders.

That was all right. At the very beginning, Kristin had sweetly told the girls that she did know their Billy. She also told them what had happened to her father—and that she wished that she were anything other than what she was: a citizen of a country whose people tore one another to shreds.

Josephine and Mary had turned away from her in amazement, but then the next day they had been friendly. They respected her right to have a passionate stand—even if it was a strange one.

And when Cole's name was mentioned, Mary acted just the way Shannon did. "Ooh! You're really married to him?" she gushed.

It seemed that Cole had been to dinner once at their house with Bill when he had first started out with Quantrill. But they didn't know very much about him, only that there was some deep secret in his past.

"He can be real quiet like, you know!" Mary said.

"But, oh, those eyes!" Josephine rolled her own.

"It's such a pity he left Quantrill!" Mary told her fiercely. "Why, he'd have cleaned out half of Kansas by now; I just know it."

Kristin assured them that Cole was still with the Confederate Army—in the cavalry, like his brothers. Then Shannon went on to tell them about their brother Matthew and how he had gone off to join up with the Union Army after their father's death.

Mary and Josephine thought that was a terrible tragedy, but they understood that, too. "I'm surprised he didn't become a jayhawker, because that's how it goes, you know! They say that old John Brown was attacked way back in '55, that one of his sons was killed. So he killed some Missourians, and some Missourians went up and killed some more Kansans. But you two—why, I feel right sorry for you! Missourians, with a brother in blue and your husband in gray. It's a shame, a damned shame, that's all."

It was a good thing they were able to come to an understanding. All summer long, General Ewing, the local Union commander, had women picked up so that their men couldn't come to them for food or supplies. There were a great many of them living at very close quarters. The authorities holding them weren't cruel, and the women weren't hurt in any way. A number of the young officers were remarkably patient, in fact, for the women could be extraordinarily abusive when they spoke to their captors. But though the men behaved decently toward their prisoners, the living conditions were horrid. The building itself was in terrible shape, with weak and rotting timbers, the food was barely adequate, and the bedding was full of insects.

Kristin wanted desperately to go home. At first she had been angry. She had fought and argued endlessly with various commanders, and they had all apologized and looked uncomfortable and shuffled their feet, but none of them had been willing to let her go. And finally she had become resigned.

She grew more and more wretched. She had often been sick in the first weeks of her captivity and she had thought it must be the food. She was still queasy much of the time, but, though she hadn't told anyone, she knew why now. She was pregnant. Sometime in February of the following year she was going to have Cole's baby. She had been stunned at first, but then she had taunted herself endlessly. Why should she be surprised, after all. Children were the result of a man being with a woman.

She wasn't sure how she felt. Sometimes she lay there and railed against a God that could let her have a baby in a world where its blood relations were destined to be its mortal enemies, in a world where murder and bloodshed were the order of the day.

Then there were nights when she touched her still-flat belly and dreamed, and wondered what the baby would look like. And then, even if she was furious with Cole, even if she had convinced herself that he was as evil as Zeke, she knew she loved him. And she did want his child. A little boy with his shimmering silver eyes. Or a girl. Or maybe the child would be light, with her hair and eyes. Whoever the child took after, it was destined to be beautiful, she was certain. Cole's baby. She longed to hold it in her arms. She dreamed about seeing him again, about telling him.

And then there were times when she sank into depression. Cole probably wouldn't be the least bit pleased. He probably intended to divorce her as soon as the war was over, she thought bitterly. She was imprisoned for being the wife of a man who intended to divorce her.

Then not even that mattered. She wanted the baby. She wanted the baby to hold and to love, and she wanted it to be born to peace. The war could not go on forever. She didn't care who won. She just wanted it to be over. She wanted her baby to be able to run laughing through the cornfields, to look up at the sun and feel its warmth. She wanted peace for her child.

And most of all, she wanted it to be born at home. She did not want to bear her baby here, in this awful, crowded place of degradation.

Kristin looked up from the letter she was writing to her brother asking if there was anything he could do to get the authorities to free Shannon and herself. The three other women in the room looked as if they were preparing for a ball.

Josephine stepped back. "Oh, Shannon, that just looks lovely, really lovely."

"Why, thank you, ma'am," Shannon said sweetly. Then she sighed. "I wish I could see it better."

Mary dug under her pillow and found her little hand mirror. "Here, Shannon."

Suddenly the room fell silent. One of the young Federal officers, a Captain Ellsworth, had come in. The women looked at him suspiciously.

His dark brown eyes fell on Kristin. "Mrs. Slater, would you come with me, please?"

She quickly set aside her paper and pen and rose, nervously folding her fingers in front of her and winding them tightly together.

A middle-aged woman called out to the captain, "Don't walk too hard on this here floor, sonny! Those Yankee boots will make you come right through it!"

He nodded sadly to the woman. "Sorry, Mrs. Todd. The place is awful, I know. I'm working on it."

"Don't work on it!" Mary Anderson called out gaily. "You tell them to let us go home. You tell them that my brother will come after them, and that he'll kill them all."

"Yes, miss," Captain Ellsworth said, staring straight at her. "That's the problem, Miss Anderson. Your brother already does come to murder us all." He bowed to her politely. Then he took Kristin's elbow and led her out of the room. He preceded her down the groaning staircase to the doorway of the office below. Kristin looked at him nervously.

"It's all right, Mrs. Slater. Major Emery is in there. He wants to talk to you."

He opened the door for her, and Kristin walked in. She had never seen Major Emery before. He was a tall, heavyset man, with thick, wavy, iron-gray hair and great drooping mustache to match. His eyebrows were wild and of the same gray, and beneath them his eyes were a soft flower blue. He seemed a kind man, Kristin thought instantly, a gentleman.

"Mrs. Slater, sit, please." Kristin silently did so. The major dismissed Captain Ellsworth, then smiled at Kristin. "Can I get you some tea, Mrs. Slater?"

"No, thank you." She sat very straight, reminding herself that, no matter how kindly he looked, he was still her captor. He smiled again and leaned back in his chair.

"Mrs. Slater, I'm trying very hard to get an order to have you and your sister released."

A gasp of surprise escaped Kristin. Major Emery's smile deepened, and he leaned forward again. "It will take a few days, I'm afraid."

Kristin and Shannon had been here almost three months. A few more days meant nothing.

"Because of my brother?" Kristin said. "Did Matthew find out that we were here? I didn't want to tell him at first because I didn't want him going into battle worrying, but I was just writing to him—"

"No, no, Mrs. Slater. I haven't heard anything from your brother at all."

"Oh, I see," Kristin murmured bitterly. "You've finally decided that a woman who had her father killed by some of

Quantrill's men is not likely to give aid and comfort to the enemy, is that it?''

Major Emery shook his head. "No. Because of your husband," he said quietly.

"What?" Kristin demanded suspiciously. "Major, I'm in here because I'm married to Cole Slater. No one seems to believe me when I say that he isn't with Quantrill anymore."

Major Emery stood and looked out the window. Then he turned back to Kristin. "Do you believe it yourself, young lady?"

"What?" She was certain she was blushing, certain her face had turned a flaming red.

"Do you believe in him yourself, Mrs. Slater?"

"Why... of course!" she said, though she was not at all sure she did.

Emery took his seat again and smiled. "I'm not sure, Mrs. Slater, I'm not sure. But that doesn't really matter. You see, I do have faith in your husband. Complete faith."

Kristin stared at him blankly. She lifted a hand in the air. "Do go on, major. Please, do go on."

"I'm wiling to bet I know your husband better than you do, Mrs. Slater. In certain ways, at least."

She tightened her jaw against his mischievous grin. He was a nice man, she decided, a gentle, fatherly type, but he seemed to be having a good time at her expense at the moment.

"Major..."

His smile faded. He looked a little sad. "He was a military man, you know. He went to West Point. He was in the same class as Jeb Stuart. Did you know that?"

Yes, he had said something to Shannon about it. To Shannon. Not to her.

"I know that he was in the military, yes."

Major Emery nodded. "Cole Slater was one of the most promising young cavalrymen I ever knew. He fought in Mexico, and he was with me in the West. He's good with the

Indians—fighting them and, more importantly, talking with
them, making truces. Keeping truces. Then the war came.''

"And he resigned," Kristin murmured.

"No, not right away. He didn't resign until they burned
down his house and killed his wife.''

"Killed? His wife?'' She didn't realize that she had gotten to her feet until Major Emery came around the desk and
gently pushed her back into her chair. Then he leaned
against the desk and crossed his arms over his chest, smiling down at her kindly. "I reckoned you might not know
everything. Cole is a closemouthed man. Tight-lipped, yes
sirree. He was an officer in the Union Army when South
Carolina seceded from the Union. That didn't matter none
to the jayhawkers. He was a Missourian. And Jim Lane had
sent out an order that anybody who was disloyal to the
Union was to be killed. The boys got pretty carried away.
They rode to his place and they set it on fire. Cole was out
riding the range. I imagine he was giving his position some
pretty grave thought. Anyway, Jim Lane's jayhawkers rode
in and set fire to his place. His wife was a pretty thing, real
pretty. Sweet, gentle girl from New Orleans. She came running out, and the boys grabbed hold of her. Seems she
learned something about gunfire from Cole, though. She
shot up a few of them when they tried to get their hands on
her. Cole came riding in, and by then she was running to
him. Only some fool had already put a bullet in her back,
and when Cole reached her, she was dying. She was expecting their first child right then, too. She was about five
months along, so they tell me. Of course, after killing his
pregnant wife, none of the men was willing to let him live,
either. Someone shot Cole, too, and left him for dead. But
he's a tough customer. He lived.''

"And he joined up with Quantrill," Kristin whispered.
She swallowed. She could almost see the fire, could almost
smell the smoke, could almost hear the screams. She suddenly felt ill. As if she were going to throw up.

"Oh, my God!" she whispered, jumping to her feet. Major Emery, too was on his feet in an instant, yelling for a pail and some water.

To her horror, she *was* sick. Major Emery was a perfect gentleman, cooling her forehead with a damp cloth and then insisting that she have tea with lots of milk to settle her stomach. When it was over and they were alone again, he said to her, "You are expecting a child, Mrs. Slater?"

She nodded bleakly.

"Well, my point exactly. I just don't think you should be here anymore. And I don't think Cole is still with Quantrill, because it just isn't his style. Ma'am, I want you to know that I find our jayhawkers every bit as loathsome as the bushwhackers. They're all murderers, pure and simple. Cole isn't a murderer. I think he went with Quantrill to try to get the man who led the attack on his ranch, and only for that reason. Only he wasn't easy to find, because he retired along with Lane. Hell, Lane is a U.S. senator! But the man who attacked Cole's place is back in the center of Kansas, and like Lane, he owns a lot of things, and a lot of people. Cole knew he couldn't get to him, not with Quantrill. And he knew that what Quantrill was up to was murder. He's regular army now, all right."

Kristin swallowed some of her tea and nodded painfully. She hurt all over, inside and out. She had despised Cole, despite everything that he had done for her, just because Bill Anderson had told her that Cole had ridden with Quantrill. She desperately wanted to see him again. She wanted to hold him. She wanted to make him forget, if only for a moment, what had been done to him.

It made men hard, this war did. It had made her hard, she knew, and it had made him harder. She realized anew that he did not love her, and now, she thought, he never would. He had loved his first wife.

"Mrs. Slater?"

Kristin looked at the major. "Yes . . . yes I think that he's in the regular army. That's—that's what he said."

The major frowned suddenly, his hands flat on his desk. He looked up at the ceiling.

Then Kristin felt it. There was a trembling in the floor beneath her, in the very air around her.

"Hellfire and damnation!" Major Emery shouted. He leaped to his feet, hopped over his desk and pulled her out of her chair. He dragged her over to the door and kicked it open, then huddled with her beneath the frame, shielding her with his bulk.

Suddenly floorboards and nails were flying everywhere and great clouds of dust filled the room. Dirt flew into Kristin's mouth and into her eyes, and she heard screams, terrible screams, agonized screams.

The whole building was caving in. The awful place had been faulty structurally and decaying and now it was actually caving in.

"Shannon!" Kristin screamed. "Shannon!" She tried to pull away from the major, but she couldn't. He was holding her too tightly. The rumbling continued, and inside was chaos. Boards were falling and breaking and clattering on the floor. A woman's body fell right next to Kristin, who was able to pull away from the major at last to kneel down by the girl.

It was Josephine Anderson, and Kristin knew instantly that she was dead. Her eyes were wide open, glazed as only death could glaze them. "Jo!" she cried out, falling to her knees. She touched the still-warm body and closed the pathetic, staring eyes. Then she looked up from the body to the gaping hole above her. "Shannon!" she screamed. She twisted around to look at what had been the hallway and the stairs. Only the bannister was left. Everywhere, the floor had crumbled. Tears and screams filled the air. "Shannon!"

"Mrs. Slater! You must remember your child!" the major urged her, grabbing her arm.

"Please!" She shook herself free and stumbled through the wreckage that littered the floor. She found Mary, her body grotesquely twisted beneath a pile of boards. "Mary!" After clawing away the debris, Kristin knelt and felt for the other woman's pulse. Mary was alive. She opened her eyes. "Jo?"

"It's Kristin, Mary. Everything... everything is going to be all right." She squeezed the girl's hand and turned around, searching for someone, anyone. "Get help here!" Kristin shouted, suddenly choking back tears. Where was Shannon? The girls had all been together.

Several young medics rushed in. Kristin moved away as they knelt over Mary. There were clanging bells sounding from outside, and the sound of horses' hooves was loud as a fire hose was brought around.

"Mrs. Slater!"

The major was still trying to get her out.

"Shannon!"

An arm was protruding from a pile of lumber. Kristin began to tear away the planks. This was the worst of it. The woman beneath was dead. Kristin inhaled on a sob and turned away.

"Kristin!"

She looked up. Shannon, deathly pale, was clinging to a board that looked as if it were just about to give way.

"Shannon! Hold on! Just hold on a little longer—"

There was a cracking sound. The board began to break. Shannon's toes dangled ten feet over Kristin's head. "Hold on!"

"No, Miss McCahy, let go now! I'm here. I'll catch you!"

It was Captain Ellsworth. He stepped in front of Kristin and reached out his arms to Shannon. Shannon still clung to the board. "Come down, now! Please, before it breaks!"

Kristin saw the problem. If the board broke, Shannon could fall on a splinter in one of the beams that had been exposed, and she would be skewered alive.

"Shannon! Where the hell is your courage? Jump!" Kristin called out. She watched as Shannon's eyes fell on the splintered beams below her. But then Shannon looked down at her and she grinned. "What the hell! We can't all live forever, now, can we? Thumbs up, Kristin. Say a prayer."

Shannon released her hold on the board. She fell, her skirts billowing out around her, and suddenly, Captain Ellsworth was falling, too. He had caught her and the impact had brought him down with her.

"Get them both out of here!" Major Emery shouted. He picked Kristin up bodily and carried her outside. Captain Ellsworth swept Shannon up and followed. When they were finally out in the street, Kristin and Shannon hugged each other, sobbing.

"Jo—"

"Jo is dead," Kristin said softly. Then they stared at one another as they realized how lucky they were to be alive. And they just hugged one another again and sobbed, and listened to the chaos as more women were carried from the building, some alive, some injured . . . and some dead.

A week later, Kristin and Shannon were in the home of Captain Ellsworth's sister, Betty.

Four women besides Josephine Anderson had been killed. Rumor had it that Bill Anderson had gone berserk, foaming at the mouth, when he had heard that one of his sisters had been killed and the other had been seriously injured. Many Confederates were saying that General Ewing had purposely ordered that the women be incarcerated in the ramshackle building so that just such a tragedy might occur. There would be repercussions. To make matters worse, General Ewing had issued his General Order Number Ten, ordering all wives and children of known bushwhackers to move out of the state of Missouri.

That night, Major Emery rode out to the small house on the outskirts of the city with Captain Ellsworth beside him. It was quite apparent that an attachment was forming between Shannon and the captain, and Kristin didn't mind at all. After all, the young captain had come valiantly to her rescue. Kristin liked him herself. He was quiet and well read and unfailingly polite. And Shannon was eighteen, a young woman who already knew her own mind.

But though both the captain and the major were charming in Betty's parlor, Kristin knew that something was very wrong. The major called her onto the porch.

He looked at the moon, twirling his hat in his hand. "Quantrill attacked Lawrence, Kansas, yesterday."

"Oh, God!" Kristin murmured.

"It was a massacre," Major Ellsworth said grimly. "Almost the entire town was razed to the ground. At least one hundred men were killed...one twelve-year-old boy was shot down for being dressed up in an old Union uniform. And Quantrill only lost one of his boys. A former Baptist preacher named Larkin Skaggs. He was too drunk to ride away with Quantrill. An Indian found him and shot him dead, and then the survivors ripped him to shreds." Major Emery was silent for a moment. "What is it coming to? None of us, not one of us, it seems, is any better than a bloody savage."

Kristin wanted to say something to comfort him. A lot of good men were experiencing the same despair, she knew. But she could think of nothing to say.

He turned around and tipped his hat to her. "You're free, young lady. I'm going to see to it that an escort takes you and your sister home.

"But how—"

A grin tugged at his lower lip. "Someone got through to your brother, and he raised all kinds of hell with the higher-ups. And then..."

"And then?"

He shrugged. His eyes twinkled. "Well, you see, Kristin, I know Cole. And a lot of other cavalry boys know Cole, so we know damned well that he isn't any outlaw. But people who don't know him, well, they're still convinced that he's a bad 'un. At the moment, that's all right, because there's a rumor out that he's heard about you and Shannon being held up here and that he's steaming. After everything that's happened, well . . . we can't have troops everywhere. Some folks are afraid he might ride in here and destroy the town just to get to you. I decided not to dispute that with any of them. I thought you deserved the right to go home if that was what you wanted."

Kristin stared at him a long time. Then she kissed him on the cheek. "Thank you."

"You see Cole, you tell him I sent my regards. You tell him I miss him. I never did meet another man who could ride or shoot like him."

She nodded. "Thank you. Thank you so much. For everything."

"Be there for him. He probably needs you."

Kristin smiled ruefully. "He doesn't love me, you know. You see, he only married me because he felt he had to. To protect me."

"Love comes in a lot of ways, young lady. You give him a little time. Maybe this war will end one day."

He tipped his hat to her again, and then he was gone.

In retaliation for the attack on Lawrence, General Ewing issued General Order Number Eleven, which forced almost everyone in Missouri to leave. People were given fifteen days to leave their property. The exodus was a terrible thing to watch, one of the worst things Kristin had seen in all the years since the fighting had begun. Poor farmers were forced to leave behind what little they possessed, and others were shot down where they stood because they refused to leave. Because the McCahy ranch belonged to Matthew, a soldier serving in the Union army, Major Emery was able to keep his promise and send Kristin and Shannon home, however.

The young lieutenant who escorted them was appalled by what he saw of the evacuation. Once he even told her that it was one of the cruellest measures he had ever seen taken. "This war will never end," he said glumly. "We will not let it end, it seems. The people who do not fight are ordered to leave, and the bushwhackers will come through here when they're gone, stealing whatever they leave behind!''

It was true, Kristin discovered. Even when they were home, when it seemed that they had returned to something like a normal life, Peter often came to her at night to tell her that he had seen another house burning somewhere, or that he had found cattle slaughtered, a sure sign that guerrillas had been in the area, living off the land.

In the middle of September they had a letter from Matthew. He was trying to get leave to come and see them, but so far he hadn't been able to manage it. He explained:

But the Rebels are in worse shape than we are. I think that perhaps by Christmas I will be able to come home. There was a battle fought in a little town in Pennsylvania called Gettysburg. Kristin, they say it was the most awful yet, but General Lee was stopped, and he was forced to retreat back to the South. Since then, there has been new hope that the war may end. Some of these fellows say that they will force the South to her knees. They do not know Southerners. I cannot imagine your husband on his knees, nor do I ever quite forget that I am a Missourian myself. But I pray for it to end. I watched another friend die yesterday of the dysentery, and it seems that we do not even have to catch bullets to drop off like flies. John Maple, who was injured in our last skirmish, had to have his leg amputated. Kristin, if I am caught at all by shot, I hope that the ball passes straight to my heart, for those operations are fearful things to witness. There was no morphine, but we did have some whiskey, and still, John screamed so horribly. Now we must all pray that the rot does not set in, else he will die anyway.

Kristin, forgive me, I wander again into subjects that do not fit a lady's ears, but you are my sister. I am still so grateful that you and Shannon are home. Every man who heard of the incident in Kansas City was appalled, and none was proud. That you might have been killed there chilled me to the bone, and I waited very anxiously for the news that you were safe.

As I said before, the Rebs are hurting badly. They have good generals, and good men, but those that die cannot be replaced. I am telling you this, aware that you must be worried for your husband. If you do not see him, you must not instantly fear the worst. They have probably refused to give him leave. They are desperate now to hold on to Virginia, and perhaps they are keeping him in the East.

Kristin set her brother's letter down and stared out the window. She wondered if Cole would come if she thought hard enough about him. Then she wondered, not for the first time, if he had been at the battle of Gettysburg. They talked of it constantly in Kansas City. It seemed that the death toll had been terrible there, but she had read the lists endlessly, looking for his name, and she had not found it. She had thought, too, that he might have been with John Hunt Morgan, along with Malachi, but she had read that Morgan had been captured in July, though what had become of his men was unknown. She had checked the lists of the dead again and again. Once her heart had nearly ceased to beat when she had read that a Slater had been killed, but it had been Samuel Slater from South Carolina, no relation, she hoped, to Cole.

Looking out the window would not bring Cole back to her. Wishing for him to appear would not help, either.

Every night she left a light burning in the window, hoping he would return. Even if he were to try, it would be hard for him to do so, she knew. The Union was getting a firm grip on the area. There were almost always patrols somewhere in the vicinity.

Every night she stood on the steps before going up to bed, and she lifted her chin, and she felt the breeze, and she waited. But it was all to no avail.

All to no avail...

Until one night in late September.

There had been no breeze all day, but there was the slightest whisper of one now. The night had been still, but now a tumbleweed lifted from the ground. Fall was coming, and in the pale glow of the moon the world was dark brown and pale gold and rich orange.

She thought she had imagined the sound at first. The sound of hoofbeats. But she had learned how to listen, and she closed her eyes, and she felt the wood beneath her feet shiver.

She stumbled out onto the porch and down onto the bare earth. She felt the hoofbeats more clearly. A rider was approaching, a single rider.

She needed to run into the house. She needed to grab one of the Colt six-shooters, or her rifle. The breeze was cool, and she was standing there barefoot on the cold ground, dressed only in a white cotton nightgown. The wind swept the gown around her and molded it to her breasts and hips and thighs. The breeze picked up the tendrils of her hair and sent them cascading behind her.

Then she saw the horse, and saw the rider, and she was exhilarated and incredulous and jubilant.

"Cole!"

"Kristin!" He reined in his horse, cast his leg over the animal's haunches and slid quickly to the ground. He frowned at the sight of her there, but she ran to him, laughing, and threw herself into his arms.

They closed around her.

Cole felt her, felt her soft and fresh and fragrant and clean, the way he had dreamed her, the way he had imagined her, the way he had feared he would never feel her again. The road home was always long and hard and dangerous. He had been riding for days, trying to avoid the Union patrols that were all over the place.

But now she was in his arms. There were no questions, no answers. She was in his arms, whispering his name. He be-

gan to shake. Her hair spilled over his hands like raw silk.
She pressed against him, and she was so feminine and sweet
that he nearly lost his breath. He breathed deeply, and her
scent filled him, and it made his heart pound and his loins
quicken.

"Kristin—"

She caught his face in her hands and kissed him. She
kissed him as if she had starved for him, she kissed him
deeply, passionately, like a woman. She kissed him with the
fullness of her mouth and with the fullness of her body. Her
tongue was wickedly sensual, touching all of him, plunging
deep into his mouth. When his tongue invaded her mouth
in turn, she moaned and fell against him, suddenly weak.
After a long time he lifted his head to stare down into her
eyes, eyes as blue as sapphires beneath the moon.

"What are you doing out here?"

"Waiting."

"You couldn't have known I was coming."

"I'm always waiting," she told him, and she smiled. It
was just the slightest curve of her mouth, a rueful admis-
sion that left him feeling as if the earth trembled beneath his
feet. He swept her hard against him again, heedless of
whether she felt the emotion that racked him.

"I heard about Kansas City. I tried to come for you.
Malachi and Jamie knocked me flat. Then I heard about the
building, and I heard they let you go at the same time—"

"Hush!" She pressed a finger to his lips. She smiled
again, and it was a dazzling smile. She was so soft, all of her.
Her arms wound around him. Her thighs molded to his,
naked beneath the gown. Her breasts pressed against his
chest, against the gray wool of his uniform. "It's all right.
We're home. Shannon and I are home, and you've come
home now, too."

It wasn't his home. He could have told her that. But he
didn't want to. Not tonight. She might not understand.

He wove his fingers into her hair, savoring the feel of her. Then he swept her up into his arms and stumbled up the steps, somehow keeping eyes locked with hers.

It seemed to take forever to reach their room, and it was not until much later that he wondered if his poor horse had managed to wander to the trough and into the barn. If not, the animal had known much worse nights upon the road.

For the moment, all that he knew was the woman in his arms and the sweetness of his homecoming.

When they were alone in their room he set her down. With trembling fingers, he undid the buttons of her nightgown and let it float to the floor. He stared at her. He wanted this moment to be etched in his memory forever, and he wanted the memory to be as incredible as the reality. Her eyes luminous. Her smile welcoming. Her breasts full and round and firm, more entrancing even than he had remembered. Her legs long and beautifully shaped.

Then he touched her.

And he wanted, too, to remember the feel of her skin against his fingertips, and so he touched her again and again, marvelling at the softness of her. And he kissed her, for he had to remember the taste of her. He kissed her lips, and he kissed her forehead, and he found the pulse at the base of her throat. He kissed her breasts, and the desire inside him grew. He savored the taste of her shoulders, of the little hollows there. He turned her around and kissed her back, trailing his fingers down the beautiful line of her spine and over the curve of her buttocks. He had to touch and taste and feel all of her. He went on and on, drinking deeply of her, until the whole of his body shook and trembled, until she cried out his name with such anguish and passion that he came to his feet, crushed her in his arms and lifted her again, bearing her to the bed.

Whispering to him, telling him how much she wanted him, how she needed him, how she desired him, she feverishly helped him out of his clothes, desperate to touch him as he had touched her. Soft as a feather, gentle as a breeze, sensual as the earth, she touched and petted and loved him. Then, at last, they came together, a man and a woman meeting in a breathless fusion.

All that night she felt she was riding the wind, an endless, sweet, wild wind that swept away the horrors of the world and left her drifting on the clouds of heaven. Anticipation had sown its seeds, and their first time together was erratic and wild and thunderous for them both. Barely had they climaxed before he touched her again, and again the clamor of need rose quickly in them. They were slower this time, easier, for the first desperate hunger had been appeased.

And still the night lay ahead of them.

She never knew just how many times they loved that night, never knew when she slept and dreamed, never knew when she awakened to find that he was holding her again. She only knew that it was heaven, and that however long she lived, however old she grew, she would never, never forget it, or the crystalline beauty of the desire that surged between them.

It was morning before they spoke.

Dazed and still delighted, Kristin lay in his arms, wondering lazily how to tell him about the child. She wondered if he could tell by the subtle changes in her body. He hadn't said anything. She smiled. His need for her had been too great for him to have noticed anything. She thought to speak then, but he was speaking already. He was talking about the war, and his tone was cold.

"Stonewall Jackson was the greatest loss. Lee might have taken Gettysburg if he hadn't lost Stonewall. It was the first battle he had to go into without Jackson. God, how I shall miss that man!"

"Sh..." she murmured. She drew a finger across the planes of his face, and she felt the tightness there, and the pain. It was a strong face, she thought, a striking face. And it was so hard now.

"And Morgan . . . God help Morgan. He has to escape." He shook his head. Then he turned to her and took her in his arms, whispering, "How can I say these things to you? You've been through so much already, you've witnessed so much. That horror in Kansas City . . ."

"The deaths were terrible," Kristin admitted. She drew away, smiling at him. "But Major Emery was very kind."

Suddenly Cole was stiff as steel, and every bit as cold. "Emery?"

She didn't understand the abrupt change in him. "Yes. He said that you had been with him, before the war. He—"

He sat up and ran his fingers through his hair. "He what?" She didn't answer, and he turned, setting his hands firmly on her shoulders. "He what?"

"Stop it! You're hurting me!" Kristin pulled away from him. "He told me about—he told me about your wife."

Cole smiled suddenly. It was a bitter smile. "I see," he said softly.

"What do you see?" she demanded.

"Nothing, Kristin, nothing at all." He tossed the covers aside and stood and wandered around the room, picking up his clothes.

"Cole!"

He stepped into his gray trousers and pulled on his shirt. Still ignoring her, he sat and pulled on his boots. She frowned when she realized that he was putting his uniform back on—something he wouldn't be doing if he was staying.

"Cole, you can't be leaving already?"

He stood up, buckling on his scabbard. He nodded gravely. Then he walked to her and stroked her chin. "I only had five days. It took me three to find my way through the Federal troops. I have to pray I can make it back more quickly." He bent down and touched her lips lightly with his own. "You are so very beautiful, Kristin," he murmured to her. But he was still distant from her. Very distant.

"Cole—" She choked on his name. Her heart was aching. There were so many things that needed to be said, and none of them mattered. She had said or done something to offend him and she didn't even know what it was. "Cole, I don't understand—"

"Kristin, I don't want your pity."

"What?"

"Pity, Kristin. I don't want it. It's worthless stuff, and it isn't good for anyone. I wondered what last night was all about. You were barely civil to me when I left in May. Hate me, Kristin. Hate me all you want. But for God's sake, Kristin, don't pity me!"

Incredulous, she stiffened, staring at him, fighting the tears that stung her eyes.

"I've thought about having you and Shannon move to London until this thing is over with. I had a little power with Quantrill, but I'm afraid my influence with the Yankees is at a low ebb. This is a dangerous place—"

"Go!" Kristin said.

"Kristin—"

"Go back to your bleeding Confederacy!" Kristin said heatedly. "I've already met with the Yankees, thanks, and they were damned civil."

"Kristin—"

"I'm all right here! I swear it. We are fine."

He hesitated, then swept his frock coat over his shoulders and picked up his plumed hat.

"Kristin—"

"Cole, damn you, get out of here! You don't want my pity, you want my hatred! Well, then, you've got it! Go!"

"Damn you, Kristin!"

He came back to the bed and took her in his arms. The covers fell away, and she pressed against the wool of his uniform, felt the hot, determined yearning of his kiss. She wanted to fight him. She wanted to tell him that she really did hate him. But he was going away again, going away to the war. And she was afraid of the war. The war killed people.

And so she kissed him back. She wound her arms around him and kissed him back every bit as passionately as he did her. And she felt his fingers move over her breast, and she savored every sensation.

Then he lifted his lips from hers, and their eyes met, and he very slowly and carefully let her fall back to the bed.

They didn't speak again. He kissed her forehead lightly, and then he left her.

PART 4

The Outlaw and The Cavalier

13

He never should have come to Kansas.

Cole knew he should never have come to Kansas. A scouting mission in Kentucky was one thing. He could slip into Virginia or even Maryland easily enough. Even in Ohio he might be all right. In the East they were slower to hang a man as a spy. In the East they didn't shoot a man down where he stood, not often, not that Cole had heard about anyway.

He should never have come to Kansas.

But the war effort was going badly, very badly. First General Lee had lost Stonewall Jackson. Then Jeb Stuart had been shot, and they had carried him back to Richmond, and he had died there. Countless men had died, some of them brilliant men, some of them men who were perhaps not so brilliant but who were blessed with an endless supply of courage and a fine bravado, even in the face of death.

Jeb was the greatest loss, though. Cole could remember their days at West Point, and he could remember the pranks they had pulled when they had been assigned out west together. The only comfort in Jeb's death was the fact that his little daughter had died just weeks before. They said that when he lay dying he had talked of holding her again in heaven. They had buried him in Hollywood Cemetery. Cole had been with Kristin when they had buried him, but he had visited the grave when he'd come to Richmond, and he still found it impossible to believe that James Ewell Brown Stuart, his friend, the dashing cavalier, could be dead. He had visited Flora, Jeb's wife, and they'd laughed about some of their days back in Kansas, but then Flora had begun to cry, and he had thought it best to leave. Flora had just lost her husband, a Confederate general. Her father, a Union general, was still fighting.

The war had never been fair.

Cole had to head out again, this time to the Indian Nation, to confer with the Cherokees and Choctaws who had been persuaded to fight for the Confederacy. The Union armies were closing in on Richmond, and Lee was hard pressed to protect the capital without Jackson to harass the Federals as they made their way through the Shenandoah Valley.

When he had left Virginia Cole had gone to Tennessee, and from Tennessee he had been ordered to rejoin his brother's unit. The noose was closing tighter and tighter around the neck of the Confederacy. John Hunt Morgan had managed to escape his captors, and he needed information about the Union troops being sent into Kentucky and Tennessee from Kansas City. Cole had taken the assignment in the little town outside the big city for only one reason—he would be close to Kristin. He had to see her. It had been so long, and they had parted so bitterly. He'd received a few letters from her, terse, quick notes telling him that they were all fine, telling him that the Union was in firm control of the part of Missouri where the ranch sat, that he was better off away and that he should take care.

Jamie and Malachi had received warmer letters. Much warmer letters. But still, even to his brothers, Kristin had said very little. Every letter was the same. She related some silly little anecdote that was sure to make them laugh, and then she closed, telling them she was praying for them all. She thought there might be a wedding as soon as the war was over or maybe even before. Shannon was corresponding regularly with a Captain Ellsworth, and Kristin said she, too, thought he was a charming gentleman. He was a Yankee, but she was sure the family would forget that once the war was over. They would all have to, she added forcefully, if there was to be a future.

Cole wasn't sure there could be. There was that one part of his past that he couldn't forget, and he never would be able to forget it, not unless he could finish it off, bury it completely. Not until the redlegs who had razed his place and killed his wife were dead could he ever really rest. No matter how sweet the temptation.

Sitting at a corner table in the saloon, his feet propped and his hat pulled low, he sipped a whiskey and listened to the conversation at the bar. He learned quickly that Lieutenant Billingsley would be transferring eight hundred troops from Kansas to Tupelo and then on to Kentucky by the following week. The saloon was crowded with Union soldiers, green recruits by the looks of them—he didn't think many of the boys even had to shave as yet—but they had one or two older soldiers with them. No one had paid Cole much heed. He was dressed in denim and cotton, with a cattleman's chaps and silver spurs in place and a cowhide vest. He didn't look much like a man who gave a damn about the war one way or the other. One man had asked him what he was doing out of uniform, and he'd quickly invented a story about being sent home, full of shrapnel, after the battle of Shiloh. After that, someone had sent over a bottle of whiskey and he'd set his hat low over his forehead and he'd listened. Now that he had his information, it was time to go. He wanted to reach his wife.

His wife.

He could even say it out loud now. And only once in a while did the bitterness assail him. His wife... His wife had been slain, but he had married a little spitfire of a blonde, and she was his woman now. His wife.

He tensed, remembering that she knew, knew everything about him, about his past. Damn Emery! He'd had no right to spill out the past like that for her. Now he would never know...

Know what? he asked himself.

What her feelings were, what her feelings really were. Hell, it was a damnable time for a marriage. He could still count on his fingers the times he had seen her....Kristin. He'd been impatient with her, and he'd been furious with her, but he'd always admired her courage, no matter what, and from the beginning he'd been determined to protect her.

Then he'd discovered that he needed her.

Like air. Like water. Like the very earth. He needed her. When he'd been away from her he'd still had the nightmares, but time had slowly taken them away. When visions of a woman came to haunt him while he slept, it was Kristin's delicate features he saw, her soft, slow smile, her wide, luminous eyes.

He'd never denied that he cared for her.

He just hadn't wanted to admit how much.

He didn't want a wife feeling sorry for him. He didn't want her holding on, afraid to hurt a traumatized soldier. The whole thing made him seethe inside. He'd swear that he'd be quit of her as soon as the war was over, and then he'd panic, and he'd pray that everything was all right, and he would wish with all his heart that he could just get back to that little patch of Missouri on the border where he could reach out and just touch her face, her hand....

And if he did, he wondered glumly, what good could it do him? He could never stop. Not until one of them lay dead. Him or Fitz. Maybe Fitz hadn't fired the shot that had killed his wife, but he had ordered the raid on Cole's place, and he had led it. In the few months that he had ridden with Quantrill, Cole had managed to meet up with a number of the men who had been in on the raid.

But he'd never found Henry Fitz.

His thoughts suddenly shifted. He didn't know what it was that told him he was in danger, but suddenly he knew that he was. Maybe it was in the thud of a new pair of shiny Union boots on the floor, maybe it was something in the air. And maybe he had lived with the danger for so damned long that he could smell it.

He should never have come to Kansas.

It wasn't that he wasn't armed. He was. And the poor green boys in the saloon were carrying muzzle-loading rifles. He could probably kill the dozen or so of them in the room before they could even load their weapons.

He didn't want to kill them. He'd always hated that kind of warfare. Hell, that was why Quantrill had been able to run circles around the Federals for years. Quantrill's men were so well armed that they could gun down an entire company before they could get off a single shot.

He prepared to leave, praying that the newcomer wasn't someone he knew. But when he saw the man's face beneath the brim of his hat, his heart sank.

The man was his own age, and he wore a lieutenant's insignia. He had dark hair and a long, dark beard, and the lines that furrowed his face said that he should have been older than thirty-two.

It's been a long hard war for all of us, Cole thought bleakly.

The Union officer's name was Kurt Taylor, and he had ridden escort and trails out in the Indian country with Cole when he had been with Stuart. Another West Pointer. They'd fought the Sioux side by side many times.

But now they were on opposite sides.

When Cole stood, Taylor saw him. The men stared straight at one another.

Cole hesitated. He wasn't going to fire, not unless he had to. He didn't cotton to killing children, and that was about what it would be. He looked at the boys standing at the bar. Hell, most of them wouldn't even have started school when the trouble had started in Kansas.

Do something, Taylor, Cole thought. Say something. But the man didn't move. The two of them just stood there staring at one another, and it was as if the world stood still.

Then, miraculously, Taylor lifted his hat.

"Howdy," he said, and walked on by.

Taylor had recognized him. Cole knew it. He had seen the flash of recognition in his eyes. But Taylor wasn't going to turn him in.

Taylor walked up to the bar. The soldiers saluted him, and he told them to be at ease. They returned to their conversations, but they were no longer as relaxed as they had been. They were in the presence of a commissioned officer now.

But Kurt Taylor ignored the men, just as he was ignoring Cole. He ordered himself a brandy, swallowed it down quickly and ordered himself another. Then he turned around, leaned his elbows on the bar and looked out over the room.

"You know, boys," he said, "war itself, soldiering, never did bother me. Joining the army seemed to be a right noble position in life. We had to defend American settlers from the Indians. We had to keep an eye on Mexico, and then suddenly we had our folks moving into Texas. Next thing you know, our great nation is divided, and we're at war with our Southern cousins. And even that's all right, 'cause we all know a man's gotta do what a man's gotta do." He paused and drained his second brandy. He didn't look at Cole, but Cole knew damned well that Taylor was talking straight to him.

"Bushwhackers!" Kurt Taylor spit on the floor. Then he added, "And bloody murdering jayhawkers. I tell you, one is just as bad as the next, and if he claims to wear my colors, well, he's a liar. Those jayhawkers we've got up here, hell, they turned half of Kansas and Missouri against the Union. Folks that didn't own no slaves, that didn't care one way or another about the war, we lost them to the Confederacy because they so abhorred the murder that was being done. Quantrill's boys started up after Lane and Jennison began their goddamn raiding.''

"Pardon me—'' one young man began.

"No, sir! I do not pardon you!'' Kurt Taylor snapped. "Murder is murder. And I hear tell that one of the worst of our Kansas murderers is right here, right here in this town. His name is Henry Fitz. He thought he could make himself a political career out of killing Missourians. He forgot there were decent folk in Kansas who would never condone the killing of women and children, whether it was done by bushwhackers or jayhawkers.'' He stared straight at Cole, and then he turned his back on him.

He knew Cole wouldn't shoot him.

He knew Cole wouldn't shoot a man in the back.

Cole was trembling, and his fingers were itching. He didn't even want to draw his gun. He wanted to find Fitz and wrap his fingers around the bastard's throat and choke the life out of him.

"Give me another brandy there, barkeep. Boys, you watch your step while Fitz is around. He's down Main Street at the McKinley barn with his troops. I'd say there's about a dozen of those marauders. Yep, I think you ought to steer clear of the area.''

He tossed back another brandy, and then he turned and looked at Cole again.

And then he walked out of the saloon.

Cole left a few minutes after Taylor did. He wondered if his old comrade in arms had put on the performance he had so that Cole would get out of town or so that he would stay in it.

He came out on the steps and looked up at the noonday sun, and he smiled. He came out to the hitching post and mounted his horse, a bay he had borrowed from Malachi because he had been afraid his own stallion was too well known here.

Taylor had even told him where to find Fitz. Straight down Main Street.

Cole started the bay at a walk. Within seconds he had urged the horse to a trot, and then to a canter, and then to a gallop. The barbershop whizzed by him, then the savings bank, the newspaper office and Ed Foley's Mercantile. He passed rows of neat houses with white picket fences and summer gardens, and then he was on the stretch of road leading to the farms beyond the town limits.

He must have headed out in the right direction, because suddenly there was a line of troops coming toward him. Redlegs, so called for the color of their leggings. Raiders. Murderers. Jim Lane had led them once. Now Senator Jim Lane was in Washington, and even Doc Jennison, who had taken command of them after Lane, had gone on to new pursuits. But Henry Fitz was still leading his band, and still striking terror into the hearts of innocent men, women and children.

Cole slowed the bay to a walk as the men approached. Henry Fitz sat atop a piebald, dead center. He had narrowed his dark little eyes, and he was staring down the road at Cole.

Cole kept moving. He had to do this. He had to kill Fitz. And if he died, too...

Would Kristin care? he found himself wondering. He had never doubted her gratitude, but he wondered now what she would feel if she heard that he had been gunned down on a Kansas road. Would she shed any tears for him? Would she miss him? Would she revile him for dying a senseless death, for leaving her alone?

He closed his eyes for a moment. He had to do this. If they were to have any kind of a future together, he had to do this. Now.

For a moment he remembered the flames, remembered them clearly. He remembered the crackling of the fire and he remembered the acrid smell of the smoke. And he remembered her, running, running to him. He remembered reaching out and touching her, and he remembered the way she had looked into his eyes and smiled and died. And he remembered the blood that had stained his hands . . .

I loved you! his heart cried out. I loved you, Elizabeth! With all my heart and with all my soul.

And in that moment he knew at last that he loved Kristin, too. He had to bury the past, because he longed for a future with her. He had been afraid to love again. He had not wanted to destroy Elizabeth's memory by loving again. Yet he knew now that if Elizabeth could speak to him she would tell him to love Kristin, to love her deeply and well, in memory of all they had once shared.

He brought the bay to a halt and watched the road. The redlegs were trotting along easily, none of them expecting trouble from a lone man atop a single bay horse. But in the center of the group, the frown upon Henry Fitz's face was deepening. Another five feet—ten—and he would recognize Cole.

"Howdy, there," Fitz began, drawing in on his reins. The rest of the party stopped along with him. His hat was tilted low over his thickly bearded face, and his eyes seemed to disappear into folds of flesh. "I'll be damned!" he said suddenly. Then he laughed. "Come all the way to Kansas to die, boy?"

And he reached for his revolver.

Cole had been fast before the war. He had been fast in the West. He was faster now.

Fitz had been the inspiration that had taught him how to draw faster than sound, faster than light. He had always known that someday, somehow, he would meet up with this man.

And he did now, guns blazing. Holding the reins in his teeth, he tightened his thighs around the bay and rode into the group.

He watched Fitz fall. He saw the blood stain his shirt crimson, and he watched him fall. The rest of it was a blur. He heard men and horses screaming as he galloped through their midst. A bullet struck his saddle, and then the bay went down beneath him. Cole tasted the dust roused by the multitude of horses. He jumped away from the fallen bay, grabbed his rifles and fired again. The gunfire seemed to go on forever.

Then there was silence. He spun around, a cocked rifle in either hand.

Three men remained alive. They stared at him and raised their hands. Their faces meant nothing to him.

He hurried away from his fallen horse and leaped into the saddle of a large, powerful-looking buckskin. Warily eyeing the three men, he nudged the horse forward. The buckskin had been a good choice. It surged forward, and Cole could feel the animal's strength and sense its speed. He raced forward, his heart pounding, adrenaline pumping furiously through his system.

He was alive.

But as he raced toward the town he saw the soldiers. Rows of blue uniforms. Navy blue. On both sides of the road. He slowed his horse to a walk. There was nowhere to go. It was over. They would build a gallows in the middle of town, and they would hang him as a bushwhacker.

Suddenly Kurt Taylor was riding toward Cole. "Hear there's been some shooting up at the end of town, stranger. You might want to hurry along and let the army do the picking up."

Cole couldn't breathe. Taylor lifted a brow and grinned at him. Cole looked down at his hands where they rested on the pommel. They were shaking.

He saluted Taylor.

Taylor saluted back. "Someone ought to tell Cole Slater that the man who killed his wife is dead. And someone also ought to warn him that he's an outlaw in these parts. Someone ought to warn him that he'd best spend his time way, way deep in Dixie. I know that the man isn't any criminal, but there aren't many who served with him like I did. The rest think he ought to wear a rope around his neck."

"Thank you kindly, sir," Cole said at last. "If I meet up with him, I'll tell him."

He rode on, straight through the ranks of blue uniforms. He kept riding. He didn't look back, not even when he heard a cheer and realized that the Union soldiers were saluting him, that Kurt Taylor had won him a few friends.

His thigh was bleeding, he realized. He had been shot after all, and he hadn't even known it. It didn't matter much. He had to keep riding. He wanted to get home. Night was falling. It was a good time to ride.

A little farther down the road he became aware that he was being followed. He quickly left the road and dismounted, whispering to the buckskin, encouraging it to follow him into the brush.

He was being followed by a single horseman. He hid behind an oak tree and listened to the hoofbeats. He waited until the rider was right by his side. Then he sprang up and knocked the man to the ground.

"Damn you, Cole Slater! Get off me."

"Taylor!"

Cole stood and dragged Taylor to his feet.

"You son of a bitch!" Taylor laughed, and then he clapped Cole hard on the shoulders. "You damned son of a bitch! Hasn't anybody told you that the South is going to lose the war?"

"It wouldn't matter what they told me," Cole said. "I can't much help what I am." He paused a moment, and then he grinned, because Kurt really had been one damned good friend. "Thank you. Thank you for what you did back there. I've seen so many men tearing one another to shreds. The truth meant more to you than the color of a uniform. I won't forget that, Kurt. Ever."

"I didn't do anything that God wouldn't call right," Kurt said. "You got him, Cole. You got that mangy bastard. 'Course, you do know they'll shoot you on sight now and ask questions later."

"Yes, I know that."

"You're heading south, I hope?"

"East, and then south."

"Don't stay around the border too long," Taylor warned him. "Even to see your boy. Major Emery said that if I ever came across you I was to warn you—"

"What?" Cole snapped, his hands on Taylor's shoulders.

"I'm trying to tell you. Major Emery said—"

"The hell with Emery! What boy?"

Taylor cocked his head, frowning. "Why, yours, of course. Born last February. A fine boy, I understand. Captain Ellsworth gets out there now and again, and he reported to the major that both mother and child were doing fine. Don't rightly recall what they named him, but Ellsworth says he's big and healthy and has a head of hair to put many a fine lass to shame. Cole, let go, you're about to snap my damned shoulder blade. Oh, hell! You mean you didn't know? Listen to me now. Don't you go running off half-cocked after everything that happened here today. You move slow, and you move careful, you hear me, Slater? Most of the Union boys would shoot me if they knew I let you slip through my fingers. Cole?"

"I'll move careful," Cole said.

Yes, he'd move careful. He'd move damned careful. Just to make sure he lived long enough to tan Kristin's sweet hide.

Why in God's name hadn't she told him?

It was hot and humid on the Fourth of July, 1864. Scarcely a breeze had stirred all day.

It had been a difficult day for Kristin. She had learned long ago to keep her mind off her worries, to try not to think too much, to concentrate on her tasks. Anything was better than worrying. If she worried all the time she would drive herself mad.

But the fourth was a particularly difficult day.

There were celebrations going on everywhere. Union soldiers letting off volleys of rifle fire, ranchers setting off fireworks. Every gunshot reminded Kristin that her husband could meet her brother on the field of battle at any time, that they were still at war, that the nation celebrating its birthday was still bitterly divided.

There was smoke in the air, and the noise was making the baby restless. She'd had him with her down in the parlor, and Delilah's Daniel, almost three years old now, had been laughing and entertaining the baby with silly faces. But then Cole Gabriel Slater had decided enough was enough, and he had jammed one of his pudgy little fists into his mouth and started to cry.

"Oh, I've had it with the entire day anyway!" Kristin declared to everyone in the room and to no one in particular. She picked up the baby and started up the stairs. Delilah, sewing, stared after her. Shannon, running her fingers idly over the spinet, paused. Samson rolled his eyes. "Hot days, yes, Lordy, hot days," he mumbled. He stood up. "The hands will be back in soon enough. I'll carry that stew on out to the bunkhouse."

Upstairs, Kristin lay down with her fretful baby and opened her blouse so that he could nurse. She started, then smiled, as he latched on to her nipple with a surprising power. Then, as always, an incredibly sweet feeling swept through her, and she pulled his little body still closer to her. His eyes met hers. In the last month they had turned a silver gray, just like Cole's. His hair was hers, though, a thatch of it, blond, almost white. He was a beautiful baby, incredibly beautiful. He had been born on the tenth of February. Stroking his soft cheek, she felt her smile deepen as she remembered the day. It had been snowing, and it had been bitterly cold, and she had been dragging hay down for the horses when she had felt the first pain and panicked. It would have been impossible for Dr. Cavanaugh to come out from town, and it would have been impossible for her to reach town. Pete had been terribly upset, and that had calmed her somehow, and Delilah had assured her that it would be hours before the baby actually came.

Hours!

It had been awful, and it had been agony, and she had decided that it was extremely unfair that men should be the ones to go off to war to get shot at when women were the ones stuck with having babies. She had ranted and raved, and she had assured both Delilah and Shannon in no uncertain terms that she despised Cole Slater—and every other living soul who wore britches, as a matter of fact—and that if she lived she would never do this again.

Delilah smirked and assured her that she was going to live and that she would probably have half a dozen more children. Shannon waltzed around in a daydream, saying that she wouldn't be complaining one whit if she were the one about to have the baby—if the baby belonged to Captain Ellsworth.

The pain subsided for a moment, and Kristin had smiled up at her sister, who was pushing back her soaked hair. It was "colder than a witch's teat," as Pete had said, but she was drenched with sweat.

"You really love him, don't you, your Captain Ellsworth?"

Shannon nodded, her eyes on fire. "Oh, Kristin! He saved my life. He caught me when I fell. He was such a wonderful hero. Oh, Kristin! Don't you feel that about Cole?"

She hesitated, and she remembered how happy she had been to see him. And she remembered how they had made love, how tender he had been with her, how passionate. With a certain awe she remembered the way his eyes had fallen upon her, how cherished that look had made her feel. And she remembered the ecstasy...

But then she remembered his anger and his impatience, and how he had grown cold and distant when she had mentioned his past. He was in love with another woman, and though that woman lay dead, she was a rival Kristin could not best.

"Cole was a hero!" Shannon whispered. "Kristin, how can you forget that? He rode in here and he saved our lives! And if you think you're having a difficult labor, well, then ... that is God's way of telling you you had no right to keep the information about this baby from your husband!"

I meant to tell him.... Kristin almost said it. But if she did she would have to explain how he had acted when she had mentioned his past, and she would have to think about the fact that he didn't love her, right in the middle of having his child. She shrugged instead. "What can he do? There is a war on."

A vicious pain seized her again, and she assured Shannon that Cole was a rodent, and Shannon laughed. And then, miraculously—for it had been hours and hours, and it was nearly dawn—Delilah told Kristin that the baby's head was showing and that it was time for her to push.

When he lay in her arms, red and squalling, Kristin knew that she had never imagined such a love as swelled within her.

And she prayed with all her heart that her son's father was alive, that he would come home to them all. She vowed that she would ask no questions he could not answer, that she would not ask for anything he could not give.

Lying with the baby, nursing him as she did now, was the greatest pleasure of her life. Kristin forgot the world outside, and she forgot the war, and she even forgot that his father probably did not know he existed. She loved his grave little eyes, and she loved the way his mouth tugged on her breast. She counted his fingers endlessly, and his toes, and she thought that he was gaining weight wonderfully and that he was very long—even Delilah said he would grow to be very tall—and that his face was adorable. He had a little dimple in his chin, and Kristin wondered if Cole had a dimple like it. She had seen all of his body, but she had never seen his naked chin. He had always had a beard.

Delilah had warned her to let Gabe, as they called him, nurse only so long at one breast. If she did he would ignore the other, and she would experience grave discomfort. Consequently she gently loosened his grasp on her left breast, laughing at his howl of outrage.

"Heavens! You're more demanding than that father of yours!" she told her baby, cradling him against her shoulder and patting his back. Then, suddenly, she realized that she was not alone. She had been so engrossed with her son that the door had opened and closed without her noticing it.

A peculiar sensation made its way up her spine, and suddenly she was breathless. She dared to look at the door, and found him standing there.

Her hero.

He was in full dress uniform, tattered gray and gold, his sword hanging dangerously from its scabbard. He was leaner than she remembered him, and his face was ashen, and his eyes...his eyes burned through her, seared into her.

"Cole!" she whispered. She wondered how long he had been standing there, and suddenly she was blushing, and it didn't matter that he was the child's father, she felt awkward and vulnerable and exposed.

He pushed away from the door and strode toward her, and despite herself she shrank away from him. He reached for the baby, and she clung to her child. Then she heard him speak, his voice low and hoarse.

"My God, Kristin, give him to me."

"Cole—"

She had to release the baby for Cole meant to take him. She nervously pulled her dress together but he had no eyes for her. He was looking at the baby. She wanted to shriek his name, wanted to run to him. It had been so long since she had seen him last, and even that had seemed like a dream. But she couldn't run to him, couldn't throw her arms around him. He was cold and forbidding. He was a stranger to her now.

He ignored her completely, setting the squalling child down on his back at the foot of the bed, freeing him from all his swaddling so that he could look at the whole of him. Kristin could have told him that Gabe was perfect in every way, but she kept silent. She knew he had to discover it for himself. Suddenly she was more than a little afraid of her husband. Should she have written to him? What good would it have done? Cole shouldn't be here even now. There were far too many Union troops around. Was that the real reason? she wondered. She had hesitated once because he had made her angry, because she had realized that he did not love her. But she hadn't written, she knew, because she had been afraid that he would be determined to come home, and that that determination would make him careless.

For a moment Gabe quieted and stared up at his father. He studied Cole's face as gravely and as purposefully as Cole studied him. His little body was perfectly still.

Then he had had enough of his father. His mother was the one he wanted. He lifted up his chubby little legs and screwed up his face and kicked out and howled in outrage all at once. The cry brought a surge to Kristin's breasts that soaked the bodice of the gown she held so tightly against her. Cole covered his son again, then picked him up and set him against his chest. Kristin reached out her arms.

"Please, Cole, give him back to me. He's...he's hungry."

Cole hesitated, staring at her hard. Then he handed the baby to her. Kristin lowered her head and wished he would go away, but then she remembered that he had just come, and that if he went away again he might be killed this time. Color spilled over her cheeks, and she remembered just how they had gotten the baby, and she touched the baby's cheek with her finger and let her bodice fall open and led his little mouth to her breast. He latched on with an awful, piglet-like sound, and she found that she couldn't look up at all, even though she knew that Cole was still in the room and that his eyes were still on her.

The room was silent except for the baby's slurping. Then even that stopped, and Kristin realized he had fallen asleep. She lifted him to her shoulder and tried to get him to burp, but he was sleeping too soundly. Biting her lip, she rose and set him in the cradle that Samson had brought down from the attic. All the while she felt Cole's eyes on her.

Still, he didn't touch her, and he didn't speak to her. He stood by the cradle and stared down at the child. He was going to touch him again. Kristin bit her lips to keep from protesting. She watched in silence as Cole's long fingers tenderly touched the tiny cheek. She tried to button her bodice, then realized that she was drenched and that it was a foolish gesture. Flushing, she hurried to change her gown, but it didn't matter. Cole didn't seem to have noticed. She wondered if she should tiptoe away and leave him alone, but the moment she started for the door he was on his feet, and she realized that he had noted her every movement.

"Where do you think you're going?"

His voice was low, but there was real anger in it, and real menace.

"I thought you might be hungry."

He was silent. His gaze fell over her. Then he took a step toward her, and she almost screamed when his fingers gripped her arms and he shook her. "Damn you, Kristin! Damn you a thousand times over! You knew! You knew— and you didn't tell me! What right did you have to keep him from me?"

She tried to free herself, but she could not. She looked in his eyes, and she hated what she saw there, the uncompromising hardness.

"What rights have you got!" she choked out. "You ride in whenever you choose.... You may feel you have obligations, but that is all you have! I—"

"I ride in when I can get here!" he snapped, shaking her again. Her head fell back, and her eyes, glazed suddenly with tears, stared into his. "Lady, there is a war being fought out there! You know that. Of all women, you know that. I have done everything that is humanly possible, I have given you everything—"

"No! No, you have not given me everything! You have never given me the least little part of your—"

"I could have been killed. I don't know how many times I could have been killed on some stinking battlefield, and I wouldn't even have known I had a son!"

"Let me go!"

"No!"

"Please!" He was so close to her, and he felt so good. He was so warm, and she could feel the hardness of his body, and the touch of his hands. She wanted to touch his face and soothe away the lines around his eyes, and she wanted to fill the emptiness in his heart. She wanted to see his eyes alight with passion again. As she thought of the passion they had known together, her breasts seemed to fill again, but it was not for her child this time, it was for him. She needed to be held, to be touched.

To be loved.

"Please!" she repeated softly. She was so glad to see him, and their time together should be a precious respite against the war that raged on around them.

"Cole, I wanted to tell you when you were here, but all of a sudden we were fighting, because Major Emery had committed the horrible sin of telling me that you had been hurt. Mr. Cole Slater had been hurt, cut open and left bleeding, and he just couldn't bear that! Well, you are human, Cole, and you're supposed to bleed! And I should hurt for you, too, because damn it, what happened was awful!"

"Kristin, stop—"

"No! No, I will not stop! What have you got now? One week, one day? One lousy hour? Not long, I'll warrant. There are too many Federals around. So you stop, and you listen to me! I am grateful to you, Cole, eternally grateful. And I've been glad of this bargain of ours, heartily glad.

You have fulfilled every promise you ever made me. But don't you dare yell at me now! I didn't write because I didn't want you getting killed, because I was afraid of your temper."

"My temper! I would never—"

"Yes, you would! You would have taken foolish chances to get here. You would have been afraid because of what happened to you with—"

She broke off, remembering that Emery had said that his wife had been pregnant when she had been killed.

"Oh, God, Cole, I'm sorry. I just realized that you would probably rather that she...that I..."

"What the hell are you saying?" he asked hoarsely.

Kristin shook her head miserably. "Your wife, your first wife... You were expecting a child. I'm sorry, you must be thinking of her, that you would prefer—"

"That she had lived? That you had died? My God, Kristin, don't you ever say such a thing, don't you even think it, do you hear me?" He caught her against him. He threaded his fingers roughly through her hair, and suddenly he lowered his head and buried his face in the fragrant strands. "Don't you ever, ever think that!" he repeated. Then he looked at her again, and he smiled. It was a weary smile, and she saw how much the past few years had aged him, and her heart ached.

"He is a beautiful boy. He is the most wonderful child I've ever seen. And he is mine. Thank you. Thank you so very much."

"Oh, Cole!" she whispered. She was dangerously close to tears. He saw it and his tone changed.

"I'd still like to tan your hide for keeping the truth from me!"

"Cole, I really didn't mean to. I was afraid. I'm always afraid, it seems."

"I know, I know." He held her against him.

"Cole, you must be starved. Let me go down and have Delilah—"

"No, not now."

"Cole, you must need—"

He stepped away from her.

"I need my wife," he said. "I very, very badly need my wife."

He bent his head and kissed her, and then he lifted her into his arms and they fell upon the bed together.

"We have a son, Kristin," he said, and she laughed. "We have a son, and he's beautiful, and . . . and so are you."

It was a long, long time before either of them thought of any other kind of sustenance.

14

The days that followed were glorious for Kristin. It wasn't that anything had been settled between them. It was just that for a time they seemed to have achieved a private peace, and it was wonderful.

They did not stray far from the house. Cole explained how hard it had been to elude the patrols to reach her. But Kristin knew her own land, and she knew where they could safely travel. They picnicked on the banks of the river with the baby, and while he slept they splashed in the deliciously cool water. Kristin was first shocked and then ridiculously excited to dare to strip away her clothes in the broad daylight and make love in the water.

In the evening they sat beneath the moon and felt the cool breezes play over them. Kristin listened while Cole and Samson talked about what was left of the herd, and it seemed that everything that was said began with the words "When the war is over . . ."

At night, lying curled against her husband's body, Kristin asked him if he thought the war would ever end. He hesitated a long time, stroking her hair.

"It's ending now, Kristin. We're being broken down bit by bit, like a beautiful animal chewed to bits by fleas. We never had the power. We never had the industry. We never had the men. It's going to end. If the Confederacy holds out another year I'll be surprised. Well, we went a long way on courage and tactics. But that Lincoln is a stubborn cuss. Tenacious. He's held on to his Union, so it seems."

He sounded tired, but not bitter. Kristin stroked his chest. "Can't you just stay here now? If you know you're losing..."

"I can't stay, Kristin. You know that."

"I don't know anything of the kind! You've done your best for the Confederacy! You can't—"

"Kristin, Kristin!" He caught her hands. "I'm an outlaw as long as the war is on. If I stay here, I'll be in terrible danger. If some glory-seeking commander hears about it, he might just waltz in and string me up. If I'm going to die, I'd rather it be fighting than dangling from the end of a rope!"

"Cole, stop it—"

"And it isn't over, Kristin. I'm in the game and I have to stay with it. If I don't go back, Malachi will come here and shoot me for a traitor."

"He would not!"

"Well, someone would," he said.

"Cole—"

"Kristin, I have to go back."

"Cole—"

He rolled over and swept her into his arms and kissed her and then looked into her eyes. "When I ride now, I will think of my son. Thank you for Gabe, Kristin. Thank you." He nuzzled her lips and kissed her forehead and her throat and the valley between her breasts. She tried to keep talking, to keep arguing, but he nuzzled his way down the length of her torso, and she grew breathless and couldn't speak. When he had finished she couldn't remember what she had wanted to say, only that it was terribly important that she hold him as long as she could.

The next day Kristin was overjoyed when Matthew arrived unexpectedly. He quickly warned her that both he and Cole could be shot if they were caught together. Still, for a few hours, it was a wonderful homecoming. Matthew admired his nephew, and Shannon clung to her brother, and Delilah managed a fine feast. Then Cole and Matthew shut themselves up in the library together. Kristin finally had to force her way in.

"You're discussing me, I know it, and I will know what is going on!" she insisted.

"Cole has to leave," Matthew told her. "Right away. Tonight."

"Why?"

Matthew looked unhappily at Cole. Cole shrugged and gave her the explanation. "Matthew is putting the ranch under the protection of a Federal troop."

"But—"

"I can't be here, Kristin. And Quantrill's group has split up."

"What?"

"During the spring," Matthew explained, "Quantrill and his men got into some heavy feuding in Texas. Bill Anderson has some men under him, and George Todd has a group, too. Quantrill still has his followers. Bill attacked some Federals during the summer, and Archie Clements scalped the men he murdered. The situation is frightening, and no one knows where Zeke Moreau is, or who he's with. So you see, Kristin, Cole has to get out of here. And you have to be protected."

Tears stung her eyes, and she gritted her teeth to keep from spilling them. She turned away from the men.

"I fixed the tear in your frock coat, Cole. And Delilah has been washing everything. The two of you, sometimes your clothes smell as if you'd been sleeping with skunks for a year. I'll see that you're packed up and have Shannon wrap up a supply of jerky."

She stumbled into the hallway. Cole found her there and swept her into his arms and took her upstairs to their room. She cried the whole time they made love, her tears spilling over his shoulders and his chest and dampening his cheeks.

Then he kissed her and held the baby tightly. She insisted on coming down with him, and when he was mounted he leaned down to kiss her again. Holding their child close to her breast, Kristin waved as he left.

That night some Union soldiers moved into the bunkhouse. Kristin supposed it was necessary. But it was still hard.

The bushwhacker situation grew much worse. On the thirtieth of September Kristin was surprised when she came out on the porch to see that Major Emery was riding toward her. She stood and smiled, ready to greet him, but her smile died when she saw his face. She went pale herself, and the world spun, and she was afraid that she was going to faint.

"Oh, my God, it's Cole—"

"No, no, Mrs. Slater," he assured her hastily, taking Gabe from her. "He's a fine boy, ma'am. A fine boy." He looked around uncomfortably. "I don't think your sister should know the whole of this, ma'am, but... Captain Ellsworth is dead."

"Oh, no!"

"That damned Bill Anderson! Since his sister died they say he froths at the mouth every time he fights. Fights—bah!" He spat into the dirt. "He tore up Centralia. He made twenty-five unarmed soldiers strip, and then he shot twenty-three of them dead. The troops that went out after him fared worse. It was a massacre. At least a hundred killed. Stripped, scalped, dismembered, their bodies mutilated as they died—"

"Oh, God! Oh, God!"

They both heard the scream. Kristin turned around to see that Shannon was standing in the doorway. She had heard every word. She knew.

"Oh, God! No!" she shrieked. Major Emery took a step toward her, barely managing to catch her as she pitched forward in a dead faint.

"Could you take her to her room for me, please?" Kristin whispered.

Major Emery nodded and carried Shannon upstairs. "We've a company surgeon out in your bunkhouse. I'll send him over and see that he gives her something."

The doctor didn't come soon enough. Shannon awoke, and she started to cry. She cried so hard that Kristin was afraid she would hurt herself. Then she was silent, and the silence was even worse. Kristin stayed with her, holding her hand, but she knew that she hadn't reached her sister, and she wondered if anyone ever would again.

Fall came, and with it more tragedy for the South. General Sherman was marching to the sea through Georgia and the Carolinas, and the reports of his scorched earth policy were chilling. In the west, the Union bottleneck was almost complete.

On the twenty-first of October George Todd died when a sniper caught him in the neck. Five days later Bill Anderson was killed in the northwestern corner of Missouri.

Kristin was alarmed to see how eagerly Shannon received the news of their deaths.

Thanksgiving came and went. It was a very quiet affair. Kristin was Matthew McCahy's sister, but she was also Cole Slater's wife, and so it didn't seem right to invite any of the Union men in for a fancy supper.

Matthew made it back for Christmas Day, and Kristin was delighted to see him. She asked if he had heard anything, and he told her that the last he had heard, Cole Slater was still at large. John Hunt Morgan, the dashing cavalry commander, had been killed late in the year, and Matthew hadn't heard anything about where Cole or Malachi or Jamie had been assigned.

She cried that night, cried because no news was good news. It seemed so long since she had lost her father, and she could hardly remember Adam's face. She didn't want to lose anyone else. She could hardly stand to see Shannon's pale face anymore. She hadn't seen her sister smile since Captain Ellsworth had been killed. Not once.

After Christmas dinner, Kristin sat before the fire in the parlor with her brother and her sister. She began to play a Christmas carol on the spinet, but Shannon broke down and ran upstairs to her room. Kristin sat staring silently at her hands for a long time.

Finally Matthew spoke.

"Kristin, nothing's going to get better, not for a long, long time, you know."

"They say it's almost over. They say the war is almost over."

"The war, but not the hatred. I doubt they'll fix that for a hundred years, Kristin. It isn't going to be easy. The healing will be slow and hard."

"I know," Kristin whispered.

"You just make sure, Kristin, that if Cole comes around you get him out of here fast. He isn't going to be safe anywhere near this place, not until some kind of a peace is made, and then only if amnesty is given."

Kristin's fingers trembled. She nodded. "He won't come back. Not until . . . not until it's over."

Matthew kissed her and went upstairs. Kristin stared at the fire until it had burned very low in the grate.

In February Gabriel had his first birthday. The news that month was good for the Union, grim for the Confederacy. Sherman had devastated the South. Robert E. Lee was struggling in Virginia, and Jefferson Davis and the Confederate cabinet had abandoned Richmond half a dozen times.

By March, everyone was talking about the campaign for Petersburg. Grant had been pounding away at the Virginia city since the previous summer, and the fighting had been fierce. The Union had tried to dig a tunnel under the Confederate lines. Mines had exploded, and many Confederates had been killed, but then they had rallied and shot down the Union soldiers who had filled in the crater. The soldiers shuddered when they spoke of it.

Kristin had become accustomed to the men who had made their headquarters on her land. They were mostly farmers and ranchers, and more and more she heard them speak wistfully of the time when the war would be over, when they could go home. The Confederate general Kirby-Smith was still raising hell in the West, and the Southern forces were still fighting valiantly in the East, but the death throes had already set in for a nation that had never had a chance to truly breathe the air of independence. Major Emery came one day and sat with them on the porch while the first warmth of spring touched them. Morosely he told Kristin that the death estimates for the country were nearing the half-million mark. "Bullet, sword and disease!" He shook his head. "So many mothers' sons!"

When he left her that afternoon, Kristin had no idea that she would never see him again alive.

April came. General Lee's forces were gathering around Richmond for a desperate defense of the capital. Gabe was learning to walk, and Kristin had agreed with Samson and Pete that he might be allowed to try sitting on top of a horse.

Kristin came outside one April afternoon, and she knew instantly that something was wrong. There was a peculiar stillness in the air.

There should have been noise. There should have been laughter. The dozen or so Union troops billeted on the ranch should have been out and about, grooming their horses, hurrying here and there in their smart blue uniforms with their correspondence and their missives.

Pete was nowhere in sight, and neither was Samson.

"Samson?" Kristin called out.

Then she heard the barn door creak as if the breeze had moved it, but there wasn't any breeze. She looked toward it, and she saw a hand. Its fingers were curled and crumpled, and it was attached to a bloodstained blue-clad arm. Kristin felt a scream rising in her throat, but she didn't dare release it. She wrenched Gabe into her arms and ran for the house as fast as she could.

"Shannon!" she screamed. In the hall she found a gun belt with the two Colt six-shooters Cole had insisted she keep loaded and ready. With trembling fingers she wound the belt around her waist and reached for the Spencer repeating rifle Matthew had brought at Christmas.

"Shannon!" she called again.

Her sister came running down the steps, her eyes wide, her face pale.

"Something is wrong. Take Gabe—"

"No! Give me the rifle!"

"Shannon, please—"

"I'm a better shot than you are, damn it!"

"Maybe, yes! But I'm not as desperate and reckless as you are!" Kristin snapped. "Shannon, for God's sake, you are the best shot! So for the love of God take Gabriel and get upstairs and try to pick them off if they come for me."

"Who?"

She didn't know how she could be certain, but she was.

"Zeke is back. He's out there somewhere. Shannon, please, don't let them get my baby!"

With that she pushed Gabriel into her sister's arms and started out the door again. Shannon watched her. Gabriel began to cry, and she pulled him close and hurried up the stairs.

"Holy Mary!" Private Watson muttered. "Will you look at that? Fool Yankee, he's all alone and coming right at us!"

Cole looked up from where he sat polishing the butt of his rifle. His eyes narrowed as he watched the trotting horse. Judging by the way the man riding it sat, he was injured, and injured pretty badly.

"Should we shoot him?" someone murmured uncertainly.

"Somebody already done shot him," came the wry answer.

"Leave him be, boys," Cole said, rising curiously. Cole had been promoted to Colonel, which made him the highest-ranking officer in the group. Malachi was now a major and Jamie a captain. The three of them were with a small company of men simply because small companies were all that was left in their sector of the West. They had decided to find Kirby-Smith, wherever he was, and join forces with him, but for the last month they had kept a field headquarters in this abandoned farmhouse deep inside an overgrown orchard.

"I know that man," Cole muttered suddenly. He hurried forward, his brothers and his ragged troops at his heels.

He reached the horse, and the Yankee fell right into his arms. Cole eased him down to the ground, wresting his own scarf from around his neck to soak up the blood pouring from the wound beneath the man's shoulder blade.

"Matthew McCahy, what the hell happened to you, boy?" he said gruffly. He looked at Captain Roger Turnbill, the company surgeon, and then he looked down at Matthew and wondered how the hell his brother-in-law had found him. Then he decided it didn't matter, not until Matthew was looked after.

"Let's get inside the house," Captain Turnbill said.

The men started to lift him. Matthew opened his eyes, huge blue eyes that reminded Cole painfully of his wife, so very close by, so endlessly far away. Matthew reached up and clutched the lapel of Cole's frock coat.

"Cole, listen to me—"

"You know this blue belly well, colonel?" Captain Turnbill asked.

"He's my wife's brother. I know him well enough."

"Then let's get him inside. He's bleeding like a stuck pig."

"Matthew—" Cole gripped the hand that clutched him so tightly. "Matthew, the captain is going to help you. I swear it." Cole wondered if Matthew was delirious, or if he was merely wary of the Confederate surgeon. Doctors on both sides had been known to boast that they had killed more of the enemy than all the artillery shells in the service.

"Cole! For God's sake, listen to me!" Matthew rasped out. His fingers held Cole's like a vise. "It's Zeke—"

"What?"

Matthew swallowed painfully. "We met up with him southeast of here, in a little two-bit place called James Fork. We were a small detachment, thirty of us, heading over to Tennessee. I went down, I was knocked out and they took me for dead. I heard him talking over me. Said he couldn't wait to get to the McCahy place and tell Kristin McCahy that he'd managed to murder her brother now, too. They spent the night at James Fork. I waited till they were drunk and I found a horse, and here I am—"

Cole was ashen and tense. He didn't realize how hard he was gripping Matthew's shoulders until Captain Turnbill said softly, "Ease off, colonel."

"How did you find us?" Jamie asked carefully. He was the only one who seemed to be capable of rational thought at the moment.

Matthew smiled. "Your location isn't exactly a secret, gentlemen. Kurt Taylor was out here with a scouting party a few weeks ago. Some of the higher-ups know where you are.... They're just hoping the war will be over before they have to come in and clean you out." His smile faded, and he choked and coughed and then groaned in pain.

"Get him up and in the house!" Turnbill ordered. A half-dozen men quickly obeyed him, Jamie Slater tensely and carefully taking Matthew's head and his wounded shoulder.

"Slater! You've got to get there. You and your men, you've got a chance. Riding straight west—"

Cole followed after him. "There's a dozen Yankees on the ranch," he said tensely. "I know it."

"So does Zeke Moreau," Matthew gasped out.

Then he was suddenly silent.

"Is he dead?" Malachi asked tonelessly.

Turnbill shook his head. "Passed out from loss of blood. It's amazing that he made it here."

Cole didn't follow any farther. He paused in the yard in front of the farmhouse and looked around at the men who remained with him. Besides his brothers and the doctor, he had one sergeant, two corporals and twenty-two privates. They had survived a hell of a lot. How could he ask them to die at this point?

"I've got to leave you, boys," he said. The soldiers who hadn't helped carry Matthew into the house ranged silently around him. "This is a private battle, and some of you might say it's being waged against one of your own—"

"Hell, Quantrill and his kind were never one of my own," Bo Jenkins, a shopkeeper in peacetime, said. "My kind of Southerner ain't never shot down a man in cold blood."

"Glad to hear it, private," Cole said quietly. "But still, I can't rightly ask you to come along and get killed—"

"Hell, colonel, how's this any different from all the other times?" Jenkins said.

His brother John stepped up beside him. "Seems like we've been following you a long time, sir. We'll keep on doing that. I mean, what the hell, colonel? You think we all want to live forever?"

Cole felt a smile tug at his lips. "Then let's get ready. We've got to ride fast. We've got to ride like the wind."

Armed and ready, Kristin came out of the house and moved quickly toward the barn, toward the bloody hand lying in the spring sunshine.

She paused at the gaping doorway and flattened herself against the wall. Then she kicked open the door and stepped inside, both her Colts cocked and ready to fire.

She heard nothing, saw nothing. She blinked in the dim light, then she saw that at least five men in Yankee blue lay on the ground and in the hay. Their killer or killers had interrupted them in the middle of a poker game. The cards were still sitting on a bale of hay in the center of the barn.

Someone had been holding a full house.

Kristin swallowed painfully.

"Drop 'em," came a sneering voice from behind her. It was one of Zeke's men. She didn't know his name, but she recognized the voice from its jeering tone. She had heard the man's raucous laughter when her father had died.

She froze, aware that she hadn't a chance in hell of turning quickly enough to kill the man. She wondered whether she shouldn't turn anyway and die quickly. Zeke surely no longer desired her. All he wanted was revenge.

Suddenly there was an explosion right over her shoulder. She screamed, stunned, wondering if she'd been hit. She hadn't. She stared toward the center of the barn, and there lay one of the Yankee soldiers she had thought were all dead. Blood was pouring from his temple, but he was smiling at her, and his pistol was smoking. She whirled around. The man behind her lay dead, very dead. There was a black hole burned right into his chest.

She slammed the Colts back into the gun belt and ran over to the Yankee who had saved her life, falling down on her knees beside him. "Bless you! What can I—"

"Lady, you can save yourself!" the man whispered, and he winced. "If all goes well, then you come back for me. Damn it to hell, but I can't help you no more now. My leg is all busted up. You go careful. He's in the house."

Chills swept up her spine. "He's . . . where?"

"Moreau, their leader. He's up in the house."

He was in the house, with her sister and her child. Kristin raced for the doorway. She found Samson and Pete slumped against the far wall of the barn. Pete was dead, his eyes wide open and staring. Samson was still breathing, a thin stream of blood trickled from his forehead.

She paused for a split second to tear apart her skirt and dab at the wound. She lowered him to the ground and pressed the hastily made bandage against his forehead. Then she raced into the yard, across the paddock and toward the house, easing the Colts from the belt once again.

Suddenly there was a shot. She stopped where she stood, feeling the dust rise around her feet where a bullet had bitten into the earth. She looked up, way up, to her bedroom window.

Zeke was standing there, a handful of Shannon's hair caught in his filthy fingers.

"Drop the guns, Mrs. Slater," Zeke drawled. "Drop 'em right now, else I'll let this pretty gold stuff in my fingers run red with McCahy blood."

Kristin stared up at him in despair. She heard a shuffling around her, and she knew that his men were emerging from the bunkhouse, from the far side of the house, from behind the watering trough. She looked around, and the faces spun before her. How many of them were there? Twenty? Thirty? It was hard to tell.

"Drop 'em in the dust, Kristin, slow and careful!" Zeke laughed then, fingering Shannon's hair. "She sure did come along nicely, Kristin. Why, I think she's even prettier than you are. Hard to tell, though. You're both nasty as rattlers."

Shannon cursed and bit Zeke's hand savagely. Zeke swore in turn and cuffed her hard. Suddenly Gabe began to cry. Kristin cried out involuntarily and bit her lip.

Shannon screamed as Zeke tore at her hair. Zeke, shouting insanely, addressed Kristin again.

"Drop the guns or else I'll kill the kid first. Slow. I'll blow off his legs one by one, and then his arms and then, if he's still alive, I'll cut off his ears!"

Kristin set the Colts on the ground. She heard Zeke's wild laughter, and then he and Shannon disappeared from the window. The shuffling around her began again. She closed her eyes and tried to ignore the soft jeers and the horrible smell as the men moved closer and closer.

The door to the house burst open, and Zeke appeared, shoving Shannon before him. Shannon was white, but

Kristin was, perhaps ridiculously, glad to see that her sister's hatred seemed to outweigh her fear. There would be plenty of time for fear.

Zeke, keeping his punishing grip on Shannon's hair, forced her into the center of the circle. He came close to Kristin, and he smiled. "I'm going to tell you about the afternoon, Kristin. Just so you can anticipate it all. Every sweet moment. See Harry over there? The guy with the peg leg and the rotten teeth? He's had a real hankering for you, so he gets to go first. I'm going for little sister here. Fresh meat. Then, well...hell, we've learned to share and share alike. We are going to make sure you stay alive, though. At least until we've had a chance to fire the house and the barn. You should get to hear the horses scream. That's a real fine sound. Then—maybe—Harry will scalp you. He learned the art real well from little Archie Clements himself. But we'll see how the afternoon goes. We may not have time for everything. There's lots of Yankees in these parts. Did you know that, Mrs. Slater? Sure you did. Your brother's a turncoat Yankee, ain't he? But don't worry about him none. I killed him last night."

Kristin's knees sagged, and she fell into the dirt. Matthew! It couldn't be. No!

Zeke started to laugh.

Something inside her snapped. She catapulted from the ground, flying at him in a fury. Shannon screamed but quickly rallied, and together they fell on him, biting him, tearing at him with their nails. Zeke screamed but none of his men moved to help him at first. And they couldn't shoot. They might kill him.

Then they heard it. The unmistakable sound of hoofbeats pounding the Missouri earth, pounding like thunder, coming closer and closer.

"Take cover!" one of the bushwhackers shouted.

Zeke let out a terrible growl and threw Shannon down hard in the dirt. He slammed the back of his hand against Kristin's cheek, and when she reeled, stunned by the blow, he caught her by the hair and dragged her up the steps to the porch and behind the oak rocker.

The hoofbeats came closer, thundering like a thousand drums. "Bastard!" Zeke muttered. "How could they know..."

It was only then, as Zeke aimed his gun through the slits in the back of the rocker, that Kristin got her first glimpse of the riders.

They were dressed in gray, and they might have been a sorry sight had they not ridden with such grace and style. A rebel yell suddenly rose up in the air, and the horses tore around the front of the house. Dust flew everywhere. Gunfire erupted, and Kristin bit back a scream.

Cole was leading them, whirling his horse around, his head held high. Malachi was there, too, and Jamie.

The Union army had failed endlessly against the bushwhackers because the bushwhackers were so well armed and so fast. But now they were fighting a man who knew their ways. A man who was faster. A man with a company of soldiers who were every bit as well armed as they were, a company of soldiers who were determined to salvage something of honor and chivalry from a war they were destined to lose. They fought their own kind, for their own kind had defied the very code of the South that so many had fought to preserve.

Kristin couldn't see for the clouds of dust the horses and the gunfire had churned up. All she knew was that Zeke was dragging her viciously along the porch.

She fought him. He swore he would turn around and shoot her, but she didn't really care. He had murdered Matthew, and he had murdered her father, and he was probably going to murder her. All she dared hope for was that Delilah had hidden somewhere, and that she had found Gabe. She wanted her son to live. She wanted something good to rise from the dust and ashes of this war. She wanted her child, Cole's child, to live, to remember, to start over.

"Damn you!" Zeke screamed. He twisted her arm cruelly behind her back, and she cried out in pain. He pushed her to the front door and then into the house. He pushed her toward the stairs, and the pain in her arm was so piercing that she had to stumble up the steps.

"Maybe we do have a little time. Maybe they'll all stay real busy out there for a long, long time. I wouldn't mind having you on Cole Slater's bed while he chokes on his own blood down below."

Suddenly the front door flew open and Cole was standing in the doorway. Zeke whirled, and Kristin stumbled and almost fell, but Zeke caught her and held her in front of him.

Framed by the doorway, the sunlight behind him, Cole was frightening and yet strangely beautiful. In his left hand he held his cavalry saber, and with his right he aimed his Colt.

"Put it down nice and easy, Slater, nice and easy," Zeke said. He pulled Kristin close against him, so close that she could breathe in the reek of his breath and feel the sweat of his body.

"You get your filthy hands off my wife, Zeke."

"You know, Slater, I started in with Quantrill late. That's why I didn't remember you the first time we met here. But now I remember you real well. And I've thought about this moment. I've dreamed about it. So you put the gun down. See how I've got this beautiful silver barrel aimed right at her throat? Think about how her blood will pour out where the artery's cut...."

Suddenly they heard a cry. It was Gabriel, crying in fear and rage. Delilah must have him in a closet close by, Kristin thought.

Her stomach twisted, and she saw that Cole had gone white. She sensed that Zeke was smiling. Now Cole was forced to think not only about her but about his son.

"That's a real fine boy you got there, Slater," Zeke drawled. He moved the barrel of the gun against Kristin's cheek. "A real fine wife, a real fine boy. You want to see them live, you'll set that gun down, slow and easy. No fast moves."

"No fast moves," Cole echoed tonelessly.

Gabe was still crying. Kristin bit into her lip. As soon as Cole set the gun down, Zeke would shoot him, and there was so much she had to tell him. Gabe was walking now, could say so many words. She had taught him to say papa. He had the most wonderful laugh in the whole world, and his eyes were so very much like his father's. . . .

"Cole, no!" she cried out.

He smiled at her. "I have to do this, Kristin."

Zeke laughed. "Yeah, he has to."

Cole was looking at her. A curious smile touched his lips. "I never got a chance to tell you that I loved you, Kristin. I do, you know. With all my heart."

"Oh, God, Cole!"

"I love you. I love you. Duck, Kristin."

"What?" she gasped,

He didn't drop his Colt. He aimed it right over her head. She screamed, and the world exploded.

15

Kristin fell, and it was as if the earth had opened up beneath her feet. All she knew was that Cole had fired.

And that Zeke had not.

Zeke's body was tumbling down the stairs after hers. Kristin came to a halt at the landing, and something fell hard on top of her. She stared up at Zeke, at his wide, staring eyes, at his forehead, where flesh and bone had been ripped away. She pushed away from him, desperate to get him away from her.

"Kristin, Kristin!"

Strong arms were around her, pulling her up from beneath him. She couldn't tear her eyes away from him. His face was still frozen in a sneer, even in death.

"Kristin!"

Cole turned her into his arms. "Kristin!" She looked up and saw his face, his eyes. Concern furrowed his brow as he eased his knuckles over her cheek. "Are you hurt?" he asked anxiously.

She shook her head. She couldn't speak. She stared at him blankly, and then she shrieked out his name and threw herself against him and started to cry. He stroked her hair and murmured comfortingly to her. Then he held her away from him and studied her anxiously. She struggled desperately for control.

"Oh, Cole! How did you know to come? They slaughtered all the Yankees.... Oh, no, a few of them might still be alive. You have to help them. Him. One of them saved me." Tears flooded her eyes. No matter how hard she tried, she couldn't keep from crying. "Cole! He killed Matthew! He found my brother and he killed him."

"Hush, Kristin, hush," Cole murmured. He pulled her against his body again and smoothed back her hair. Then he tilted her chin and sought her eyes. He had to make sure she understood. "Kristin, Matthew is fine. Well, I'm sorry, I suppose he's not fine. He's injured, but he's alive, Kristin. I would never have known—" He was suddenly unable to speak. It was all over, and now he was suddenly paralyzed by the fear. His hands trembled as he held her. "Kristin, Matthew's company was attacked. Zeke left him for dead, but he wasn't dead, and he got away in the night. Thank God, the Yanks knew where I had my men all along, and Matthew knew the area so well that he came straight to me."

Her eyes were wide with hope, with a joy she dared not feel. "Oh, Cole! Please, don't tell me that unless—"

"It's the truth, Kristin, I swear it."

"But they didn't come after you? The Yankees, they let you be?"

"I have a few friends in the right places," Cole said with a wry smile. "It gives me hope. Maybe, when this thing is over, some of the hatreds will be patched up. Some of them won't be. But, oh, God, I want it to end. I want it to be over!"

He pulled her against him again and she felt the beating of his heart. The rough wool of his frock coat tickled her cheek, and she had never been so glad of anything in her life. She wanted to look at him again. She wanted to study his features, and she wanted to see him smile, because he was young again when he smiled. She wanted to see the silver light in his eyes when he held her, and most of all she wanted to hear him speak again. She wanted to hear him say he loved her.

Of course, this wasn't really the right time. There was a dead man at her feet, and though the guns had gone silent outside the house, dead men littered the earth there, too,

and—please God—a few living men, too. She had to go
back to the barn for the young Yankee who had saved her
life, and she had to find her son.

"Kristin—" Cole began, but he was interrupted by an
outraged cry.

"Miz Kristin! Mister Cole! Why, thank the Lord," Delilah called. She was at the top of the stairs with Gabe, who
was struggling fiercely to free himself from her grasp. Cole
stared at his son with the awe of a parent who has not seen
his child in a long, long time. Gabe might have been a grown
man the way Cole was staring at him.

Kristin's eyes twinkled. "He walks now. And he talks. I
taught him how to say papa."

Delilah hurried down the stairs. She saw Zeke's body, but
she didn't pause. She spat on it and stepped over it, and then
she set Gabriel down. He tottered for a moment. Kristin
watched Cole as he went down on his knees and reached out
for the boy. Gabe waddled carefully over to inspect the
stranger.

"Say papa!" Kristin urged him.

Gabriel wasn't interested in saying anything. He turned
away from the stranger who was his father and buried his
face in his mother's skirts. He reached out his arms, and
Kristin laughed and picked him up. Then, suddenly, she
crushed him against her, so hard that he cried out in protest. "Oh, Gabriel!" she murmured, holding him tight.

Cole came to his feet and rescued his screaming son. He
lifted Gabriel very high and silver eyes gazed into silver eyes.
"I'm your papa, little man!" He laughed. "And you'd best
get used to the idea."

Gabriel couldn't possibly have understood what Cole had
said to him, of course, but he smiled anyway, as if he had
decided to accept the stranger in gold and gray. Cole lowered him at last and set him on his hip, smiling at Kristin.

Suddenly there was an awful commotion at the door.

"Put me down, you piece of trash!" Shannon shrieked.

Malachi—Shannon thrown over his shoulder—came through the doorway, his face dark and thunderous. "I don't mind bushwhackers, and I don't mind the damn Yankees, but Cole, I will be damned if I'll be responsible for this brat!"

"Put me down!" Shannon screamed.

He did. He dumped her in front of Cole, and she was thrashing and flailing, trying to get her balance. She rolled over and came face-to-face with Zeke Moreau's body.

"Oh!" she gasped, and fell silent at last.

Kristin looked at Malachi and arched a brow.

He sighed with great patience. "Kristin, I didn't know what the hell was happening in here. I didn't want her barging in to get shot, or to cause you or Cole to get shot. Mainly. It would be her own damn fault if she did get shot, but since she is your sister, I thought I'd try to save her sweet, darling, precious little life!"

For once Shannon didn't reply. She was still staring at Zeke's face. She began to tremble uncontrollably, and then she burst into tears.

Kristin started toward her sister, but Cole pulled her back. Malachi was kneeling beside Shannon, and he pulled her up and away from the body.

"It's over! It's all over!" he told her roughly. "Don't go falling apart now."

Shannon stiffened momentarily, and then she hiccuped. Malachi gave her his handkerchief, and she dried her face, nodding an acknowledgement. Then she jammed it back into his hand.

"I never fell apart, you backwoods bastard!"

"Well, good. Get your derriere out there and start helping!"

"Helping?"

"There are injured men out there. Unless you're too damned prissy to help the men who were willing to die to save your miserable life."

"Miserable?"

"Go!"

"I am going, Malachi Slater! I'm going because those are fine men out there—even the rebels! I'm going for them, and I'm going because I choose to go, and I'll never, never do anything because you tell me to, do you understand?"

With an elegant toss of her golden curls, she swept past him. It was a splendid exit except for one thing. Malachi smacked her rump soundly as she went past. She yelped in outrage and slapped him hard across the face. He caught her by the elbow and turned her toward him, his face dark with rage.

"Malachi! Please! She is my sister," Kristin reminded him sweetly.

Slowly, his eyes narrowed, he released Shannon. "Why, thank you, kind sir!" she said. Then she kicked him hard in the shin and raced out the door.

Kristin began to smirk, and then Cole laughed, and the baby giggled. Delilah laughed along with them, but then her laughter faded, and she gasped, "Samson! My man! Oh, Mister Slater—"

"The barn," Kristin said quickly, her eyes on Cole. "He was breathing—"

Cole ran out the door, Delilah hard on his heels. Kristin followed but when she stepped out on the porch she stood there stunned, her son in her arms, staring at the scene of destruction.

There were bodies everywhere. Men in gray were collecting them, dragging them away. A weary-looking young man nodded to her in grim acknowledgment as he passed her. She swallowed and caught his arm. "Thank you. Thank you for coming here."

He smiled and tipped his hat. "I'd go anywhere Colonel Slater invited me, ma'am. I'm right glad we got here in time."

He had work to do, and he went back to it. Dazed, Kristin stepped down into the yard.

Then someone called out, asking for water. She hurried over to the trough and found one of Cole's boys behind it, clutching his shoulder and trying to stand.

"Here, here!" she whispered, ladling up some water. Gabe gurgled. He seemed to think they were playing.

"Thank you, ma'am," the soldier said. Then he winced, and she saw that he had a ball lodged in his flesh.

"Help me over here!" she called. Another soldier lifted the wounded man, and within minutes she had him in the house and on the couch and she had Cole's men scurrying around, boiling water, ripping up sheets for bandages, setting up the parlor as a temporary infirmary.

Gabriel refused to sleep, so she set up a little playpen in the parlor and busied herself with the injured. Shannon was at her side and Delilah, too, now that she knew that Samson was all right. He had been knocked cold, and he had a blinding headache, but otherwise he was none the worse for wear.

Samson was out on burial detail now. Zeke Moreau's body had been removed from the house.

There had been a scene when that had happened. Shannon had followed them out. She had stood on the porch and begged the men, "Please . . . please! Don't bury that man's body anywhere on this property!"

"Miss McCahy—"

"Please! Let the vultures eat him, let the wolves finish him, but I beg you, don't bury him near here!"

And so some of the men had set out with a wagon, and they were taking Zeke and the bodies of the other bush-whackers far, far away. Pete was dead, and he was family, and three of Cole's men had fallen, and there were the Yankees that the bushwhackers had killed. They were being laid to rest with infinite tenderness in the family plot, beside Kristin's mother and father.

By nightfall, most of the traces of the gun battle had been cleared away. Delilah managed to produce a hearty stew in abundance to feed everyone.

At ten they heard the sound of a wagon creaking along. Cole had just finished eating, and he was sipping a brandy on the porch. Gabriel was in bed, and Kristin was sitting at Cole's feet, listening to a sad tune being played on a harmonica somewhere nearby.

She felt Cole stiffen. Then she realized that he had sentries posted, for there was something like a Rebel yell in the darkness, and then the wagon came through.

"Cole?" Kristin murmured.

"It's a surprise," he said, squeezing her shoulder. She followed him down the steps and out to the yard. There was something lumpy in the back of the wagon, something cried out plaintively, "Kristin, Shannon?"

"Matthew!" She screamed her brother's name and flew to the wagon. She kissed him, and she held him so tightly that he muttered, "Kristin, I survived being shot, you're going to kill me here in my home at last with kindness!"

"Oh, Matthew!"

Then Shannon was flying down the steps. The three McCahy's greeted one another, and the men looked on, and then the harmonica player started up again, with "Lorena" this time bringing tears to eyes that had nearly run dry in all the years of bloodshed.

Matthew was brought in and put to bed in his own room. Once he was tucked in, he caught his sister's hand, and Kristin smiled and kissed him on the forehead again and told him to rest.

"Kristin!" He pulled her back. "Kristin, there'll be a bunch of Yankees here soon. They'll find out that Major Emery and his men were slaughtered, and they'll know that Cole and his men came in for the cleanup, and they'll be damned glad. But there's still a war on. They'll have to take them prisoner, or else they'll have to fight, and a lot of men will die needlessly. They're true heroes—to both sides, probably—but that won't make any difference. Kristin, are you understanding me?"

No, she wasn't. Or perhaps she was and she wanted to deny it. She couldn't have her husband taken away from her so soon.

"Kristin, Cole is considered an outlaw. Worse than ever before."

"Why? What do you mean?"

"He'll have to explain that to you himself. But be prepared. They need to sneak away now, tonight."

She felt weak, as if she had been drowning and she had reached and reached for a rope and it had been viciously wrenched away.

"Thank you, Matthew," she told her brother.

She blew out the lamp and left him. She hesitated, leaning against the door.

When she came back downstairs, she quickly discovered that everything that Matthew had said was true. The Confederate surgeon who had so carefully tended to her brother was checking the men she had sutured and bandaged—and preparing them for travel. He smiled at her when he saw her.

"Your brother is going to be just fine. Keep the wound clean. Never use the same sponge twice when you're cleaning out a wound. I'm becoming more and more convinced that rot travels that way. Seems we have been doing better with sanitation than the blue bellies." He paused, and she thought that he, too, looked weary. "He's a fine young man, your brother. You take care of him."

"Thank you, Captain Turnbill," said Kristin. He was about to turn away, but she stopped him with a hand set lightly upon his arm. "Captain, are you sure these men are fit to travel?"

"The worst wounded are the Yankees we found in the bunkhouse and the barn, and they don't have to travel anywhere. My men have one broken arm, a broken leg, some shot in the shoulder and two concussions. They'll be all right." He paused, looking at her unhappily. "Mrs. Slater, they'll be a lot better off traveling now than they would be in a Yankee prison camp. I'm not a man to say that all

Yanks are butchers, but there's not much good to be said about prison camps, whether they're Yankee camps or Confederate camps."

The able-bodied men were walking past her, making ready to leave. Kristin couldn't see her husband anywhere.

Malachi came around behind her and squeezed her shoulders. He turned her around. "Hope Cole won't mind," he said, and he hugged her and gave her a kiss on the cheek. "Hell, I don't care if Cole does mind!" he said, and he kissed her again. She didn't know there was a tear on her cheek until he wiped it away.

"Oh, Malachi..."

"It's all right. We won't be far away."

"Not far away at all."

It was Jamie who spoke. He was right behind Malachi, and he took her from his brother and kissed her cheek, too. "You take care of yourself, little sister, you hear? Take good care of that nephew of mine, too."

She nodded, unable to speak for a few seconds.

"Cole—"

"Cole is right here," her husband said. Tears blurred her vision. He took her in his arms. "Hey!" he whispered, his lips nuzzling her throat. "Stop that! You can't send my brothers away with tears in your eyes."

"Your brothers..."

She whirled around in his arms. Cole looked over her head. Malachi tipped his hat and grinned, and Cole grinned back. The two of them went out, and the house slowly fell silent. "I'm not leaving tonight, Kristin."

"What?" she whispered.

There was a bit of a commotion outside. Shannon was saying goodbye nicely to Jamie, and not so nicely to Malachi. Cole grinned, and Kristin grinned back, her eyes searching his. Then the door slammed, and Shannon whispered. "Oh, excuse me!"

Neither of them turned around. They heard Shannon tiptoe into the parlor to stay with the Union injured.

He was beautiful, Kristin thought. He was the most beautiful man she had ever seen. He was leaner than he had been that first day she had seen him. Strands of gray were creeping into his hair and into his beard, but somehow they were beautiful, too. They went well with the silver light in his eyes, with the handsome, dignified planes of his face.

"Oh!" she whispered heatedly. "You have to leave! Matthew says they consider you an outlaw—"

"They won't know I'm here, Kristin. My men are gone. They've taken my horse. They've learned how to disappear with the night. And for now I'm staying with my wife."

"Oh!"

"If she'll have me."

"Oh!" She touched his cheek, tenderly moving her fingertips over the coarse beard there. "Oh, she will have you!" she breathed.

He caught her hand and kissed her fingertips. Silently he led her up the stairs and through the doorway to their bedroom. Then he leaned against the door, and she smiled as she watched him.

"I never thought I would be here with you now!" he whispered.

"But you are," she said.

"Yes, I am."

Kristin walked over to him. She lifted off his hat and tossed it on the floor, and she unbuckled his scabbard and his gun belt and cast his weapons aside. Studiously, she unbuttoned his frock coat and his uniform shirt, and when his shoulders and chest were bare she felt the sweet thrill of anticipation invade her. Her fingers grew awkward, and she found that she was trembling. She whispered his name, and she pressed her lips to his chest and to the pulse at the base of his throat. He caught her lips and kissed her hungrily, tasting and tasting her mouth, trembling with ever-greater ardor. She was breathless when he released her and turned her around to work at the tiny buttons of her dress. He was shaking as badly as she, but was more practiced, and more determined, and she was startled when the dress fell quickly away from her, and then her chemise, and then her petticoats. He lifted her up with her stockings and shoes still on and carried her quickly to the bed, pausing with a rueful laugh to check on Gabriel, who was sleeping sweetly in the little bed in the corner.

Then he tossed her on the bed and fell upon her, and she threaded her fingers joyously through his hair. He groaned and kissed her again, and then he kissed her breasts, staring at them, savoring them, easing his tongue over each nipple, then his teeth, then the fullness of his mouth.

"Oh, Cole!" Her head tossed from side to side, and lightning swept through her, embedding a sweet, swirling heat at the apex of her thighs, a dizzying need for him. He filled it, touching her with a light and tender stroke and then with a demanding one, watching her eyes, watching her body, feeling the thunder of the desire that grew and grew within him.

He kissed her belly, and he stroked her thighs, and he played his touch over the golden triangle at their juncture, and then he delved within it. He made an incredibly sensual act of taking off her shoes, peeling away her garters and hose. Then he rose boldly above her. He drew a steady pattern with the searing tip of his tongue from her throat down the valley between her breasts to her navel and into the very heart of her fire. And she cried out for him, and he came to her.

Then he hovered, just above her, and she opened her eyes wide, waiting, pleading, wondering why he denied her. A great sound of agony escaped him, and he buried his head against her breasts.

"I do love you, Kristin. I do love you."

"Oh, Cole!" she said, clinging to him. "Please . . ."

He pushed away from her, and stared at her. "Well?"

And then it dawned on her what he wanted, and she pressed hard against him, arching to meet his need. "Cole,

I have loved you for ages! I love you so very much. I could never admit it, I was so afraid, I knew you didn't love me.''

"I just didn't dare admit it," he said softly.

"Say it again!" she demanded.

"I love you. I love you, Kristin McCahy Slater, and I swear that I will do so until the end of time."

"Oh, Cole!" She buried her face against his chest. It was hot and sleek and damp with perspiration. And he chose that moment to plunge deep, deep within her, and even as he did he was whispering again, the sweet words over and over again.

He loved her.

Later that night—much later, for making love took on a sweet new dimension when the words were spoken, and they were tempted to explore that dimension again and again— Cole held her in his arms and told her everything. First he told her about the day the jayhawkers had come, and how they had burned down his home and killed his wife. She heard the agony in his voice, but she didn't stop him, because it was important that he say everything, that he lay his soul bare for her, as she had hers. He needed to trust her in that way, and, Kristin thought, he needed the healing power of words. His heart needed the cleansing.

She listened, and she was not afraid of the past, merely saddened. Then she listened as he told her what had happened in Kansas, how his old friend Kurt Taylor had been there and how he had purposely alerted Cole to the fact that Henry Fitz was in town with his jayhawkers.

"I killed him, Kristin. I knew what I was doing. I knew exactly what danger I was riding into, but I had to face him." His arms tightened around her. "If we were to have a future, I just had to do it. Can you understand that?"

She didn't really have to answer him. She planted little kisses over his chest, and he groaned, and his hands rode roughly over her hair, and then they were in one another's arms once again. They were still so desperate, so hungry, so determined to have all that they could of one another, to cherish, to hold, to keep always for their dreams.

It was near dawn before they dozed off. Kristin was startled when she awoke almost before she had slept. Day was breaking, bright and fresh as a rainbow. Pink light fell upon her.

She heard the sounds of hoofbeats below.

With a soft gasp, she rose and raced to the window.

Down by the well she saw a single Union officer. She glanced at Cole, and he seemed to be asleep. He seemed at peace, the lines of strain erased from his features at last.

Kristin struggled into her gown and left the room without stockings or shoes, closing the door behind her. She padded silently down the stairs and hurried out to the well.

She couldn't imagine how she looked to the man, her face pale, her blue eyes wide, her hair in complete and lovely disarray around her fine-boned, very worried face.

He smiled at her and looked her up and down. He suddenly envied Cole Slater very much.

"Good morning, ma'am. This the McCahy ranch?"

"It is. My brother, a Union officer, is inside, recovering from wounds."

And your husband, a Southern officer, is inside, too, I'd wager, he thought, but he was silent.

"This is sweet, clear water. Thank you."

"You're very welcome to it."

"Zeke Moreau came here and gunned down most of the men?"

Kristin swallowed and nodded.

"There's a detachment of medics coming for the injured later today."

"That's fine. We're doing our best."

"I'm sure you are."

"Would you like to come in?"

He shook his head. "No thanks. I'm not here officially." He spoke softly. "I came here to tell you that the war is over. Well, all but the shouting. I'm sure it will take a while for all the troops to surrender. Kirby-Smith is a tenacious soul. Proud man, fine fighter, but—''

"The . . . the war is over?" Kristin breathed.

"Yes, ma'am, like I said, all but the shouting. Two mornings ago, on April twelfth, General Robert E. Lee surrendered the Army of Northern Virginia to General Ulysses S. Grant at a little place called Appomattox Courthouse. Word has it that President Lincoln is determined that this great nation must unite in peace and brotherhood as quickly as possible, and he seems determined that there be brotherhood between North and South again."

She was shaking. She had to sit down. He saw her lips and her limbs tremble, and he came around to her and helped her over to the porch. He gave her a sip of water, and she nodded her thanks.

"The war . . . is really over?"

"Really over." He smiled. "I hear tell that Colonel Slater and his men came in here yesterday. Yep, I hear tell they cut down Zeke Moreau and his bloody bushwhackers. That must have been a fine piece of work, yes, ma'am. I'd have liked to have been here. No doubt the Union commanders—and the law—will hear about it." He smiled at her again. "'Course, Slater's men are gone, I take it?"

Kristin nodded. "Yes . . . they're gone."

"You his wife?"

"I'm his wife."

"Someone ought to tell him that the war is over. 'Course, they should warn him that he needs to take care. Some people still don't take kindly to a few of his exploits. Once with Quantrill, you know, and then there was Kansas . . ." He shrugged. "If you should happen to see him, Mrs. Slater, you might warn him to lie low for a while. Ride on to Texas, maybe. Fitz had a brother, and he's sure to make an outcry. But tell him that he has to remember—the war is over. It will all come right. You hear? Tell him Kurt Taylor said so."

Kristin nodded.

"Thanks for the water. That's mighty good water."

"You're welcome, sir. Mighty welcome."

Kristin stood and waited. She waited until the Union officer in his blue uniform had disappeared on the dusty Missouri horizon.

Then she turned and screamed, "Cole! Cole!"

She tore up the stairs. He was up. He had been watching her and the officer from the window. Kristin threw herself at him, sending him flying across the room.

"It's over, it's over! The war is over! Lee has surrendered! Oh, there are still troops that haven't surrendered yet, but they're saying it's over! Oh, Cole!" She caught his face between her hands, and she kissed him. She kissed his throat and his shoulders, and she was so alive and vibrant that even though he had been worried and wary he had to laugh.

"Kristin, Kristin, it can't be that easy—"

"No, it isn't that easy," she said solemnly, and she told him what the man had said. "His name was Kurt Taylor, and he said you should head for Texas."

"I will," Cole said.

Kristin corrected him. "We will."

"We will?" he asked her, arching a brow. "I do seem to recall that there was once a woman who would not leave this ranch. She sold her honor to a disreputable rebel in order to stay right here on this property."

Kristin smiled at him. She had never felt so deliciously alive and sensual and vibrant and aware of all the world around her. It was spring—and the war was over. Over.

"It isn't my ranch. I was just holding on to it for Matthew, and Matthew is here now. You see, it's time to move on, anyway. And I consider that my honor was sold for a fair price. It was rather useless, you see, while my son—he's just magnificent. And—"

"And?"

"Well, there is this other minor thing. I fell desperately in love with that disreputable rebel. Even when I wanted to hang him myself, I was very much in love."

"Very much?"

"Incredibly, inestimably, most desperately in love."

"Really?" He laced his fingers through hers and bent his head and kissed her. She felt a shudder rake through him, and she sought his eyes.

"Cole?"

"We really have a future."

"Yes!"

"We can watch Gabriel grow, and we can have more children. And I can hold them when they are little tiny infants—"

"And you can change their little bottoms, too," Kristin informed him sweetly.

He smiled, and he kissed her again, and she let out a sweet, shuddering sigh. "Cole?"

"My love?"

She smiled, slowly, lazily, sensuously. "If you go to Texas, I will follow you wherever you may lead. But for the moment..."

"Yes?"

"We've never made love in peacetime before. Never," she told him with very wide eyes. "We've never made love in peacetime, whispering that we love one another!"

He threw back his head and laughed, and his eyes sizzled, silver and mercury, into hers, and she thought that he would always be her cavalier, the tall, dark stranger with the plumed hat who had stepped into her life like a hero, taking her from darkness into light. They weren't clear of the darkness yet. There would be pain. There would be time to mourn Pete, who had always been her friend, always at her side. There would be time to mourn Major Emery, who had been their friend, too, noble and caring, until the very end.

For now, though, they had one another.

Cole grinned wickedly. "Then," he said, "we must make love at peace, and whisper that we love one another. Kristin!"

"Yes?"

He came close against her lips, his mouth a breath away from hers.

"I love you!" he whispered fervently. "I love you, I love you, I love you!"

And though they were at peace they soared into the sweetest tempest, and through it all they never ceased to whisper the words.

The sun entered their room, and a new day had truly dawned.

Cole stroked his wife's beautiful hair, luxuriating in the sweet satisfaction she brought him. He stared at the ceiling, at the new light of day.

It would take the country a long time to heal, he knew. A long, long time. A long time to unite.

But she had brought healing to him, and his heart was united with hers now. "A new age," he murmured.

"What?"

"I said I love you!" Cole lied, and he turned to her again.

The war wouldn't end as easily as Kristin thought. Life was never as easy as that. But they did have a future.

And Texas could wait just a little while longer.

_____ Author's Note

The war did not end easily, and especially not in the West, on the Kansas-Missouri border where it had really begun, long before shots rang out at Fort Sumter.

General Kirby-Smith was determined, and he held out with his troops until the twenty-sixth of May, holding the last Southern command to stand in the field.

William C. Quantrill died on June 6, 1865, fatally wounded by Union troops while conducting a raid on Louisville, Kentucky. On his deathbed he swore that if he had captured Jim Lane, leader of the jayhawkers before Doc Jennison, he would have burned him at the stake.

Jim Lane himself fired his last shot on July 1, 1865—with his revolver in his own mouth.

Frank and Jesse James and the Younger brothers—Quantrill's men—went on to find a separate infamy.

For Cole and Kristin, all those things were in the future. Cole was to have his own problems.

But those are really part of Malachi and Shannon's story, and must be told by them.

Take 3 of
"The Best of the Best™"
Novels FREE
Plus get a FREE surprise gift!

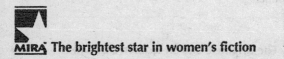

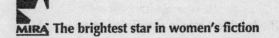

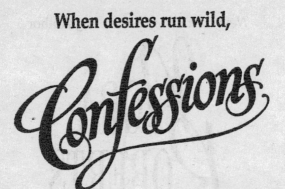

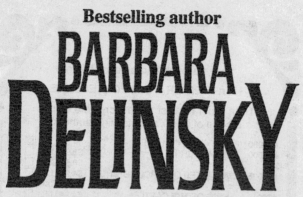